C000048112

'Fine clothes and fine manners make good partners!'

'Not in my experience,' said Piero, in the manner of one handing down a judgement from on high. 'Poor clothing and even worse manners appear to surpass them if your own behaviour is anything to go by.'

There was a dreadful silence at this home truth until Bianca, stamping one ill-shod foot, angrily blazed out, 'Oh, you are impossible, Messer Piero, quite impossible.'

'Why, lady,' he replied, and his smile was sweet poison, 'I do but take my cue from you, as a good guest should.'

Dear Reader

We welcome new author Marie-Louise Hall to the list—she has treated us to a look at Napoleon's retreat from Moscow, and a tempestuous love story for Tristan and Angèle! After two excellent Regencies, Paula Marshall has moved to fifteenth-century Tuscany in her new story. Piero is a wonderful hero, and the blossoming of Bianca is a delight! Despite a six-month gap, Paula has not been idle, and there are excellent books by her scheduled for next year—look out for them.

The Editor

Paula Marshall, married with three children, has had a varied life. She began her career in a large library and ended it as a senior academic in charge of history in a polytechnic. She has travelled widely, has been a swimming coach, and has appeared on *University Challenge* and *Mastermind*. She has always wanted to write, and likes her novels to be full of adventure and humour.

Recent titles by the same author:

AN IMPROPER DUENNA
COUSIN HARRY

THE FALCON
AND THE DOVE

Paula Marshall

All the characters in this book have no existence outside the imagination of the Author, and have no relation whatsoever to anyone bearing the same name or names. They are not even distantly inspired by any individual known or unknown to the Author, and all the incidents are pure invention.

All Rights Reserved. The text of this publication or any part thereof may not be reproduced or transmitted in any form or by any means, electronic or mechanical, including photocopying, recording, storage in an information retrieval system, or otherwise, without the written permission of the publisher.

This book is sold subject to the condition that it shall not, by way of trade or otherwise, be lent, resold, hired out or otherwise circulated without the prior consent of the publisher in any form of binding or cover other than that in which it is published and without a similar condition including this condition being imposed on the subsequent purchaser.

*First published in Great Britain 1992
by Mills & Boon Limited*

© Paula Marshall 1992

*Australian copyright 1992
Philippine copyright 1992
This edition 1992*

ISBN 0 263 77922 X

*Masquerade is a trademark published by
Mills & Boon Limited, Eton House,
18–24 Paradise Road, Richmond, Surrey, TW9 1SR.*

*Set in 10 on 10½ pt Linotron Baskerville
04-9211-87928*

*Typeset in Great Britain by Centracet, Cambridge
Made and printed in Great Britain*

CHAPTER ONE

BIANCA DI SAN GIORGIO was on her hands and knees
cleaning a stain on the stone floor of the outer hall of her
brother's tower which dominated the little town of San
Giorgio, the centre of her brother's lordship, when Piero
de' Manfredini and his train arrived on that bright day
in 1430.

She had left the shabby apartments in which she and
her brother lived to see that the stain, which she had
noted earlier that day, was still there, untouched, and
that Lucia, the servant, had slopped water about to no
avail and was now about to traipse off. Bianca had given
an exasperated snort and a piece of her mind to Lucia,
and when Lucia had mumbled resentfully, 'Too difficult,
madonna, for a poor girl to shift,' she had said, abruptly,

'Give me your apron, the bucket, the brush and the
soap,' and had then plumped down on her hands and
knees to remove the offending thing herself. There was
no task in the tower—it could hardly be called a castle—
however menial, that Bianca had not, at some time,
performed. Poor noblewomen were driven to such shifts
to keep up appearances—particularly if they were as
fiercely proud as Bianca and possessed a shiftless brother
like Bernardo, who did not know what pride meant.
Someone had to see that San Giorgio and the tower did
not decline into the kind of lordship which appeared so
defenceless that any marauding mercenary company, or
neighbouring acquisitive lord, might decide to attack it
without warning.

She was so deep in her task, which soon took in the
rest of the grimy floor, that she did not hear the noise
outside which told of the arrival of someone important.
Neither did she hear the approaching footsteps, and even

if she had done so she would have thought that it was
merely some of her brother's men-at-arms approaching.
When, at the last moment, she became aware of the
newcomers, her belief that it was some of the San Giorgio
retainers was so strong that, assuming that, as usual,
they would walk straight through her work unless fore-
warned and shouted at, Bianca continued her scrubbing,
flinging inelegantly over her shoulder the words, 'Be off
with you. You can just keep your great plate feet out of
my work if you know what is good for you!'

Almost before she had finished speaking she felt a
hand seize her right ear and pull, hard, so that she was
forced to rise to her feet, and once on them was spun
smartly round to face the hand's owner.

White with rage, except for her ear, which, alas, was
flaming scarlet, Bianca found her eyes on a level with a
tall man's chest, and looked up to find herself staring at
the most coldly handsome face she had ever seen. Short
golden hair fell in loose curls about a tanned face. His
eyes were a brilliant blue, his nose aquiline, and his long
shapely mouth was twisting derisively as he looked down
at her. He appeared to be in his early twenties.

'I am not,' said the hand's owner—and oh, distress-
ingly, his voice was beautiful, too—'accustomed to be so
addressed by scrub women. If I have a mind to perform
a Turkish dance on your damned floor I shall do so.'

'Oh!' began Bianca furiously. 'How dare you?'

'How dare I? An impertinent scrub woman, indeed.
You presume on your lack of looks, my girl,' he said
lazily, letting go of her ear, and stepping back to survey
her—which gave her the opportunity to further survey
him. His body was as beautiful as his face and his
clothing equalled them both. He was altogether too
impossibly perfect, Bianca thought, rage building inside
her at the sight of him.

He was clad from head to foot in black, with a ruby in
his right ear, rubies in the clasp of his long cloak, and in
the buckle of the gilt belt which circled his slim waist.

His hose and boots were perfect, too. The only weapon he wore was a dagger in the belt, and that was a work of art, as well as a deadly weapon. Altogether he was as apparently rich as the San Giorgios were poor. He made Bianca feel even more plain, ill-dressed and neglected than she actually was. It was enough to make a self-respecting sixteen-year-old want to spit.

Her disgust was so evident that it was written on her face. He leaned forward and took her by the ear again. 'A little respect,' he began, 'would be becoming,' and then as her eyes blazed at him he laughed softly, and said to the older man at his side, '*Per Dio*, Lodovico, even the servants at San Giorgio are dispossessed royalty,' and his look as he said this was so dismissive that she almost exploded.

'Release me at once, Ser.'

'Oh, willingly, when I am ready,' he drawled. 'Why should I keep you? A fish to throw back in the sea, I think. A little punishment for insolence is required, but what? A kiss? But a kiss would punish *me*.'

Bianca found herself trembling violently, and, shamingly, unwanted tears were threatening to fall.

'Oh, you are vile, vile,' was all that she could manage.

'So everyone tells me. But why should the scrub woman—child—be original?'

Bianca was suddenly aware that behind the stranger and the man he had called Lodovico was a train of equally well-dressed attendants and soldiers, added to, now, by some slovenly-appearing San Giorgio men-at-arms, laughing and snickering at the sight of the lord's high-tempered sister being put in her place at last.

'Tell him to take himself to Gehenna, lady,' one of them bawled.

The stranger's eyebrows, thin, dark and arched, climbed. 'Lady,' he said, and finally released her, laughing. 'The jest, at least, is original.' He gave her a mock bow.

'Oh,' raged Bianca, almost jumping up and down. In

all her sixteen years she had never been so angry. She was painfully aware of the disadvantage she was at. How could he know that she was the lord's sister? How could she tell him? It was so unlikely when she was wearing a brown canvas apron, was holding a brush, and was standing over a pail of dirty water. She had a mind to throw the contents of it over him. That would ruin his impossibly perfect appearance, and no mistake.

Her tormentor saw her eyes change, and his own glittered sardonically. 'Oh, no, and I've no mind to be baptised in dirty water, either.'

He bent down, and before Bianca could stop him he picked up the pail and handed it to Lodovico, who by his expression did not entirely approve of what his lord—for lord he must be—was doing.

'Dispose of that for me, Lodovico, before this hell-cat does more than spit,' he said cheerfully.

'You are no gentleman, Ser who-ever-you-are, to tease a poor girl so. You shall pay for this, I promise you.' She was now far too angry and embarrassed to inform him that he was in the presence of the lady of the tower, was dismally aware of how little of a lady she looked or sounded, and could only imagine what mordant witticism from him would greet this unlikely news. Never before had she so regretted her small size, her lack of physical development, for she was as thin and flat as any boy despite her age, and had as little presence as could be expected from a girl who looked like a filleted herring, as her brother, Bernardo, had once unkindly said, adding, 'No wonder Agneta tells me that your courses have not yet begun.'

'True that I am no gentleman, and I doubt me that I shall pay,' the stranger went on. 'Now, child, tell me where to find your lord, and quickly. He is expecting me.'

Was he, indeed? And if so, why did she not know? Bernardo was neither a kind nor a thoughtful brother, but she usually knew what he was about, and she had heard nothing of a visitor. Almost, now, she told him who she was, but then thought better of it. Let him be the more shamed when he found out she was the lady of the tower. On second thoughts this was too foolish a notion to entertain. He looked as if nothing and nobody could ever shame him.

She bobbed a perfunctory curtsy. 'If you would but give me your name, lord. . .' The title nearly choked her, but she got it out somehow. 'I will inform him of your arrival.'

'You may tell him that Messer Piero de' Manfredini, Lord of Astra, is here, at his service.'

Bianca could not stop herself. Her heart fell into her serviceable but ugly shoes when she heard with whom she had been trifling—and who had been trifling with her.

'The Golden Falcon. . .'

'A well-informed scrub woman. Run, child, tell your master I am here.' His hand was in the purse at his belt. 'And here's a coin for your damaged ear, and for your errand,' and he held it out to her. His hand was as beautiful and deadly as the rest of him. . .and his reputation.

Bianca had not thought him to be so young, to be a mercenary soldier, a captain, a *condottiero* of such note. A man who had won a series of victories for his Florentine masters, and whose one defeat had not really been a defeat at all, for he had somehow managed to save his *condotta*—his army—whose crest and badge was the golden falcon, and come out of it with his reputation enhanced, since he had almost managed to fight off no less than three companies hired to oppose him, so fearful of him was the opposition. A man who was noted for his cunning as well as his bravery. A man who had made fools of the older men who had opposed him, and whose tongue was said to be as cutting as his sword. But the offered coin completed her humiliation. He might be the cleverest and the most ruthless blade who had ever cut a swath across Italy, but she would not take it.

And then, yes, she took the coin, looked at it scornfully, and, holding it at arm's length, dropped it into the pail of dirty water which Lodovico was holding. 'And that is what I think of your money, lord,' she said, as it plopped satisfyingly down below the scum which had gathered on the water's top. 'You may keep it—if you care to fish it out, that is.'

His hand shot out again, like lightning, or a snake striking—she was to find that such speed of reflex action was typical of him—caught her by the chin and tipped her dirty, defiant face towards him. Bianca did not know that her face was dirty, would not have cared if she had known. Would have preferred it to be dirty if only to spite his impossible perfection, to show that *she* would never emulate it.

'Let me see you, girl,' he said. 'A rich scrub woman, to refuse my bounty. Lodovico may give the coin to the tower's priest when he has disposed of the water.' He spun her around, smacked her hard on the backside, 'Now, run, child, run, tell the Lord Bernardo I am here, lest worse befall.'

Oh, the monster! He would pay for this—he would, he would! But as she scurried away to find her brother the monster's light laughter pursued her until she was in the corridor, away from him and his impossible perfection.

Old Agneta, Bianca's woman, came in to her room to find her staring horror-stricken at her dirty face, revealed in her small Venetian glass hand-mirror, one of her few beautiful possessions.

'No wonder he thought that I was a scrubbing wench,' she moaned. The hair which she had screwed on to the top of her head to be out of the way while she worked had come down, and hung in lank black wisps about her brown, thin face—and her dress! Dear God, her dress looked like a rag under the hideous overall. And she—

what did she look like? No figure, flat-chested, hips like
a boy's—and a small boy's at that. She saw the amusement on his face again. Knew why it was there. Such
impossible perfection doubtless demanded the equiva-
lent in women. Even when God finally made her a
woman—and when would that be?—she would never
look remotely like anything Messer Piero de' Manfredini
might be interested in.

'A bath, Agneta,' she said feverishly, 'I need a bath.'
At least she could be clean, if nothing else, when she
next saw him.

'A bath, lady? Now?'

'At once, woman, and quick about it. And a dress.
Have I no better than this to wear when my brother has
noble guests at his table?'

Agneta went on to her knees before the press—the
chest in which Bianca's few clothes were kept. It had St
Sebastian, stuck about with arrows, crudely painted on
the lid, and garlands of flowers decorated the sides. *He*
had not looked at all like the dark, emaciated saint, but
like the beautiful figure of the warrior archangel St
Michael, part of the fresco in the tower's chapel. Why
did she keep on thinking about such a creature? He did
not deserve her consideration, and shortly she was to
meet him again, and she must look better than she had
done, on her knees, in the hall.

By now Agneta was hauling clothes out, sniffing
loudly, and rejecting them one by one. Too small, too
shabby, not appropriate for such a grand occasion—she
soon came to the end, hands empty, sitting back on her
heels. 'Naught there for banquets and grand lords, lady.
The finest you have is nothing, and will be too small.'
And she picked up again a gown in blue and silver
brocade.

'When I have bathed I will try it on,' said Bianca,
breathlessly, thinking, Sweet Mother of Christ, have I
nothing fit to wear? And the note of despair rang sour in
her head.

'I told your lord brother not once, but many times, that you had nothing fit to put upon your back. He said that he could afford nothing better until you looked more like a woman, and less like a stunted boy.'

'He can afford to put treasure on Giulietta's back, so that she can lie on it for him,' said Bianca savagely and improperly as she ripped off her soiled clothing while Agneta and the other maids brought in water, and filled the wooden tub in the corner. She thought with anger of her brother's mistress, the last in a long line. Not even remarkably pretty; but the poverty-stricken Lord of San Giorgio could afford no better.

The soap she used to clean herself was not even scented, but from the kitchens. The water was tepid, and she shivered in it. There was no liquid perfume or aromatic oil to pour in to sweeten it. The chroniclers— Plutarch, was it?—said that Cleopatra bathed in asses' milk to make herself more beautiful. Perhaps if she, Bianca di San Giorgio, bathed in it, she too might become beautiful and alluring, and reduce the Sultan of Turkey to gibbering desire as Cleopatra had seduced Antony, causing him to lose his empire.

Despite her annoyance at herself and at impossibly perfect Piero, this brought on a fit of the irreverent giggles, for her satiric wit was never far from the surface, and embraced herself as well as others. And wishes are horses and beggars will ride, she ended, as she vigorously soaped herself. Face it, Bianca, you are doomed to be a dark-eyed, brown girl whatever God does to give you proper curves—that is, if he ever does, and your temper will never improve, as both Father Luca and Bernardo have often prophesied.

Agneta, never short of words, alternately lamented the lord's poverty, and her charge's lack of charms; she had been Bianca's nurse before she became her waiting woman.

'So thin you are, so flat. Why, they say this lord who is visiting is single, has made himself rich, despite his youth, and needs a wife. But, the Lord God be praised, he will want something to fill his arms, as well as his bed—and look at you.'

'No,' said Bianca, standing up, and waiting for Agneta to raise the threadbare towel to put it about her as she climbed out, 'do not look at me, I beg of you. And as for the Lord Piero, I would not marry him if he were as beautiful as an angel, as rich as Croesus, and went on his bended knees twenty times a day to ask me, so do not speak of him either.'

Agneta sniffed again. 'Well, well, perhaps some day. . .' she began, and left the despairing sentence unfinished. And then, 'Perhaps if you had not spent so much time with Father Luca, learning your letters, reading Latin, reading Greek, you might have turned into a woman sooner. Why should a woman read Greek? What point is there in a woman knowing such things? You will never need to read—that will not help you in bed, or in the kitchen, either.'

She had lamented at the priest in similar vein, and he had replied in his gentle way, 'The lady must have something in her life. Her mind is sharp. It needs occupation.'

After that she had taken her lamentations to Bernardo, and he had listened wearily to her complaints: 'The priest is ruining her, Latin he teaches her, and other heathen things not fit for a woman to know.'

'So long as she can do all the things the Lady of San Giorgio ought to do, I do not care,' he had snapped at her. 'And, so long as he keeps her quiet, he may teach her Hebrew and the Black Arts. She nags me else.'

For Bianca was like his conscience, a clear eye for all her youth, which saw how idle he was, how self-indulgent, lacked courage, stamina, cunning, all the virtues which an Italian nobleman needed to survive and keep his lordship in the harsh world of the city states. He had only hung on to San Giorgio because it was too poor to attract the wolves around him. Piero de'

Manfredini was such a one, Bianca knew, as, rejecting Agneta's complaints, she allowed her to try on her thin person the rich brocade, tarnished with age. But, of course, it did not fit her, was too small, had been made for a San Giorgio lady years ago, and was thoroughly out of fashion into the bargain.

Finally, Bianca wrenched the gown from Agneta's hands, ripped it down the back, and said briskly and practically, 'Sew me into it, and I shall wear a lace shawl to hide the stitches. No, for the sweet Lord's sake, do not argue with me; I must wear something, and this is all I have.'

So Agneta did as she was told, and, staring at herself in the mirror afterwards, Bianca thought that she looked little better than the scrub woman Piero de' Manfredini had thought her, but it would have to do. Turning herself about for Agneta to add final useless touches to her inadequate toilette, she heard a rapping on the door. It was Raimondo, Bernardo's steward, and the moment that Agneta admitted him he began haranguing her, and she was screeching back at him. He was imperturbable. 'The lord wishes his sister at table. She is inconveniently late. He has noble guests present, needs her, at once.'

Bianca walked to the door, put her hands on her hips and admonished Raimondo, 'Tell the lord that if he honoured his sister with decent garb she would not be so long in the preparing of herself. I will be with him presently.' She allowed Agneta to put a jewelled comb in her thick hair. I look ridiculous. A child dressed as a woman—will I ever have a proper body? Why was I not a boy if this is all I am to be? ran through her mind as she left the room, toiled up the stairs, Agneta attending her, and wailing behind her,

'Your stocking has a hole in it, your slippers are a disgrace.'

'Sweet Jesu, keep quiet,' she finally snapped, as she pushed open the heavy oak doors to her brother's private quarters where they were dining.

She had spoken so loudly that *he* must have heard her. Bernardo was lounging in his great chair—the one with arms, and the insignia of Saint George, San Giorgio, on its back, a faded red cross and a lance—the lance of the saint—embroidered on it. There were carved SGs and lances all over the tower, remnants of the days when the family had been rich and powerful, owned all the land as far as the eye could see from the top of the tower itself, and much further, instead of a mere few plots outside of the town. Power and wealth all gone, and the San Giorgios, too. Only Bernardo and herself were left.

Piero de' Manfredini was standing before the big stone fireplace, empty now, and filled with early summer flowers thrust into a copper urn, tarnished like everything else in San Giorgio.

Early though it was, it was apparent that Bernardo had already been drinking, the goblet seldom having left his hand. Piero's was before him on the table, full. He had thrown off his cloak to reveal a golden falcon, a ring in its beak, embroidered on the front of his tunic. His eyes raked Bianca as she entered, and amusement made his mouth curl up as he recognised the scrub woman from the outer hall.

Beside him Bernardo looked even more slovenly and careless than usual. His doublet was stained and greasy, his hair unwashed, his linen, as usual, yellow where it was not grey. 'My sister——' He gestured at Bianca, not even doing her the honour of rising. 'Late, as ever. Bianca, this is Ser Piero de' Manfredini, Lord of I forget where.'

He always had a nice line in insult. Was a master of that, if of nothing else.

'Astra,' said Piero, his slight smile never faltering. 'No matter. Lordships come and go.' And that was a warning, if you cared to take it as such, thought Bianca, and a rebuke to Bernardo, too. He added, bowing slightly to her as he spoke, 'Your sister and I have already met. You have had a bath, I see.'

Oh! How dared he remind her of her dirty face and hands, that she had been scrubbing the floor when he arrived? Her gown felt even tighter and more ridiculous under that cool stare, his mouth curling again at the sight of her, as it had done in the hall. But he came forward, all elegant gracefulness, like a great hunting cat, took the hand which hung limp by her side—she had not even the presence of mind to offer it to him as she ought—kissed it, and said, 'Your servant, lady,' but the blue eyes told her quite a different tale as he dwelt a little on the word servant, before letting go of her hand. She wrenched it back as though she had been stung, and saw the mouth twitch again. Did he see everything?

'Have you nothing better to wear than that?' said Bernardo kindly.

'No, or I would wear it,' returned Bianca furiously, conscious of what a scarecrow she looked beside the cool perfection of the man before her. She had never before minded how she appeared—clothes were merely things to keep you decent, not to decorate yourself with. Why did she mind so much now?

'Ser Piero is here on business.'

'He is?' said Bianca. 'And what business is that?'

'Nothing for little girls to know,' said her brother, grinning infuriatingly at her, and wishing that his sister were big and brassy, a counter he could use in his feeble games to revive San Giorgio's power. Only yesterday he had looked at her and said, 'Sweet God, do you not eat, that you are so plain and scrawny? Were you a beauty like Isabella da Trente I could scrape a dowry together and sell you to some lord who wanted a bride, but who would want you? Even ugly old Marucci, desperate for a wife, laughed in my face when I offered you to him. No taste for boys, he said, or women who looked like them. Who do you take after, I ask myself? Our mother was beautiful—God rest her soul—and our father not unhandsome,' and he had subsided into drunken sobbing.

He waved a hand then shouted to the steward at the door, 'My sister has deigned to appear. Tell Jacopo to bring in the food.' And to de' Manfredini, 'Sit, man, and drink up some of the good wine. You have scarce touched a drop. Even falcons must drink, I presume?'

Piero shrugged, waited for Bianca to seat herself, Agneta standing behind her, before sitting in an armchair not quite so magnificent as Bernardo's, the rest of the company following suit once he was at table. His wine, Bianca noticed, remained untouched on the cloth before him. Whoever was going to get drunk that night, it seemed unlikely Messer Piero would be among the number. She disliked excess, and this should have pleased her, but in some mysterious way merely served to add to the count against him.

To Bianca's surprise the food was good. Far better than their normal fare, and the wine was also of the finest—and where *that* had come from she could not guess. When he began to eat their visitor produced a small silver implement from the purse at his belt and used it to hold his meat while he cut it with the knife which Bernardo had provided.

Bianca could not prevent herself from staring at it. He saw her looking—she was correct, he saw everything—and said with a smile and a touch of pity, 'A useful tool, lady, is it not?'

The pity infuriated her, but the curiosity and interest with which Bianca always faced the world gripped her. 'I see that it keeps the grease from your fingers and clothes, Messer Piero. What is it called?'

'A fork,' he said. 'It is a new thing.'

'The old ways are best,' said Bernardo patronisingly.

Stick in the mud will always stay there, thought Bianca nastily. Piero de' Manfredini made Bernardo look even more shopsoiled than ever, and provoked her own shrewishness—which didn't need provoking, seeing that it was always with her.

The meal wore on. She could not prevent herself from

eating everything put before her with the greatest gusto, if not to say greed, from the boar's meat, which was the crown of the meal, to the marchpane sweetmeats at the dinner's end. She was unaware that Piero, who saw everything, saw that, too. It was pitifully evident that the lord's sister seldom dined on such good fare. Bianca was too busy enjoying herself to notice his interest in her. Perhaps, she thought, taking yet another sweet, if I ate like this every day I might grow a bosom and a bottom, and she licked her sticky fingers vigorously. Mustn't waste any of the good food, she told herself— the Lord God knew when she might get any again.

Watching her unashamed pleasure, Piero disguised the pity he felt for the lord's sister, a pity he had felt from the moment she had walked in and he had learned that the half-starved-looking scrub woman was the lady of the tower. By her manner and demeanour he knew that she would fiercely reject it, and the dislike he had for the boorish Lord of San Giorgio, which he had felt from the moment he had met him, grew even greater as he watched the lord's plain sister, and guessed, correctly, that she rarely ate as well as this. His impatience with Bernardo increased, particularly as he was now also aware that his errand here was a wasted one.

'And you are still serving Florence, Messer Piero?' remarked Bernardo, mouth full. 'Good paymasters, but fussy, I have heard.'

Piero inclined his head. 'True,' he said, 'and they inflict a commissary on you, who not only wants to keep his accounts straight, but demands a share in battle strategy, too. Diplomacy as well as martial arts are needed to wage war today.'

Bernardo laughed. He had asked the Golden Falcon to visit him for a number of reasons. They ranged from an ill-formed wish to raise a small band of his own to hire out to him, to a more ambitious design to arrange for him to recover the San Giorgios' lost lands, payment to be made when they had been recovered.

But he, why had he come? What had brought the Lord of Astra, Florence's *condottiero*, to San Giorgio? Why had he left his *condotta* to his captains? Something had drawn him, but what? This was a question which his captains had also asked themselves, but dared not ask him. They knew their leader too well for that. More than once he had come out with some scheme which seemed mad in the telling, but in the execution had come to seem quite plain and reasonable.

In the meantime he sat at table and made small talk. Lodovico beside him was silent, except when Piero called on him, as he did once, for information, or to jog his memory.

'But we are boring the lady,' he said smoothly, wishing above all to silence Bernardo's flow of ill-informed gossip with which he hoped to impress his visitor.

'No,' said Bianca truthfully, 'I like to know about the great world,' and then, in a burst of confidence, 'I should like to be part of it. San Giorgio is such a backwater these days.'

Bernardo glared at her. 'Only to you, sister,' he said. 'The great world is not for little girls.' And he continued to drink heavily, calling on his guest to do the like. Bianca, always observant, particularly so once the food had been removed, to be replaced by bowls of fruit, noticed that although Piero's wine disappeared, and his goblet was often refilled, it seemed to have remarkably little effect on him. Either he had an extremely hard head or by some means he was contriving to dispose of his wine without drinking it—or only a little.

So convinced was Bianca of Piero's villainous cunning that she was sure it was the latter—but how? Watch how she might, she could not catch him doing anything untoward. He saw her eyes on him, gave her a smile of such sweetness that she blinked in astonishment and went hot all over, while he raised his goblet to her, and said, 'A toast to the Lady of San Giorgio.'

'And who might she be,' guffawed Bernardo drunkenly, 'seeing that I am not married? Oh, you mean Bianca,' he added in some surprise, following Piero's gaze. 'Yes, I suppose you might call her that.'

This was almost too much for Bianca. She had avoided drinking very much herself—wine always had a disastrous effect on her if she was foolish enough to overindulge. She rose, and said with as much dignity as she could muster, 'I ask your leave to retire, brother.'

He waved a lordly hand. 'Aye. You may go, sister. Messer Piero will excuse you, I am sure. He must be used to livelier company than yours, and we have matters of moment to discuss, not fit for little girls' ears.' And his burst of laughter at his own wit brought the colour to her cheeks.

Well, one thing was certain, Bernardo thought, he would not be offering her to Messer Piero. Such an elegant sprig would hardly be tempted by a starveling scrap like Bianca.

Piero rose as Bianca left. His manners were as perfect as the rest of him. Courtly without being servile, and they exposed Bernardo di San Giorgio for the boor he was—or that drink and disappointment had made of him.

Bianca, Agneta behind her, walked steadily from the room. She turned at the door and looked back at the table.

Some trick of the candlelight had given Piero a golden halo around his head where its luminescence caught his hair. As though her gaze had touched him physically he swung his head around, and gave her, once again, the brilliant smile which she had seen earlier. It was something, she later discovered, which he rarely offered anyore, but he was offering it to her.

It had more effect on her than his earlier careless and parting blow when she had been in the outer hall. It was as though someone had struck her, hard, in the stomach, so that she felt faint, as though her clothes had fallen off, and an extraordinary tickling and throbbing sensation invaded her whole body. She shivered, shook her head, tried to recover herself. Lord God! I must be going mad that a smiling man whom I dislike should have such a strange effect on me, she thought.

She was so shaken that she ignored Agneta's dooming and wailings about the unsatisfactory state of her body, her clothes, her conversation, her everything, and stumbled up to bed in a daze. And once in bed, she was deaf to all scoldings, warnings and admonitions, only knew that for the first time she really, truly wished that she was incredibly beautiful, was dressed to perfection, with a body to match, and had all the talents of Venus, the goddess of love, and Pallas Athene, the goddess of wisdom, combined, so that she could dance all over impossibly perfect Piero, having rendered him mad with desire for her, and he would have no answer to make to her, because she would be even more perfect than he!

CHAPTER TWO

'So WHAT did we come to San Giorgio for, then?' said Lodovico to his commander, who sat at a table in his room, drawing a neat map of San Giorgio with a reed pen. Piero was, as usual, immaculately dressed for the day, early though it was.

'Soundings,' said Piero, without raising his head from his work.

'Soundings!' said Lodovico. 'You could have sent Van Eyck, or Bisticci to do that. Why come yourself? All the world knows that Bernardo di San Giorgio, Lord of Nothing, has nothing to offer.'

Piero said, his voice equable, still without looking up, 'Tell me, Lodovico, are you my commander now? What further advice from the depths of your generalship do you have to offer?'

'I speak only common sense,' replied the big man stiffly, walking away to the window-slit, to stare out at the sunlit landscape below. 'It is not like you to waste time.'

'No,' agreed Piero. 'Then why assume that that is what I am doing?'

His work with the map finished, he put down the pen. 'Do you have any further gems of wisdom to offer? If so, I should like to hear them.'

'Only that I expect that we shall be leaving early today. Shall I tell the men to make ready?'

'That is an expectation unlikely to be fulfilled. Do I look like a man dressed to make a longish journey on horseback?'

Lodovico looked at his captain's splendid appearance, and sighed.

'Hardly. When do you propose to leave, then?'

'Since I have not yet decided, I cannot yet inform you. Tell me, Lodovico. What troubles you? My interest in the lord, or the lord's sister?'

This last came out so drily that Lodovico sighed again. No deceiving Messer Piero about anything. He should have known that.

'I can scarce think that you are interested in either of them. But something brought you here, and now something keeps you.'

Piero yawned. He even managed to do so elegantly, and his reply was as sharp as the voice in which he made it was indifferent.

'This is a singularly pointless conversation we are having. I am as well aware as you are that we need to rejoin the *condotta* and proceed to Trani to besiege it on behalf of our Florentine masters. I am also aware that the Florentine commissary, Bruschini, will expect us to dance to his tune, and will be awaiting us with impatience. I will tell you that part of my reason for staying is to make him wait. He must learn that I rule my *condotta*, and no one else. Certainly not a book-keeping treasurer whose sole purpose in living is to save money, regardless of the success of my campaign. I will keep him informed of what I think he needs to know, and nothing more. An army cannot have two masters— the first rule in battle strategy, and the last. Will that do? For the rest you must control your impatience.'

'A dangerous strategy with both Bruschini and Florence——' began Lodovico.

Piero threw down his pen, which he had picked up again to make some minor alterations to his work, and waved the map about to hasten drying. 'If I had wanted to avoid danger I should have remained in the monastery, and stayed on my knees all my life, except, of course, when I arose to sing hymns about peace on earth and goodwill to all men. War and diplomacy are about danger. In fact, they *are* danger. Do not presume too much upon our relationship, Lodovico. I have no mind to give daily lectures to all and sundry on every scheme I contemplate. What you need to know, I will tell you. As for the men, I shall probably send them off later today under Filippo Montone. It is time he had a little independent leadership. Let him begin by taking his small troop safely back to the main army. I hope you approve, my lord and master?'

Lodovico bowed to the inevitable then turned to go. Piero's beautiful voice behind him stopped him at the door. 'And Lodovico,' it said, 'you are wrong about one thing to do with our visit here, quite wrong. I will leave you to discover what it is. It should enliven the rest of your stay here for you.'

Bianca awoke in the morning wondering why she felt so annoyed—and then she remembered. It was *him*, Piero de' Manfredini, who had cast a blight on her whole life. She did not trouble very much about being poor, plain, badly dressed Bianca di San Giorgio so long as there was no one around to see her. But that such a piece of superior manhood as Piero de' Manfredini should arrive to destroy her unthinking acceptance of her own lack of attractions was more than a high-spirited sixteen-year-old—just—could stand.

The worst thing was that it made all Bernardo and Agneta's sighings about her shortcomings abundantly reasonable. Worst of all was that she was not even yet a woman, and at such an advanced age, too, God having withheld her courses as well as a proper female's body, and having given all the beauty which she could have done with to impossibly perfect Piero as well. It was enough to curdle milk.

And after breaking her fast, and back to black bread again—no fine fare when he was not about—there he was in the outer courtyard talking to Lodovico, so splendid it was enough to make a poor girl want to spit. And although he was in deep and confidential conversation with his lieutenant he must have had eyes in the back of his head, damn him, because he said, 'God send you a good day, Madonna Bianca,' to her before he had the courtesy to turn it.

It was a pity that he had to look at her at all, because the best she and Agneta could do was dress her in her faded brown taffeta, clean but shabby, too short and the hem showing her ankles. She looked more like a servant than ever, an overgrown girl of twelve, to boot. Impossibly perfect Piero was polite, but she could have sworn that she saw his shapely mouth twitch at the sight of her.

Her annoyance grew to such a height that before she could stop herself she said, not at all courteously, not at all as the proper Lady of San Giorgio should have done, but savagely, 'I see that you are still with us, Messer Piero. You have not yet left.'

His reply was as gravely polite as her own comment had been rude, but two-edged as well, another habit she would come, in time, to recognise.

'And you, *madonna*, you are still with us?'

'Naturally I am here,' she snapped. 'This is my home.'

One eyebrow lifted and he smiled, not the brilliant one of last night, but a mere sketch of a smile, hardly there. Ah, *Dio*, how could he be so disgustingly handsome, so exquisitely turned out, everything about him in place, and in perfect order, the superb clothing complementing the superb body?

This morning he was in court dress. He was wearing over it a houppelande—an overgown or coat—of sapphire-blue, the full sleeves ending in tight cuffs of ermine fur, its deep folds falling to the ground. It was girdled with a belt of hammered silver, decorated with sapphires, as was his dagger, and purse. The houppelande's front opening revealed a lightly padded doublet of a deeper blue, ornamented, of course, with buttons of sapphire and silver. Also revealed were a pair of shapely legs, one clad in blue hose, the other in blue striped with silver. The garter below his right knee was again of silver, set with sapphires. Winking and trembling, yet another sapphire set in silver dangled from his ear, which the ruby had adorned yesterday. His golden curls were not loose as they had been last night, but were swept back, confined by a silver net, decorated with— yes, face it, Bianca, more sapphires. It was all enough to make a poor girl grind her teeth.

Bianca ground her teeth. Particularly when he said, his voice even sweeter, 'Yes, indeed, *madonna*, I am well aware that you live here. But I had supposed that you would be about your scrub woman's duties. The tower's stairs are badly in need of your attentions.'

Were they, indeed? Bianca's eyes flashed fire at him, her whole body vibrated with anger. How dared he remind her of yesterday? 'You are impertinent, Messer Piero.'

'But accurate, *madonna*. At least grant me that. To be truthful is always my aim.'

Oh, and what a lie that was! Everyone, but everyone, knew of his reputation as a trickster. Bianca waved a small hand, noticed that it was already grubby from fruitless attempts to scour her own quarters a little, and tried to hide it from the spotlessly clean monster before her. 'I would not grant you anything, Ser Piero, but permission to leave San Giorgio and its fief.' That should silence him, but no.

'Oh, I hardly need your permission to do that, lady,' he said, his faint smile still in place, the sapphire in his ear shivering and shaking in the morning light. 'I shall go in my own good time, as is my habit.'

'But not in San Giorgio's good time,' she said. 'Your greedy followers would eat us bare.'

'But you,' he returned, 'would seem to enjoy the good food your brother allows us. And besides it is hardly difficult to empty your pantry from what I have seen. Dirty stairs and a dearth of good food appear to go together.'

'Fine clothes and bad manners make good partners,

too,' Bianca snapped back sharply, both intrigued and appalled at her own nastiness.

'Not in my experience,' said Piero de' Manfredini in the manner of one handing down a judgement from on high. 'Poor clothing and even worse manners appear to surpass them if your own behaviour is anything to go by.'

There was a dreadful silence after this home truth until Bianca, stamping one ill-shod foot, angrily blazed out, 'Oh, you are impossible, Messer Piero, quite impossible.'

'Why, lady,' he replied, and his smile was sweet poison, 'I do but take my cue from you, as a good guest should.'

Now what could one say to that? She had a horrid desire to sob, to jump up and down, scream at him, hit him, rip the beautiful clothes from his back. The more she said, the worse it was. He had an answer for everything, and every answer nastier than the one before. She bit back treacherous tears. She would not cry before him, she would not. She would see him dead first. Oh, damn him, damn him to every one of Messer Dante's Hells. Let him wander among them, and she would not lift so much as a finger to save him from the eternal fires. And Messer Satan could prod him with his sharpest pitchfork and she, Bianca, would only cheer him on. Oh, the very idea made her feel better. It did. Yes, it did.

She had no idea how wonderfully she was transformed as these dreadful thoughts shot like lightning through her brain, so that the man before her saw a glimpse of what she might look like if properly fed and cared for. Her head held high, as though she were a very princess, she said, in the haughtiest tones she could assume, 'I think I had better leave you, Messer Piero de' Manfredini, before I breach hospitality's laws.'

'Oh, quite,' he said. 'I do so agree with you. Good manners are the key to a civilised life. So happy to learn that you propose to acquire some.'

May the good God grant her patience! And if only she were four inches taller, even more improbably beautiful than he, had a sweet nature, a kind brother, a vast fortune and a gentle tongue, she would show him—what? Nothing, no, she would show him nothing, not if he fell on his knees before her, this very minute, demanding pardon for so insulting her.

At this further unlikely thought she almost burst out laughing herself, but instead swept him a perfect curtsy—except that she caught her foot in the dangling hem of her dreadful dress, only just managing to prevent herself from landing on her nose in front of him at the last minute—all of which ruined what would otherwise have been a dignified exit.

'You were unkind to the child,' said Lodovico mildly. 'Your tongue is sharp this morning.'

'Oh, she would not thank me for kindness,' said Piero shrewdly, watching the small but gallant figure mount the stairs. 'She has her pride, you see, has decided that she dislikes me, and I preserved that pride for her, by confirming her dislike. Softness would destroy her. She is not accustomed to it.'

Lodovico thought that his lord, as usual, showed a painfully accurate understanding of other people and their behaviour, and not for the first time wondered how much distress it brought him to have so few illusions about anything. 'But the little one was near to tears,' he said.

'Yes, but,' said Piero, 'she will comfort herself all day with the memory that I did not set her down, and that she gave as good as she got. She is worth ten of the fat brother.' He looked thoughtful as he finished speaking, turned away, and walked slowly up the stairs himself.

Lodovico sighed for the tenth time that morning. What maggot was working now in his unpredictable lord's brain? he wondered. For all they stood to gain in San Giorgio, the leader of the company of the Golden Falcon might as well leave within the hour. But Piero had already said no to that, and one had to grant that his judgement was rarely wrong, and never perverse.

Had the Lord of San Giorgio's sister been beautiful, then he could have understood the delay. Messer Piero was no womaniser, but he did have an eye for beauty, and most women had an eye for him. Surely the Falcon could not be stooping to the poor little sparrow with her drab plumage, which even the brave spirit beneath it could not lighten?

He shrugged. Deviousness was second nature to Messer Piero, and only a fool would waste time trying to anticipate what he might later care to explain—which would then seem quite clear, however odd it had appeared earlier.

Bianca found that Bernardo did not look at all like Piero. He was heavy-eyed, yawning and bad-tempered. He had thrown his dirty clothes on anyhow, and greeted Bianca with surly rudeness. 'No wonder de' Manfredini was happy to see you leave last night. Nothing in you to attract him.'

'You are not so remarkably beautiful yourself, brother, that you can afford to taunt me for my lack of looks,' said Bianca reasonably, but tactlessly. 'And I have no desire to please Messer Piero. He is quite pleased enough with himself as it is.'

Bernardo acknowledged the truth of this statement with a grunt, and despite the early hour poured himself a bumper of wine, and added, 'I also thought of offering him you, as a bride—until I saw his expression when you came in. They say he has women everywhere—and all beautiful.'

Of course they are all beautiful. He would settle for nothing less, the lustful beast, thought Bianca coarsely, but said aloud, 'Well, I am no catch for him, that's for sure. He could hardly boast about my beauty, and as my dowry is almost non-existent he couldn't use it to help pay his *condotta* if his next campaign should fail.'

'I also told him that the sack of Trani would provide him with enough, on top of what the bankers might lend me, to fund a campaign by him to recover the San Giorgio lands for me from Marucci and the rest who have stolen them. A useful task for an enterprising young captain, one might think, with lots of ransom money from Marucci, even if the rest are not so rich. He refused that, too, damn him.'

'The bankers?' almost shrieked Bianca. 'You mean the Florentine leeches. The money-lenders. They would take San Giorgio for themselves if you failed to keep up even the first repayment. I am astonished at you, brother, and surprised that you should think de' Manfredini would show any interest in such a shady and poverty-stricken enterprise, knowing what he can command already from Florence—aye, and Milan and Venice, too.'

'Nag, nag, nag,' groaned Bernardo, as all this unwanted truth from his young sister cascaded about his head. 'Surely the man is prepared to take a little risk occasionally. He would not be a *condottiero* else.'

'A little risk. . .' began Bianca hotly, until her brother banged the table with his fist, setting the dishes rattling, as he roared,

'Enough. I will not be lectured at by flat-chested girl-children who know nothing of anything, let alone of war. And what a ridiculous nonsense that is these days. It has turned into a business, run by money-lenders and commissaries, and young sprigs like Piero think more of *that* than of gaining honour on the battlefield.'

'Money is what Messer Piero is after gaining, not honour,' snarled Bianca, who rightly thought that she knew more about everything than Bernardo, and that that was not a difficult feat, either. 'All the world knows that the Falcon besieges Trani because Trani's lord, Uberti, failed in his payments to the bankers there for the loans he raised, and now they have hired the Falcon to take Uberti's lands from him to discourage others from defaulting. I sometimes think that Florence will not rest until she owns all Tuscany. And the Falcon grows rich on the money they pay him. And where is he now, this shining morning?'

Bernardo almost spat. 'He was up with the sun, the steward said, and ate in the kitchen, he and his men. Thank the Lord, I do not have to feed the whole of his army as well. It is camped at some distance from here, on Dolci's fief, and he is bearing the expense at the moment for what he hopes to gain from the Florentines when Trani is taken. De' Manfredini's energy is indecent, and his appetite matches it—how he stays so slim, I do not know. Bad enough to feed him and his immediate staff. Your own appetite these days is monstrous, judging by the way you carried on last night.' He spoke as though he grudged her every mouthful she ate.

'I shall never improve my flat chest if you continue to groan over all I eat,' returned Bianca vigorously. 'And when does our hungry visitor depart, may I ask?'

'Tomorrow, he seems to think, and why not today, I ask myself, if he is not to oblige me? But as I invited him here I cannot turn him out, in all decency. I cannot imagine why he lingers. Tonight we shall dine together again, and—who knows?—some profit may yet accrue to us.'

'Not if your usual luck holds, and his is as good as rumour says it is. Although, personally,' she added thoughtfully, 'I think a man makes his own luck. I suppose he is as impossibly perfect at that as at everything else he does.'

Her brother watched her absently pick up the bread and begin to gnaw vigorously at it, hunger overcoming her dislike of its coarseness. His expression was as glum as a man's could be. 'You need not dine with us this evening,' he said. 'One less to find good food for, and I have no doubt that he will not miss you.'

This speech, with its mixture of sexual jealousy and brotherly spite, was almost too much for Bianca. She rose, furious. What earthly use was impossibly perfect Piero if she could not gain so much as a meal out of his unwelcome presence?

'You are welcome to his company, and his silent shadow's as well,' she said. 'I'm sure I don't want to sit looking at such a paragon any longer than I need. He reminds me of everything that I am not and never will be, unless the good Lord changes his mind and makes me blonde, buxom, and——'

'Good-tempered,' finished her brother. 'And if all this fury and offering of unwanted advice is the result of Father Luca's teaching you Latin, then you had better have remained ignorant. On second thoughts you may eat in the kitchen this evening, and have an early night. No candles so that you may take the good Father's books to bed with you. I shall tell Agneta to set you to useful stitchery. That should keep a proud stomach down. You may think yourself lucky you eat at all. I shall be thinking of nunneries for you next.'

A nunnery? The thought was so awful that Bianca managed to walk back to her room like a lady, and vow to be good and quiet in future. Perhaps old Marucci might be preferable to a nunnery, but face it, Bianca, face it—even that dried-up old stick does not want you. Oh, how I wish I had been born a boy, and then I could have joined Messer Piero's *condotta*, and made a career for myself, and no one would complain that I was flat-chested—they would expect it!

'Well, at least,' said Bianca to Agneta's wailings, as they descended the tower's stairs, 'it is something of a boon I had not expected. One more night's eating in that dress we cobbled together, and I should be ruined for life. Besides, if I had to put up with another meal with his superb lordship of Astra, I should expire of an access of bile between a too tight bodice and contemplation of such a favourite of fortune.'

'Pity it is that your brother is right about one thing,'

sighed Agneta. 'You haven't the looks to tame the Falcon, nor the money, either. Plainness such as yours can only be redeemed by money or power, preferably both.'

'Sweet-suffering Saints!' exclaimed Bianca at the top of her voice. 'Has everyone in the world but one mission and that to remind me constantly of my own lack of looks?' She had turned towards Agneta as she spoke with the result that she walked straight into the ineffable Piero, who, with his usual dexterity, kept his own balance and prevented her from taking them both head-long down the stairs.

To make matters worse, if one could make them worse, he had undoubtedly heard her last complaint to Agneta, and she had no doubt that his twitching mouth and a certain gleam in his eye could be attributed to what he had overheard.

'Your servant, lady. I trust that you came to no harm?' he said, as gravely as he could. Lodovico behind him had also checked himself, Bianca noticed savagely. His master's shadow, as usual.

'No,' Bianca snarled at him—well, at least he knew now that she had no illusions about her own lack of attractions. 'I thank you, Messer Piero. You are as handy as one of the tumblers at our annual fair.'

'Oh, hardly,' he returned smoothly, 'else we should have turned a mutual somersault at the end.'

'*You* might,' said Bianca, 'I should certainly not. Most unladylike.'

'I would not have thought that a consideration to trouble you, lady,' he returned, his face quite straight.

'No?' said Bianca, still drawing on reserves of nasti-ness which she had not known she possessed. 'But, then, one supposes you know little of how true ladies behave.'

'You would care to instruct me?' he enquired, head on one side. 'I might find it useful—if ever I encountered one, that is.'

Bianca could hear Agneta clucking behind her, 'Oh,

my lady, consider your words. . .' or some such nonsense, could see Lodovico's impassive face behind *his* amused one. Was there nothing she could think of which would silence that impertinent tongue, take the smile from his eye?

'A true gentleman always——' she began.

'Oh, then, that explains all. You cannot mean me,' he interrupted her rapidly. 'I make no claim to gentility, *madonna*. You see how well matched we are—you being no lady and I being no gentleman. The Lord God must have meant us to come together.'

'The Lord God made a mistake if he did,' said Bianca awfully, her tongue running even further away with her. 'We are not matched at all in any way that I can see, in face, or in fortune, or. . .anything.' She ran lamely out of words. Not so Piero. Of course, he wouldn't. Not he.

'When you have achieved my years,' he returned gravely, as though, Bianca thought, fascinated, he were ninety at the very least, 'you might come to a different judgement.'

'But by then you will be older, too,' said Bianca with triumphant and perfect logic. 'So you will think differently as well. Father Luca would not give much for *that* argument.'

'But I am not arguing with Father Luca,' replied Piero reasonably, 'only with your good self. Do but consider. . .'

'No, I refuse to consider anything,' said Bianca, raising her voice again to stifle Agneta's wails, which were now redoubling in vigour. 'How can we be engaging in such a ridiculous conversation and on the stairs as well? Your poor lieutenant must be tired of standing behind you, and Agneta is fretting behind me, so. . .'

'Oh, dear,' said Piero, a look of the most exquisite concern on his face. 'I had quite forgot Lodovico. Tell me, Lodovico,' he added, inclining his head gravely in his lieutenant's direction, 'are you tired of Madonna Bianca's conversation? Myself, I find it totally fascinating. You, of course, may differ. Pray tell us and relieve the lady of her worries concerning you.'

Lodovico's reply was made as plainly and firmly as though this mad question were his lord's most sensible demand. He was obviously, thought Bianca, rage nearly strangling her, used to the vagaries of the popinjay before him.

'Why, lord,' he said, 'I, too, find Madonna Bianca's remarks of great interest.'

'There, you see,' said Piero triumphantly. 'Dismiss from your mind any worries that you might be boring Lodovico. You were saying?' And he inclined his head towards her, such a ludicrous expression of interest on his face that, despite herself, Bianca began to laugh, quite unrestrainedly. She could not remember when she had last experienced such a feeling of pure joy. The silliness of the whole thing, his refusal to take her seriously, to react as everyone else in the tower did when she had a tantrum, overwhelmed her.

She was so overcome that she had to sit down on the stairs, lest she fall down them. To her astonishment, Piero sat down beside her, leaving Lodovico and a rigidly disapproving Agneta standing.

'Come,' he said, as though conversing while seated on the stairs were the most natural thing in the world, 'that's better. I thought that you were always in a state of dislike of everyone and everything. A good laugh is a great restorative, I always think.'

Bianca stopped laughing long enough to say spiritedly—he was not going to win *her* over—'You do? Perhaps you should set up as the tower's jester.' She heard Agneta start wailing again at this riposte.

'Oh,' he returned, as though this were the most reasonable remark in the word, 'I must remember that advice if I start losing too many battles. I have often wondered what might be left for me if the soldier's trade failed. Do you recommend that I practise a little?'

'You hardly seem to need it,' replied Bianca repressively. 'It seems to come naturally to you.' And she smiled sweetly at the handsome face looking so sillily earnest as she came out with these nonsensical comments.

Seen near to—she had never been so close to him before—he was overwhelming. She could see how carefully he had shaved—so unlike careless Bernardo—how the fine black eyebrows arched, how there were laughter-lines already about his mouth and eyes. And the oddest sensations began to overtake her.

A curl had escaped from the net which confined his hair, and she wanted to lean forward and gently slide it back. His mouth, near to, was quite soft, and she wanted to put a finger out, and stroke it. And his eyes—sweet Lady, his eyes!—so blue they were like the lake near San Giorgio, and she wanted to drown in them. She found herself leaning towards him involuntarily.

'Yes, Bianca?' he said softly. 'What is it you wish to say? Knowing you, I am sure that you wish to say something.' And his whole face was teasing her, and it was as though they were quite alone on the steps. Oh, why was she such a poor thing? Were she not, he might take her seriously.

'Why are we sitting here?' was all that she could find to answer. She was quite dazed.

'What a sensible remark,' he said approvingly. 'I was about to ask the same thing. Most uncomfortable, but in the interests of truth I ought to remind you that you sat down first. Seeing that I am trying so hard to be a gentleman, I considered that I ought to follow the lady's lead, and sit down myself. Stairs, I find, are rather uncomfortable for long-legged man—and there I go again; I should not have said that. You see, we are a pair after all. We both speak our minds without thought.'

Oh, what a lie, Bianca thought, standing up, rather reluctantly. It was quite plain that everything he said was most carefully considered. He followed suit, holding his hand out to assist her, and Agneta, once she was on her feet again, said, 'Oh, Lady Bianca, will you never behave properly? What would your lord brother say to conversations with a man sitting on the stairs?'

'What he says to everything I do,' said Bianca briskly. 'Something disapproving.'

'I will explain, should you be reprimanded,' offered Piero courteously, 'that it was all my fault, and that I gained the most useful advice from you. I see the tower possesses no jester. I must remember that, should I require employment.'

'Oh, you are quite ridiculous!' exclaimed Bianca, annoyed all over again now that she was free of his disturbing nearness. 'I bid you good morning, Messer Piero, and a good day. I think that we are not likely to meet again, as I am forbidden dinner with you, and you are to leave tomorrow, which will be a good thing for my temper, if no one else's.'

It was quite useless, of course. He gave her the most elegant bow. 'A pity that, lady. I find your conversation stimulating. If this is to be our farewell, I wish you joy of the future, and a husband who will enjoy your ready wit.'

This time she managed to leave him without falling over her skirts or exploding with rage, but with, she considered, the utmost dignity, and 'Come, Agneta, my brother wishes us to do some plain sewing.' Although the whole effect was somewhat ruined by Agneta's trailing behind her, dooming away about the proper behaviour of young ladies, and how far Bianca was from ever achieving it.

Piero watched her go again, the expression on his face being one Lodovico recognised with a sinking heart. What mischief was he up to now? For what conceivable reason was he concerning himself with the Lord Bernardo's sister? He remembered the last barbed words Piero had thrown at him that morning, about his being wrong over his captain's plans, and wondered if they really included Bianca di San Giorgio, and if so, why?

He gave up his unequal struggle to read Piero's mind. After all, if he were as clever as Piero he would be leading the company of the Falcon, instead of merely being one of its lieutenants, and lucky to be that.

Bianca was not sure how really pleased she would be to see Piero depart. Halfway through the morning the small troop, or *bandiera*, which had accompanied him, rode out to rejoin the main army. Only Piero and Lodovico remained behind to spend another night at the tower before they, too, rode out to leave behind them only a memory.

Bianca watched them go. A dreadful hopeless spasm racked her as she thought that he would soon take away his impossible perfection, would no longer taunt and trip her with his tongue. She ought to be pleased at the prospect—and was horrified to discover that she wasn't.

What could be wrong with her? A strange restlessness filled her all day. It was as though she was waiting for something to happen, and could not think what it was. She actually went looking for him once—yes, she must be going mad—only to discover that he and Bernardo and several others had gone hawking. Lodovico, of course, had gone with him.

'Can you not sit still for an instant?' complained Agneta. 'I shall be glad when that man and his follower finally take their leave. Your behaviour is bad enough at the best of times. Since he arrived it has become impossible. I doubt me that you will ever learn enough to be offered to anyone in marriage. A meek carriage, a low voice, a tactful ear, a shoulder for a man to lean on, speak only when spoken to—you possess none of them.'

'And don't want any of them, that's for sure,' said Bianca shortly. 'If that is what married life is to be like, I think I might prefer the nunnery after all. Bad enough to have to get into bed with him, whoever he may be. To have to do all that, and carry his children as well—ugh!'

'Oh, you will feel quite differently when you are a

woman, and a handsome young man bends his knee before you to ask you in marriage,' said Agneta sentimentally, adding more practically, 'And when all that will happen, I'm sure I don't know.'

'Then don't talk about it,' said Bianca, sewing away at a great rate, never mind that the stitches were huge and that Agneta might want to unpick them—at least the work would soon be done, and then she could go to Father Luca and do something really interesting. She had tried her hand at illuminating—the old Father possessed a small talent for it—and she had painted a dear little letter A, with a dove flying through it, and the Father had exclaimed over it, and said, yet again, what a pity she wasn't a boy, since all her talents lay in the wrong direction for a girl.

She could only imagine what Bernardo would say if he knew the half of what the Father was teaching her: philosophy and divinity, how to write a beautiful script, as well as to paint and gild. But he said that he had never had such an apt pupil, and what a pleasure it was to teach someone willing again. The good Lord had sent her to comfort his old age.

Later that afternoon the Father watched her, as, tongue protruding between her lips, she painstakingly coloured a falcon, a golden one, which she had somehow entwined round the great letter F he had left undecorated in the Psalter he was illuminating. His eyes were not what they were, and on discovering Bianca's talent, quite accidentally, he had set her to work. He felt no compunction in deceiving the coarse heathen Bernardo was these days.

Bianca felt the Father watching her, looked up at him, and gave him the happy smile she so rarely gave anyone, gesturing at her work. 'Will it do, Father? I have been watching the birds so carefully to see exactly how their wings work, and what colours their feathers are. I remembered what you said—that one should look outwards, not inwards, to copy God's creatures from life, and not from the pages of another book.'

Her eyes shone as she spoke, and her whole appearance had changed. The restlessness and impatience which usually informed her had quite disappeared, been replaced by what the Father would have called a holy calm.

'Oh, I wish, I do wish that I could do nothing but this, all my life,' she declared, and she indicated her little drawing, 'And then, Father, I have quite another wish, and I hope that it is not a wicked one. And even if it is, it is never likely to be fulfilled. There are times when I should like to go out into the great world outside San Giorgio, and see how the people who inhabit it live. Am I wrong to be dissatisfied, to want not simply to live in this tower, and then leave it only to exchange it for another one? And then I think, Why am I so restless? Agneta tells me I am wrong, that I should be quiet and good. I think that might be easier if my life were different. Pray for me, Father, pray that I might be made a better person.'

She was so earnest, so sincere, that Father Luca did not know what to say to her. He should tell her what Agneta did—basically to be quiet and to accept. But, facing her, he knew that she was a free spirit, wanted to take flight and soar into the heavens. As it was, he feared that she was doomed to the nunnery, and it was wrong of him, he knew, but he could not imagine what that would do to her.

The thought was intolerable. He rose, and, more to comfort himself than her, said, as though she were years older, and a great lady, not a hapless young girl, 'My lady, one thing in this life is sure, and one thing only. We know not what the morrow may bring, only that, while it may present us with yesterday again, yet, sometimes, it may offer us chances which we did not know existed. I shall pray for you, as you ask, that God will somehow free you to use your talents and to fulfil yourself. Ask and it shall be given unto you.'

Bianca dropped to her knees before him, took his hand, and kissed the ring on it. 'Oh, I will try so hard to be good,' she said fervently. 'If only things could somehow be different. I can only hope that the Lord God knew what he was doing when he made me as I am, and that you are right.' She hesitated. 'I also know that no matter how many times I vow to be good, I always end up being naughty again.'

Father Luca looked down at her, and said kindly, 'My child, you are mistaken if you think you are particularly sinful. If it comforts you, I think that others have no small blame in the matter. And now finish your work. God wishes us always to complete our tasks, not to leave them half done.'

'Of course,' she said, thinking, Yes, I will try to be good, and then sighing, as she knew what awful temptations would be put in her way. Easy to be good in the Father's room where there was nothing and no one to provoke her.

Provocation came later, after her evening meal. She was practising her calligraphy, writing the Lord's Prayer, when old Raimondo came in and bade her attend the lord at table.

'I am not dressed for company,' she said doubtfully, looking at her ink-stained clothes, and worn shoes.

'No matter. The lord's word was immediately. Come, lady. You know that he does not like you to keep him waiting.' He hesitated. 'He has been drinking heavily.'

'That is not news,' said Bianca scornfully. 'News would be if he had not.'

But she rose, all the same, and followed him as he wished, to be announced at Bernardo's door, formally, as never before, and she could not help wondering why that was.

'The Lady Bianca di San Giorgio at the service of her

brother, and his princely guest, the Count Piero de'
Manfredini, Lord of Astra,' was her introduction, which
she thought was overdoing it a bit, Piero hardly being a
prince—even if he behaved like one.

But to decorate the occasion she bowed low as she
stood in the doorway. She saw that Raimondo was right:
Bernardo was drunk—she knew the signs, and as she
walked in she asked herself why she was wanted, and
not for one moment would she ever have guessed the
answer to that, and perhaps it was fortunate that she did
not even try, because the correct answer would have had
her running back to her own room, calling on God and
all his Saints for protection.

CHAPTER THREE

BERNARDO'S room reeked of drink and mischief. Both men were leaning against the backs of their great armchairs, goblets in their hands, the dice and their box before them. Bernardo was undoubtedly much the worse for the wine which he had taken. Bianca was not sure about Piero, but his eyes were glittering in a way she did not like, and as she entered the room behind Raimondo they were hard on her. Raimondo vanished into the shadows behind Bernardo's chair.

Lodovico sat next to Piero, stark sober, a strange expression on his face. He seemed to be the only person in the room who *was* sober.

'You took long enough to come, lady,' grumbled her brother, over the rim of his goblet.

'You told me that I was not needed tonight,' snapped Bianca. 'I am not dressed for company, nor prepared for it.'

'You never are,' said Bernardo churlishly, taking more wine and speaking as though it were her fault that she had no proper clothes, and not his. 'We have been playing dice, the Lord Piero and I. My luck has been as bad as usual, I fear.'

'You sent for me to tell me that?' said Bianca tartly. 'Could it not have waited until tomorrow?'

Her brother's lips writhed before he spoke again.

'No, lady. Only your presence can mend matters now.' His voice took on an almost pleading note, quite unlike the usual rebuking snarl which he had been offering her.

Bianca stared at him, and at the golden man in the chair opposite whose blue eyes had never left her since she had arrived. 'You require me to throw the dice for you, then?' she said acidly. 'You are too far gone?'

Her brother heaved himself forward. 'By God, girl, you have a tongue like a snake's. I shall be glad to see it gone,' he achieved at last.

'Gone?' Bianca stared at him harder, too shaken to make a fierce riposte. 'How gone?' She saw Lodovico close his eyes as if in pain, and then open them to stare at his lord, still mute, still motionless, except that Piero put out his hand to do something with the dice before him on the table—what? Pick them up only to throw them down again, rattling and rolling across the table, noisy in the silent room, punctuating the snore of the man sleeping there.

'How gone, Bernardo? What does that mean?'

'I have lost all,' he mumbled, eyes away from her, head on chest, unable to look at his sister. 'All,' he said again. 'San Giorgio, the tower, the fief, everything. I won at first, the dice ran my way, I thought to make our fortune, and then. . .'

'The luck turned. . .and you lost,' finished Bianca swiftly. 'Did it not occur to you that he could afford to lose and you could not? What else could you gamble with but your inheritance? But how, then, shall I be gone from you? We both leave as beggars, I suppose, or shall I no longer be your sister?' She could not believe what she had just heard. Piero had destroyed them. There would no longer be San Giorgios to rule their diminished lands. Where would they go? She felt suffocated, and still he did not speak. Plainly he was leaving all for her brother to tell her.

'No,' said her brother, now looking over the top of her head. 'I shall not leave, and neither of us will be beggars—indeed, you at least, my sister, will be far from a beggar. The Lord Piero is generous. He will not claim his winnings, if, instead. . .' And he could not finish, just looked at Piero, who shook his head at him, remained mute, still refusing to help him say what had to be said. He began again. 'He will be content to cancel all my losses if you will but marry him—now—within the hour.'

It was out. Bernardo was prepared to sell her to Piero in exchange for his debt of honour being wiped out, to recover his patrimony, carelessly lost to the monster opposite. Though how honour came into this sorry business she could not imagine. And why did he want to marry her? And if he did, why this way? Why not offer for her straight, as a knightly gentleman should? But, of course, he was not a knightly gentleman; that was plain. She stood there, lost, with every eye but his away from her, and still he did not speak.

'And, of course,' ran on Bernardo feverishly, 'I said yes. I agreed. Think how pat it stands, my sister. I keep what I lost in honourable fashion, and you gain a husband you could never have hoped for. Wine, Raimondo, more wine to celebrate this happy hour. The Lady of San Giorgio settled at last.' And he clapped his hands together, still avoiding Bianca's eye. 'The Father must be sent for to celebrate the nuptials.'

The world and the room turned around Bianca. Marriage! Now, to *him*. To impossibly perfect Piero. Handed over, like a parcel—without so much as a by your leave, lady—by her brother to avoid paying his just debts, freely and stupidly lost to a man with whom his common sense should have told him he ought not to play. A man who had, for his own reasons, almost certainly cheated him in order to gain his own ends.

'Who proposed this vile bargain?' she asked, astonished that her voice sounded as it usually did.

'Why, he did,' said her brother eagerly, shame at last departing. 'Messer Piero. He truly wants you for a wife—might have asked for you without this. Will even forgo a dowry to leave the slate clean between us. Such magnanimity! Was ever a man so fortunate as I—or a girl so lucky as you? Countess of Astra, you could never have hoped for that.'

'But after he won everything, not before, he offered

this,' said Bianca cuttingly. 'Not in honourable form, as a proper knightly nobleman should, for all you prate to me of honour, my lord Bernardo di San Giorgio.' She flung his title at him as though it were a term of abuse. 'And why does he want me for a wife? Tell me that.' And still Piero did not speak.

'Why do men usually want women for their wives?' roared her brother. 'He fancies you, apparently—I admit that, looking at you and at him, it seems improbable, but there it is. So much does he desire you, he wishes to marry you within the hour. . .so eager is he to have you in his bed.'

'That I do not believe,' said Bianca steadily, 'that I have slain him with my desirability.' She was trembling, her body cold. Piero, of all men, in her bed. 'Why should I agree to this? To marry a man who has shown me only mockery, who has allowed you, probably commanded you, to do all the talking for him, who has offered *me* no word of love? Not the conduct of a man, brother, who is so mad with lust for my body that he wishes to rifle it within the hour. Why should I agree to this hasty ceremony brought about by a night's drinking and gaming? Tell me that.'

Bernardo half rose, and slammed his fist on the table, hard, so that everything on it danced.

'Now, my lady sister,' he bellowed. 'Let me tell you what is at stake here. I have decided today to marry the Lady Giulietta, and she will not have me if you still live under my roof—she wants no other lady in San Giorgio but herself, and particularly does not want you—I cannot say that I blame her, having endured your tongue for so long. So, hear this. It will not be a year after you become a woman before I send you to a nunnery if none offers for you, but immediately, tomorrow. . .'

And as Bianca stammered, face white, 'B-but you promised, Bernardo, you promised. . .' he answered her, face ugly,

'No, I will not listen to you. You have nagged me for

the last time. Here is a splendid offer. Refuse it and the only bride you will ever be will be Christ's. This I promise you.'

He sat down, took another swig from his goblet, and still Piero remained silent, although Lodovico pulled at his arm, willing him to speak, she realised; but he shook the hand off, while Bernardo, drinking over for the moment, gave another roar. 'Do not be a fool, Bianca. At one stroke you solve all our problems. The Lord Piero gets the wife he says that he needs. I can marry Giulietta, whose late husband left her enough of a fortune to enrich San Giorgio's tower, and you—you gain such a prize for a husband as you could hardly have hoped for—rich, powerful. . .and of a presence which could have gained him a Royal bride. You should thank the Lord God on your knees for such an unexpected boon instead of standing there like a clown waiting to be executed.'

'I cannot believe that this is happening,' said Bianca when he had finished. 'That you are saying this, and that he wishes it, I repeat, a man who still says nothing. This must be a jest. And the haste—I do not understand the haste.'

Piero now spoke for the first time, face expressionless. 'No jest, lady. The offer was made in good faith. Your brother was distressed at losing all, and this seemed a way of satisfying us both. As he says, we all benefit. He keeps his land and I gain a wife. I do not wish to wait for the usual idle preliminaries to be gone through before we marry, and I ride out tomorrow. For both these reasons haste is inevitable.' He spoke, thought Bianca, as though he were buying vegetables in San Giorgio's market.

'And I must go with him?' she said, turning to her brother.

'Of course you must,' snarled Bernardo, exasperated. 'You will be his wife. It is your place. You cannot expect me to go on giving you board and lodging once you are married to him. He will keep you now. Go on your knees, girl, and thank the Lord God that someone wants you, and that the someone is as powerful as he is. Failing the nunnery, I thought that I was doomed to keep you forever.'

'Instead you sell me to him in order to pay your gambling debts,' said Bianca, voice desolate. 'And I still fail to see why he wants to marry me. He could have anyone for a wife. Anyone.'

'True,' said Piero, speaking again. 'But I wished to oblige your brother. I see by what you both say that the favour I am doing him is bigger than I thought.'

Oh, despite all, nothing had changed. He was still using his nasty tongue on her. Except that she had changed. For the moment all incentive to use hers on him, to rail at him as she had done in their meetings before, to give him as good as she got, had disappeared in the face of his monstrous proposal.

'By God, girl,' said Bernardo softly, 'if you do not agree before Father Luca arrives, I shall personally give you the thrashing you have long deserved for your impudence—and hand you over to the nuns tomorrow.'

Bianca shivered. He had threatened both before, but this time it was plain that he meant what he said. She had no alternative but to surrender, to become Piero de' Manfredini's property to do with as he wished. 'Yes,' she managed. 'Yes, I will marry you, Messer Piero, but why you wish this I do not know. You have spoken no word of love to me, made no effort to woo, or even to please me. I cannot think that you want me as any sort of prize—quite the reverse. You have hardly spoken since I came in, leaving Bernardo to explain as though the matter wearied you. . .'

'I thought that he would be more persuasive than I,' said Piero gravely.

'Oh,' said Bianca, 'you mean that, had you asked me, I might have thought you installed as the tower's jester already?'

She saw Lodovico wince, saw him put down the dice

box he had been holding. She saw Piero's smile—why should he smile?—then heard her brother grumble, 'I see that you are determined to be cross-grained to the end. Does that mean that you have changed your mind? Body of God, girl, give us a plain yes or no without qualifications.'

'Yes,' she said hollowly. 'Yes,' and said no more. She watched Piero rise at last from his chair. He walked over to where she stood, still defiant, head held high, a small but gallant figure. He took her hand. It was grubby again, ink-stained, but he kissed it on the palm and, near to him, she did not think that he was drunk.

The effect of his touch on Bianca was immediate and strong. His hand on hers, his lips on her palm, seemed to pierce her to the heart. It was a sensation so strange and sweet that she thought she would faint. Did he know? Had he intended it? How had it happened? What strong alchemy was at work? Twice now he had affected her so oddly. Her trembling redoubled and, still holding her hand, he turned towards Bernardo. 'The Lady Bianca accepts me,' he said. 'And, as her brother, you agree to the marriage?'

He was as formal as though the whole ridiculous and demeaning pantomime of the last few moments had not taken place, as though they were going through the courtly ritual which normally prevailed in the marriage preliminaries of such great ones as themselves.

'I do indeed,' said Bernardo. 'Bravo. She is yours, my Lord Piero. I advise you to keep her quiet. She is like the tower clock and strikes on the quarters. But she is a hard worker, and the Father says that she is clever.'

He sounds as though he is giving me to impossibly perfect Piero to scrub his stairs, or keep his books, instead of share his bed, thought Bianca dazedly. I suppose even he can hardly think that Piero is burning to. . .to. . . And her mind shied away from what was shortly to happen to her. Share his bed, I am to be his wife, her thoughts nevertheless persisted. He will. . .he

will. . .take me in his arms and. . . Oh, I am afraid of
him if the truth be known. . . What shall I do when he
begins to take off my clothes and. . .and. . .?

It was fortunate that Father Luca arrived at that
moment or she would have bolted down the stairs,
screaming, I will go to the nunnery, yes, I will, and San
Giorgio and Bernardo and the lordship may go hang.
But it was too late. She could not back out now. She
swallowed. Bernardo was explaining to the Father why
he had been sent for, and what he was to do.

The Father's kind old eyes and his concern were only
for her, and the tall blond man who stood at her side,
magnificent in his finery, reducing everyone and everything in San Giorgio to the second-rate.

'I see that you wish this, Lord Bernardo, and the man,
too,' he said, looking at Piero sternly. 'But the Lady
Bianca, does she wish it?'

'Of course she wishes it,' said Bernardo. 'She is a fool
else. And my wishes are hers. I am her elder brother
and her lord, and I command it. That should be enough
for you or any weaseling Churchman. Make ready for
the ceremony without delay.'

'Nevertheless, I would hear the lady,' said Father
Luca, still stern. 'My child——' and his eyes were on
her '—do you consent to this? Freely consent? For you
are still but a child, not of a state to marry. Only if you
consent, knowing what marriage entails, will I marry
you to this man, and then not here, but in proper form
in my chapel.'

'You may marry her in the stables or the dungeons for
all I care, so long as you perform the ceremony, and
quickly,' said Bernardo coarsely. 'Answer him, girl. Tell
him yes, and then we may all go to bed before dawn.'

She had only to say no, and she was free. Free not to
marry him, but to be thrashed—that was nothing. She
had been thrashed before for speaking her mind, and the
hurt was fierce but was worth it to maintain her integ-
rity. But she was also free to be a nun, and that was

everything. She could not be a nun. She looked up at Piero, at the perfect and beautiful face which offered her nothing of help or hindrance, and said, 'Lord, I agree to marry you of my own will. My consent is freely given as the Father here will witness.'

Something moved in the cold face looking down at her—some acknowledgement of her presence and her courage, the indomitable will with which she outfaced life, refusing to be demeaned or put down, even in such circumstances as these. He spoke, looking across at Bernardo. 'That is your wish, lady? Freely given? If not, the bargain fails, and the evening is wiped out. No wife, no game, no debts.'

And now he was offering her her freedom, but it was too late. For freedom was the nunnery, and, what was worse, to Bianca's mind it was dishonour. It was a lie he was offering. For Bernardo *had* lost San Giorgio, and in all honour Piero could not say that what had happened had not.

'Freely given,' she said, 'to be the Lord Piero's wife. No coercion, Father,' and she swept them all a great curtsy, dipping down, down, not tripping this time, keeping herself steady, rising to put out her hand to take his, which he offered her as she rose. 'Come, my lord and future husband. We must not keep the Father waiting.'

Piero bent his blond head down to her dark one, and Lodovico behind him leaned forward and said, so low that only she could hear him, 'Piero, is this proper, is this right?' No lord, she noted, no Ser Capitan, no title, but Piero—as to a younger brother, or a child.

'My will,' said Piero, also low. 'And the child, she wills it, too.'

'No,' said Lodovico, 'not that. She is a child and does not know to what she agrees.'

'You do not know *her*,' said Piero. 'I tell you, it is truly her will. She wishes it. Has wished it since we met, and does not know it.'

So I do, thought Bianca, surprised. Perhaps not since we met, but for the last few minutes yes, and yes. And then added feverishly, I must be mad. To be his wife, to... Forget that. And then again, My imperfections will cancel out his improbable perfection. She had an insane impulse to giggle at the contrast the pair of them presented. Black and fair, short and tall, fiery and cold. What can he think he is doing? I know what I am doing—avoiding the nunnery; but at what sort of price, the good God alone knows.

'Your woman must be fetched, lady,' said Piero gently. 'She will wish to prepare you for the ceremony. Your brother will allow you time to steady yourself. And the Father will not mind a little delay—will prefer it, I think.' They were following the stumbling Bernardo and the Father out of the room, and walking in the direction of the chapel. 'Lodovico will take you to your room, and I will arrange for Agneta to come to you.'

I am not dreaming this. I am to be married to him, in this old gown, for at such short notice I have none other. I hardly know him, but that is a noblewoman's common fate. And he is not drunk. He knows what he is doing, and why he is doing it—although it is beyond me, and Lodovico, too, why he has embarked on something so improbable. Only Bernardo, who hardly knows where he is, thinks that there is nothing untoward about tonight's work. And then, he called me a child. She took her courage into both hands, and said his name as he left her to make himself ready.

'Messer Piero. Do you truly wish this?'

He turned, then stood quite still, and said softly, 'Truly, lady. Or I should not be doing it. I am accustomed to doing only as I please.' She heard Lodovico groan behind her.

'You cannot want such a small, plain thing as I,' she countered.

'Are you already to tell me what I want, lady? Even before we are married?'

But there was a smile in his voice. Behind them she thought that she heard Lodovico groan again. Useless to say more. Messer Piero would have what he willed. She knew enough of him to know that. She sighed and followed Lodovico, and presently Agneta came, exclaiming over her and her good fortune. 'And you without a dress to wear,' she lamented. 'To be married in such haste. Wait, and I will find something to serve as a veil.' And she dived into the chest, and came out with some yellowed lace, which she draped around a comb in Bianca's hair. Bianca wrenched it off.

'No, I look a mock in that. I will be married as I am, in what I wear. I must wash my hands and face.'

'You should have had a bath and scents, and everything to make you beautiful for your husband.' Agneta's litany of complaints about Bianca's inadequacies of face, body and clothes had redoubled at the news of the hasty wedding, rather than been silenced. 'Have you no sense of fitness, lady, to be wed in such a gown?'

'It is his choice,' said Bianca. 'He has willed this at such short notice, not I.' And finally, a little cleaner, but hardly more bridal than when she had entered her brother's room, she left her own room for the last time as Bianca, the Lady of San Giorgio, Agneta still talking non-stop, as they descended the stairs to carry out a wedding ceremony which, had she been told in the morning she would be engaged in at night, she would have told the bearer of the news that he had run mad, and was fit only for children to mock at.

Still moving as though she were in a dream, Bianca stood before the altar in the small, incense-filled chapel. In the short time in which she had been with Agneta—but was it short?—time seemed to have lost its meaning; Father Luca had managed to prepare himself and the room for a marriage which would be somewhat more than the hasty ceremony to which Bernardo had agreed.

Piero was already so splendid that he had been required to do little more to make himself look like a proper bridegroom, and his appearance, she thought wryly, more than made up for her own deficiencies as a bride. He came forward, took her hand, unsmiling, and she said again, because this could not be true, must be a joke, or a dream from which she would shortly awaken, 'It is not too late for you to change your mind.'

'Or you, lady,' he responded, giving her, for the first time since the dream began, his white smile.

Agneta, hearing this, moaned and clucked, threw her arms around Bianca. 'Do not argue with him. You are to be married—but what a way to celebrate your wedding,' she declared, and glared at Piero, who gently removed her arms and said, frost in his voice,

'She requires your support, woman, not your eternal tears and lamentations. Be silent.'

Agneta glared at him, and then at Bernardo. 'The poor child, to be wed in such a hole-and-corner fashion, to be sacrificed between the lot of you. . . To——'

'No, I said be silent, woman,' remonstrated Piero, and there was something so cutting in his barely raised voice that Agneta, whom nothing ever silenced, was silenced, and for once stood quiet behind Bianca, breathing heavily and looking murder at his unheeding back.

And so they were married. At one point, where push became shove, as Bernardo often said, Father Luca paused and looked at her, to give her time to change her mind, but Bianca's eyes were steady on him, unflinching, so that he sighed and continued and in a trice she was no longer the Lady of San Giorgio, the Lord Bernardo's sister, but was, instead, the Lady of Astra, the Lord Piero's wife, and much good might it do him—or her either, for that matter.

Bernardo stumbled over and kissed her on each cheek, drink heavy on his breath, Lodovico kneeled before her and kissed her hand. 'I am yours to command, lady, as I am his,' he told her, but the message in his eyes as he looked at Piero was a different one. Strangely, Piero was the last to kiss her. At the moment the ceremony ended he had stood transfixed, as though he, too, felt that he was in a dream.

Now, he bent down, took her face in both his beautiful hands and kissed her—not on the lips or cheek as she might have expected, but on the forehead, a cool kiss, barely brotherly, certainly not the kiss of a husband or a lover. 'I welcome you, wife,' he said, and, stepping back, released her to Agneta. 'You may take her to my room now,' he told her, 'but mind what you say to her. She is no longer your lady, but mine, and I will not have her distressed.'

He turned to Bernardo, who was bellowing, despite Father Luca's protests, 'Wine, wine for the groom, while the bride is prepared for bed.'

Bianca shuddered. So preoccupied had she been with the ceremony that she had almost forgotten what was to come afterwards. She let Agneta, silent for once, take her by the hand, but turned at the door to the chapel to see them all looking at her: Piero, Bernardo, Lodovico and Father Luca, their expressions ranging from Bernardo's triumph, Lodovico's vague worry, Father Luca's pity, to Piero's total impassivity.

I am impossibly perfect Piero's wife, and I am waiting for him to come to bed to. . .thought Bianca as she entered his room. It was one of the few good ones in the tower. The walls were covered with faded tapestries portraying the Goddess Diana out hunting in the forest. Actaeon, the man whom she had killed in a mixture of desire and jealousy and frustration, looked exactly like Piero, blond and beautiful, except that he had an expression of fear on his face, which she doubted Piero had ever possessed.

The bed was a massive affair, with wooden ends, covered with carvings of fruit and flowers. The linen on it was fine, and the counterpane was magnificent, embroidered in scarlet and silver with red crosses and lances. There was a prie-dieu and an illuminated Book of Hours by the window-slit. A bearskin rug lay on the floor before a great chair with a cushion on it—embroid-ered with more crosses and lances. A battered silver ewer stood on a chest in a matching bowl. A silk towel, flung down, had a razor with an ivory handle, and a small brush, lying beside it. Piero's huge broadsword, a fine and deadly thing, heavily ornamented—it needed a man of his size and strength to wield it—leaned against the wall, a decorated helmet at its foot. His leather packs, elegant but serviceable, lay on the floor. The garments he had worn the previous day hung on pegs hammered into the stone wall.

Bianca saw all this in the finest detail, as though she had never seen anything before. All her senses seemed stretched, she could almost feel the blood in her body, and each separate pulse. Agneta, after lighting the candles in their sconces, so that the room was filled with light, said, 'Sit there a moment, lady, I will be back,' and shot out of the door. Piero had managed to do something no one else had ever done—to reduce the maid's nagging and roaring to a hardly heard grumble. And how long will that last? thought Bianca, grateful for the blessed quiet.

She sat on the bed then jumped off it at the thought that he might come in to find her there, and then considered that such perfection would surely give her time to prepare herself, and climbed back on it again. A sad little smile touched her lips. Fool that I am—when he does come in, I must be in it, and then he. . .he will. . . Thought stopped. I will not anticipate it. God will give me strength; Father Luca says that he always does.

Thinking of Father Luca made her remember what he had said to her that afternoon—that they knew not what the day might bring. She sighed. Well, this day had brought her something which she could never have imagined and for which she knew that she was not ready.

She put her hands to her scarlet cheeks. I am not yet a woman. I have not even a woman's body. Perhaps he likes boys! But no, the kitchen had said that he never lacked for women, and beautiful ones, so it could not be that about her which had attracted him. Her heart was beating so rapidly that it was making her feel sick as she tried not to think of him making love to her, doing to her what Enzo, the page, had tried to force her into doing last spring, and had been branded and turned away for attempting. Why in the world should she want to have such a thing done to her, and to be used so by Piero? She was blushing and shaking all over at the very thought.

Fortunately for her sanity, Agneta returned at this point, and Bianca had never before been so grateful to see her. She was carrying a ewer of perfumed water, which she poured into the silver bowl from the chest. She also had clothes in her arms—clothes which Bianca had never seen before, and which she laid reverently on the bed, before disrobing Bianca, who felt more like a filleted fish than ever when she was completely naked.

Agneta's lamentations, loud now that her fear of Piero was fading, began once more. Their subject was Bianca's lack of bosom and hips. She threw up her hands. 'Pray God he will be gentle with you—you being so small and he so large. Pleasure there for you later, but tonight. . .' And she shook her head distressfully as she bathed Bianca's shivering body in the water.

Trickling further water across Bianca's non-existent breasts, she said dubiously, 'You know what will happen to you now, lady—when he comes to you, that is? If not, I will explain.'

'Of course I know,' snapped Bianca, exasperated. 'You have told me a dozen times already, and since Enzo, the page, tried to misbehave with me last year I cannot pretend that I don't know what a roused man looks like, although why in the world I should ever want to do such a thing, or he do it to me, is a mystery I am soon like to find out, although I would much rather not.'

'And that is no way to talk,' said Agneta, drying her

charge vigorously. 'Such a handsome man as he is and
the lucky girl you are. Every woman servant in the tower
is envying you tonight, and all that you can do is
complain. No matter—he will soon teach you different.
They say that he has women from here to Milan.'

'They say!' said Bianca. 'They say anything, and they
may all have him for me. What is that you have brought
me?' she asked, and pointed to the white garment on the
bed.

'Your mother's bed gown, lady, worn on her wedding
night, and saved for you, and who would have thought
that you would have needed it so soon? The Lord God is
watching over you, that's for sure,' said Agneta, reverently picking up the delicate thing and slipping it over
Bianca's head. It was of the finest cotton and decorated
with sheer lace panels, and had a collar like a cobweb.

'Not that you will be wearing it long,' said Agneta,
stroking both gown and Bianca, 'but a pleasure for him
to remove.' She picked up a brush and began to
straighten the tangles of Bianca's lustrous black hair—
her finest feature, Agneta had often said—brushing it
until it hung in deep waves down her back. 'And now
you are ready for this,' she decided, and picked up a
little lace cap, with tiny wings at each side, setting it on
Bianca's head, tweaking at it until she gained the effect
she wanted. She stood back proudly. 'Why, I do believe
that you look almost pretty.'

Bianca groaned. 'Blow out the candles. He will not
care what I look like so long as I am female.'

'Oh, you are a lady now, and must not talk so,'
reproved Agneta. 'He will not expect you to be forward—quite the contrary; a maiden should be shy. A
little gratitude for your pleasuring will not come amiss
at the end, however. A man likes to think that——'

Bianca interrupted her. 'By all the sweet-suffering
Saints, spare me your unwanted advice. I need it as little
as I needed a husband.'

'I do but seek to help you, lady. A good marriage goes

on as it begins. You are a deal too eager to offer your opinions. . .' She stopped as Bianca's expression grew dangerous. 'Oh, very well.' She walked over to the bed, and pulled back the covers. 'In with you, lady. He will expect you to be waiting for him. Lord God, what a poor thing this day is. Why, had you a proper wedding he would have come in with your brother, finely dressed, and his court and musicians, and the Lord Piero would have been put in with you, and your health drunk, and all the world would have offered you both good cheer before they left you together.'

'The good God be thanked that I have been spared that,' said Bianca as she reluctantly climbed in and leaned against the pillows, her face set.

Agneta surveyed her doubtfully. 'Could you not look a little more welcoming, *madonna*? You have the face of one about to receive physic.'

Bianca sighed. 'I cannot say that I want any of this, Agneta, nor him, either. But it was either marry him, or ruin, and lying in his bed is better than lying in the street. You may leave me now, and yes, leave the candles burning. I cannot face the dark, after all, even though I have no wish to see him.'

'Oh, you'll feel differently in the morning,' said Agneta, a look of infinite cunning on her face. 'I bid you goodnight, lady, but not to sleep, I hope.'

'You may bid me what you like, so long as you leave me in peace,' replied Bianca, although once Agneta had gone, still exclaiming, she wished her back again, as her thoughts were worse than Agneta's company or her lubricious gossip.

What am I doing here, and when he comes what shall I do? Suppose I scream, or run mad the way the Lady of Gavi is supposed to have done on her wedding night when her lord took her? No, I shall not do that, but I cannot hope that I shall enjoy it or him. . . She moved restlessly where she sat, hands plucking at the bedclothes.

Shall I pretend to like it, or would he rather have me truthful? I hated the idea of it that time when Enzo put his hands on me, and thanked God Agneta came so quickly when I screamed. I cannot scream today, and he—he is not Enzo, whom I never liked. But he is so splendid and perfect and I am so small and plain. Why does he not come? I should like to get it over with. No, I shouldn't. . . And her thoughts went round and round like the squirrel in its cage in the market at San Giorgio, a pitiful little thing which she had bought to set free, to be scolded by her brother for wasting money. I feel like the squirrel, and wish someone would buy me and set me free, she lamented silently.

The candle flames wavered in the draught. I can bear anything, she thought, so long as he is kind. Will he be kind? And she thought of the beautiful face which had teased her on the stairs, and her strange desire to touch it. And then she thought of the same beautiful but impassive face at her wedding, and alternately wished that he would come soon, or not at all.

Just as she was half falling asleep she heard his step in the corridor, and the door opened. She sat up again, clasping her hands under the bedclothes. May the Lord God help me to endure this—a stupid thing to ask, she thought, of a deity who hadn't shown her much mercy in her short life. She watched her husband enter. Only her indomitable will kept her from bolting from the bed.

Later she came to realise that somehow she understood Piero, and what moved him, better than anyone else. As she had known immediately, when her brother had sent for her, that, although Bernardo was drunk, Piero was not, she saw, straight away, that Piero was now drunk, although his walk was steady, and his manner still apparently sober and impassive. He reached the bed, and looked down at her. She heard him draw in his breath and wondered what he saw.

The prescience which was already making him known and feared, despite his youth, was strong in him, regardless of the drink he had taken since the ceremony. He saw not the little, dark, undeveloped girl child Bianca still was, but what she was going to be; the promise of the beautiful woman with a face full of passion and character that she would become when she at last grew up. The character and strength were already there, would still be there when her body and face matured. He sighed, sat on the bed by the child she still was, despite her sixteen years, and took her hand in his. He could feel her trembling.

'Bianca,' he began.

'Lord,' she said bravely, 'I await your pleasure,' wondering as she spoke how drink took him. Would he be surly like Bernardo, or stupid, like others she had seen?

'Yes,' he said gravely, speaking with slow care. 'I see that you are ready for me, my lady wife. But tell me, is it true what I hear? That your courses have not yet started?'

Bianca went hot all over. That they should talk together of such a thing! 'Alas, no, my lord. I am not yet a woman. They are late, you see.'

'Yes,' said Piero, looking at the flat chest and remembering the thin hips. 'You are not yet a woman, my lady. And I cannot make you truly my wife until you are. A man of honour does not bed with children, and despite your sixteen years you are still a child.'

Bianca went quite still, and inside her head something cried out in disappointment, for all that she feared him. . .and. . .it. But to be passed over was something again. Why, then, had he married her? She twisted her hands together.

'I do not please you, lord?'

Piero wished that he had not done this thing—that in a fit of recklessness, moved by he knew not what, he had suddenly determined on marriage with the Lord of San Giorgio's little sister. Or else he wished that he had been unkind enough to drink himself into a stupor on his wedding night, or brute enough to make her his wife, come what may.

He saw her twisting hands, and said gently, 'No, it is not that, my child, but later, when you are grown and truly a woman, you shall be my wife. This I promise you.'

'Then why did you marry me, lord,' she asked, lips quivering, 'and with such dispatch?'

'Because I need a wife, and you need a husband. . . and protection, and in time we shall truly be man and wife. You understand me?'

Bianca hesitated, bewildered by this new turn of events, aware that he, too, was distressed, and understood her distress. 'I cannot say that I do understand you, lord, but you are my husband even if you do not bed me, and thy will is mine.'

He had drunk to make himself able to say to her what must be said, to be able to live with himself for what he had done in taking her away from all she knew, in such a fashion. He put out his hand to stroke hers, and then to lift it and kiss it again, and she shivered again at his touch. He sighed, prescience deserting him for once: he thought that the shiver was one of fear, did not understand that his touch was producing in Bianca sensations she would only come to understand when she was fully a woman.

'I shall not share your bed tonight,' he said, 'but I have a duty to perform, and you must help me.'

He rose, walked over to his pack and fetched out a long strip of linen. He sat again on the bed, nearer to her this time, so near that she could see that his usually clear eyes were bloodshot, that weariness had left purple smudges under them. He unsheathed the dagger he wore at his waist, and extended his left arm to Bianca. 'Undo my shirt-cuff, wife. It is your first duty.'

Wondering, Bianca did as she was bidden, admiring the fine fabric and the gold button at the cuff. 'Now roll up the sleeve,' he said, 'as far as the shoulder, and then get out of the bed.'

She did so, fearful a little of what was to come. 'Now, sit down beside me, and hold the linen beneath my arm. Yes, that is right.' Once she was positioned as he wished he raised the dagger, and with a rapid movement slashed his arm with it, to the accompaniment of a gasping cry from Bianca.

'Hush,' he said, 'I have taken no real hurt,' and so saying bent over and rubbed the blood which ran down his arm on to the sheet where she had been lying, and then rapidly marked the gown which she was wearing with a great smear across the front and back.

'Now, bind the arm for me,' he said calmly, as though he had done an everyday thing.

Bianca's face flamed. 'Lord Piero, why. . .?'

'Why? I would not have you shamed before San Giorgio, wife. You understand me? Your woman will come in the morning and we shall have done our duty, you and I, and you are proved the virtuous maiden you undoubtedly are. . . No, not too tight, my wife. Too tight a bandage hinders, not heals a wound—though this scratch can hardly be called that.'

Devious. He was called devious, and truly so. He had saved her good name for her, and none would question their wedding night. She helped him, as he bade her, to staunch the blood, and bind his arm, and replace the sleeve. He praised her for her brisk and skilful handling of him, and for the calm with which she had accepted what he had done.

'Your understanding is quick, my lady,' he said, and she flushed at his kind words. 'And now you may return to your bed.'

'But where will you sleep, lord?'

'My duty by you done, where else but on the bearskin rug here, at your feet?'

'That will be hard, lord.'

'Not so hard as the earth on the night before battle.

Go to sleep, my child. You have a long day before you tomorrow, and the tower must think that you and I made a lively night of it.' She could have sworn there was a laugh in his voice.

Bianca scrambled back into bed, pulled the clothes up to her chin, and looked at him, still sitting there on the edge of the bed, the strangest expression on his face. He suddenly looked very young, and she understood that, like her, he exercised his will to control himself and try to control those around him, and that this demanded the utmost mental strength and concentration. He saw her intent gaze on him, smiled and, still smiling, rose. He bent down and kissed her on the cheek passionlessly. 'You are a brave child,' he said, and nothing more.

Bianca thought that she would not sleep, would never sleep again, but she did, and, surprisingly, after tears, for although she had not wanted him as a lover she had not wanted him to reject her either. And, too, in their last moments together, before he blew out the candles, and lay down on the bearskin rug, he had shown her, fleetingly, a different man—someone vulnerable, after all, not so much older than herself, capable of kindness.

Child, he had called her. He had married her—but not to bed her, or at least not yet. What maggot moved in his brain? What whim, that he had plucked her from San Giorgio to make her his wife? To be—what? To do—what?

The tears drying on her face, she slept, to dream only of him—of Piero, who put out his arms to her, but before he took her into them the dream faded, and she knew only oblivion. Impossibly perfect Piero and his child wife lay together, but apart, man and wife in name only, for the time being, and the future lay all before them.

CHAPTER FOUR

PIERO DE' MANFREDINI awoke in the early light, stiff, with a bad head and a worse conscience. At first he could not think where he was—unusual for him, for he always knew exactly where he was, and what he was doing—and why he had slept on the floor in yesterday's clothes, he who was so careful of his cleanliness.

Recollection flooded in as he sat up, and a strange remorse to be felt by one who had never tasted it before, claimed that he never felt it—it was for fools and half-men. He made his way to the ante-room, just off the bedroom, relieved himself, and then returned to the great bed to look at the wife he had won.

He remembered Lodovico saying to him, after Bianca had gone to his room, 'Why this, boy? Was this why you came, why you stayed?'

He had stared back at him and said, 'You are giving me orders now?' his voice as cutting as he could make it.

'Body of God,' his lieutenant had replied, 'I thought that we were here for military reasons, not for you to entertain yourself by marrying a half-formed girl, not yet a woman. Is it a new sensation you seek, to violate a child? You, who could, and should, have had anyone—a Duke's daughter even. I know you have been offered a Gonzaga princess, and you refused her because you said she was too young. Too young! She was more mature than this worthless sot's plain sister. Think what such a marriage could have done for you.'

He had reached out and taken Lodovico by the collar, and pulled him so that they stood face against face, two big men together, Bernardo too far gone to register what was happening before him.

'You do not yet know me, I see,' Piero had said.

'When will you grasp that I do not want anything "done for me"? No man or woman shall claim that what I do was done for me by them. I would not have the Emperor of Austria's daughter or France's sister if they were offered to me. Landless and no one I began, and if I finish full of years and honour and ruling my own principality none shall say they did it for me. Besides, you forget something. Consider that *she* was the one I wanted and none else, my bride because chosen and desired.'

Lodovico made no attempt to break free, but said, eyes steady, 'That I do not believe, and if I thought that you had bought her merely to use tonight for your sport. . .why. . .?'

Piero thought that if anyone else had said this thing to him he would have killed him, but because it was Lodovico, to whom he owed so much, he merely flung him away.

'Spare me your tender conscience,' he said, the more threatening because his cold expression had never altered. 'I know the child that she is, and I have no intention of touching her until she is ready. Will that do for you? Though why I should continually have to explain myself to fools. . . You try my patience.'

Well, why *had* he married her? And, for the life of him, he could not have explained why the fiery child he had first met scrubbing the tower floor should have made such an impression on him, should have filled him with such a strange mixture of feelings, pity for her neglected and derided state being the most prominent—and pity was not a feeling he wanted, liked or respected.

Whatever the reason, the impulse which had made him offer her fool of a brother such a strange bargain had led him here. He needed a bride for reasons beyond a simple need to be married, and a bride who was a noblewoman; and Bianca, for all her poverty, came from one of the noblest families in Italy. But had he needed a child, and a fractious one?

But she had not been fractious last night, and if she lacked beauty her mind was good. Brought up as she had been, she had learned none of the foolish tricks which most women were endowed with as the result of a training designed to please men. Though why men should want to marry ignorant and light-minded fools, he could not conceive. What she had learned was to survive, and the Father had taught her as he might have taught a boy, so that she had a mind as inconveniently sharp as a knife, and would cross intellectual swords with him or any man. Had that pleased him and drawn him to her?

He shrugged. What help to analyse and reflect so? Reason told him that his ability to do these two things had made him feared and respected at an age when most young men were still novices to be tutored, not great captains, such as he knew himself considered to be. She was his wife, and if she had not been fractious last night, be sure that the day would restore her. The thought amused him.

He bent down. She looked even smaller and more childlike in the great bed. She had taken off the little lace cap put on by the old dragon who tormented her— to allure him, without doubt. Her black hair was tumbled about her thin face, which bore the mark of tears.

Piero clenched his fists, and, rising again, turned away from the sight. She had cried, silently, before she slept; doubtless thought him a brute—first out of fear that he might mate with her, and then out of disappointment that he had not. He began to strip, pulled off his houppelande, his doublet, his shirt, his hose, his mutande—the fine linen underpants worn beneath doublet and shirt—until he stood naked to the world.

Without thinking he walked over to his pack, and pulled out a clean gown to wear in the bed, and as he lifted it to put it on heard her stir behind him. Bianca, too, hardly knew where she was, and raised her head, to see the naked man in the room, and remembered everything.

Despite herself she could not take her eyes from him, and in the instant that she saw him, before he swiftly assumed his gown, she registered everything about him. Oh, God, he was as fine and beautiful with nothing on as one of the broken statues that stood in the ruined temple outside San Giorgio. She had thought that she might be frightened to see a man, whole and entire, the evidence of his masculinity plain before her, the thing that made him a man, as her lack of it proclaimed her a woman. But she was not, and again the strange feelings which had taken to invading her body at the mere sight of him were stronger than ever. Like last night, after the ceremony, she suddenly seemed to see the whole world exactly and precisely.

'Wife,' he said, walking over to the bed, and bending down to kiss the wondering little face turned towards him, the pity which had worked in him from the first sight of her stronger then ever. The tear-stained cheek received his caress, and her hand rose to stroke it when he had done.

'Lord?'

'I must be in the bed with you, child, when the servants come, as they always do after the wedding night. Do not be frightened. I will not hurt you.'

Bianca sat up straighter than ever and said vigorously—he had been correct in assuming that her spirit would return with the day—'Oh, I am not frightened of you now.' He noted the 'now' wryly. 'And if we are to deceive, then I see that we must do it properly.' Mischief stirred on her face. 'Shall I giggle in your arms when they come, lord?'

'That will not be necessary,' he replied, almost stiffly, her gallantry moving him more than her fear might have done. Then, suddenly matching her mood, he added, 'A meek wifely submission, rather—if you feel equal to it, that is.'

He made another of his swift movements—like a great cat, she thought again; he was a leopard, or a tiger, not the falcon of his badge—and was in the bed with her. Bianca's heart, for all her brave words, gave a great lurch: to have a man beside her in bed, with so little on, was frightening.

Oh, he was behaving himself as he had promised, but he was so near—oh, so near. She could see where his beard had grown in the night. He had not fastened the strings of his gown, and she could see the tawny hair on his chest, the strong hand on the coverlet, and when he looked at her she almost drowned again in his blue eyes. She gasped, and then tried to control herself. It would not do to have him think her distressed by his mere presence.

'I wish to do what is correct,' she said almost primly, trying to forget that the strong and beautiful body she had just seen was here, beside her. 'I have no experience of wedding mornings, and have no idea whether newly pleasured wives are shy or forward. A little instruction would help.'

The blue eyes danced wickedly. 'Oh, I have no experience of being a newly pleasured bride, either.' He considered her gravely. 'A mixture of shyness and gratitude, perhaps. Do you think that you are equal to managing gratitude?'

'Like this?' And Bianca could not resist pulling an absurd face.

'That looks more like a surfeit of green apples than gratitude,' observed Piero, as though pronouncing on one of Euclid's theorems. 'Otherwise perfect, I should say.'

'A peculiar otherwise would be Father Luca's comment on that,' said Bianca, pursing her mouth even more. 'He preferred me to use language exactly.'

'I cannot say,' replied Piero judiciously, 'that so far your speech has been distinguished for its scholarly rectitude. Quite the reverse.'

'Ah, but,' said Bianca, 'we have met so little, and always in circumstances not designed to encourage formal rhetoric. Let us suppose that we met in the Father's cell.'

'A supposition which I find it too difficult to contemplate at the present moment, with a bad head, and a child bride who insists on talking nonsense,' sighed Piero. 'Could we suppose something a little simpler?'

'My supposition is little more remarkable than our situation,' said Bianca. 'You have won me at dice. You have not bedded me, although the apparent evidence says otherwise. My supposition is quite simple beside. . . all that.'

Piero threw himself back on the pillows, clutching his head melodramatically. 'Enough, child. And it is too late for me to reproach Father Luca for teaching you to chop logic. He has done his task too well. Tell me, how did your brother come to miss such instruction, while his sister revelled in it? The facts are usually quite otherwise. Have you no womanly virtues?'

'Such as?' said Bianca acidly. 'Pray be specific, lord.'

'Why, meekness, silence, a willingness to serve her lord without need of instruction, and, above all, a death-defying ignorance.'

'None of that would have helped me much in San Giorgio,' said Bianca with such devastating truth that Piero fell silent before it.

'On the other hand,' she added, 'I suppose that the Lady of Astra will be expected to behave like the sort of person you described.'

'And what sort of person is that?' said Piero lazily, hooding his blue eyes, and looking at her *so*, almost without intending to, turning the full force of his sexual charm on her, so that her heart suddenly jumped in the oddest way before it began beating normally again.

'You know perfectly well what I mean, lord. The one you described: meek, silent, ladylike.'

'How can that be, seeing that she will be you?' said

Piero naughtily, still bathing her in his charm. Bianca hit him. She could not stop herself, and it was not a real hit, only a pretend one, and oh, he knew that it was; she could see that. He caught the striking hand so quickly that she hardly saw him do it, and then pulled her to him, equally playfully, putting her in the crook of his arm.

Only, once she was there, he could feel her soft and warm against him, not bouncing and spiky, and a strong and shameful wave of desire for her passed over him, which he immediately tried to repress.

But Bianca had seen his eyes change, his face alter, and knew immediately, without being told, what was happening to him, even though she had never really encountered a grown man who was roused before— Enzo the page's pitiful attempt hardly counted, she was beginning to find. Her face went quite white, and she trembled in his arm, saying, 'Lord?' in an enquiring, frightened voice.

He looked down at the face turned up to him and said gently, 'No need to be afraid. You had my promise, last night.'

Almost without willing it she did the oddest thing: burrowed her head into his chest for protection, and then looked up again, saying, also without her will being involved—or was it with it?—'I am your flat-chested bride, Lord Piero, to do with as you will.'

They were both shaking now, so near to one another as they were, breast to breast, heart to heart; the playfulness of their earlier conversation was gone, replaced by something uncommonly like a mutual passion.

With difficulty Piero restrained himself. 'Ah, but I am tempted,' he said softly. 'Except that I have given you my word, and have made my vows that you will not be mine until you are ready, and here is my pledge again.' And he kissed the top of her head, this time not passionlessly, coldly, but with something of the love he would have offered a full grown and true woman. Instinctively, she turned to kiss him.

They had been so occupied with one another that they had not heard the urgent tapping on the door, and then, at that moment, impatient Agneta burst in on them.

'*Ayee*!' she screamed, seeing Bianca in Piero's arms, and the exchange of kisses. 'I do believe that the lovebirds are not yet satisfied. The Falcon has pleasured his little white Dove, and all San Giorgio rejoices with them!'

Piero looked at her over the top of Bianca's head. 'And I see that all San Giorgio will be fed every detail of my wedding night before you are done. A discreet servant would have waited until given permission to enter.'

'Oh, you were too busy to hear me knock. Would you have had me wait until midday?' cawed Agneta. 'You have been kind to my little one. No need to hide your face from old Agneta, my dove,' she laughed, for Bianca was as shy as though she and Piero had truly spent the night in each other's arms, and she turned away from Agneta's gleeful face to seek refuge against him.

Agneta gave another shriek. 'Oh, the lady has learned modesty at last. No more scoldings and roarings at us all. The Lord Piero has taught you your place. A pity that we shall be leaving so soon, lady, so that all may not gain the benefit of your schooling!'

'Oh!' exclaimed Bianca, face scarlet, angered at last. 'You are more impossible than ever. I cannot even go to bed with my own husband without you broadcasting all that we do to the world. You may leave us and not return until I send for you.'

Agneta's cackling persisted to the door. 'Willingly, lady, willingly. I had not meant to break in on your pleasure. I had thought the night sufficient for that.' And they could hear her shouting her news all the way down the tower stairs. 'They are not finished yet, the Lord be praised!'

Bianca turned her blushing face to Piero. 'You are not to laugh. No indeed. And you might as well have had your way with me. The whole world will think us run mad for one another, and all I have had is one small kiss and several sermons on my behaviour. I have had quite enough of those these last few years without having to endure marriage in order to receive more.' She scrambled out of bed, glaring at Piero, who was lying back against the pillows, laughing. He had seldom seemed more impossibly handsome, and none of it was for her. She sat down, plump, on the bearskin on which he had spent the night.

'And you were not even in my bed until the last hour,' she wailed, 'but spent the night on this mangy rug on the hard floor.' And she began to cry in earnest, although whether for herself or her new husband she hardly knew.

Piero leaped out of bed to kneel beside her on the floor. 'You are not to cry, my dove. Yes, you are my dove. The old besom tells true there. I promise you that it will not be long once you are properly fed and cared for. That will soon make you a woman.'

'I do not want to be a woman,' raged Bianca, her sobbing redoubling. 'I wish that I were a boy. I am not fit to be the Lady of Astra, or anyone's lady, and that is the truth, and you are so impossibly perfect that you make me feel sick. If you weren't so perfect you would have taken me last night, and used me without a thought, the way Enzo the page tried to do. And if you weren't so perfect I should not look so plain by comparison, and Agneta would not think it such a great treat for me to be pleasured by you—which I wasn't, and don't want to be.' She ended in another burst of sobbing, during which she threw her arms for comfort around impossibly perfect Piero—another thing which she did not mean to do, but somehow did.

Piero stared blindly over her head at the blank wall. There was little that he could do to comfort someone who didn't want to be comforted, only say gently and prosaically, 'You'd best go back to bed. I have to dress for the day, and I shall send Agneta in to help you when I have done so, and you are recovered a little. She must not see you crying. She will think that you are unhappy after all, and that would never do.'

Bianca lifted her wet face to him. Oh, he was still being impossibly perfect. 'Do you always know the right thing to do or say?' she said acidly, sniffing as she did so in a manner which no Lady of Astra ought to employ. 'It must be a great comfort to you, even if it does drive everyone around you mad.'

Piero laughed at that, a grim laugh. 'Oh, you are more right than you know, wife. And now I have added you to the number I offend.' But he was kindness itself, lifting her up, swinging her off her feet and carrying her over to the bed. He laid her gently in it, and pulled the covers over her.

'Try to rest a little, my dove. You have a long and hard day ahead of you.'

'And you,' said Bianca, snuffling a little. 'And you have spent the night on the floor, and all because of me.'

He turned at that, swiftly, a panther again, eyes glowing. 'But think how we may laugh together, as husband and wife should, over how successfully we have deceived them all! They thinking that we were so happy, while we were both so truly miserable. We are at one with the gods, my wife, because only they think such little tragedies amusing.'

And that, thought Bianca drowsily, is why I cannot hate him. Because I feel like that, too, often and often, and it is strange that we are so similar in our thoughts when we look and sound so different. Perhaps Father Luca could explain that to me later. . .but, of course, I shall not be able to ask him such things again.

And then it struck her, hard, that she would soon be gone from San Giorgio and all she knew, and she put her hands to her scarlet cheeks and willed herself not to be afraid, but to welcome all that was to come, for, after all, that was what life was about. Nor had she been so happy at San Giorgio that she could honestly ask the Lord God to let her stay within its confines. Far from it. Truth to tell, she had to acknowledge that she did not know what happiness was, since her share of it had been so small.

Perhaps if my mother had lived, things might have been different, she told herself. She would have helped me last night, not cross-grained Agneta. Oh, that was absurd, for surely her mother would never have let her come to this pass—to be used as Bernardo's counter to rescue himself from folly—and, thinking this, she fell into a doze, delighted for once not to have to rise and face the unwelcome day, but to be able to indulge herself in a comfortable and big bed, with good linen, and the sun just coming in and. . .and. . . She was asleep.

She was awoken by Agneta, clucking and chattering, and carrying a dress which she had not seen before, in green and gold, with dagged sleeves, their scalloped points dangling inconveniently, but still fashionably. It had belonged to her mother—God rest her soul, Agneta said, and had been saved for such a grand occasion as this. 'You should have worn it last night, but *he* said that you were not to be troubled by being changed. Just like a man. And now you may ride out in it.'

Bianca picked it up dubiously. It was so worn and faded—Agneta's eyes must be failing, for sure. The dress didn't seem really suitable for anyone to do anything in it, let alone mount a horse and ride a considerable distance, as she shortly must. Besides, it would not fit her properly, being made for someone with a woman's figure, not a stick like herself.

Once she was out of bed, however, Agneta shot over to it, turned back the covers which Bianca had carefully replaced, and with a triumphant squeal pulled out the blood-stained bottom sheet.

'La, la, your lord made a good night's work of it,' she cried, and before Bianca could stop her she was out of

the door with it to show the San Giorgio servants and
retainers the undoubted proof that their lady had been a
virgin, and her lord a true man. 'And her gown is
stained, too,' she screeched. 'Praise be to God!'

Bianca had a dreadful fit of the giggles at all the
misunderstandings her new husband had provoked. She
could imagine the long mouth twitching as he heard
Agneta on her processional walk around the tower. He
certainly displayed a talent for deception far beyond his
years, and for the first time she wondered exactly how
old he was, and whether she dared ask him. Best
question Lodovico, she thought—that was, if he ever
spoke: his hissed words to Piero before the wedding, and
the odd sentence or two before that, were all that she
had heard from him.

Once on, the dress was as unbecoming as she had
thought that it would be. She was lost inside it, and her
eyes looked bigger than ever—and the rest of her
smaller. Of course, he could not really want such a
sparrow as I am, she thought dismally. He called me a
dove, after Agneta did, and anything less like a dove
than I, I cannot imagine.

Her sombre thoughts were interrupted by a hesitant
scratching on the door, and when she called, 'Come in,'
it was Bernardo who slouched towards her. He looked
even more ill than he usually did after a night of it, and
she wondered that he was up at all.

'You are well, sister?'

'No thanks to you, brother,' said Bianca fiercely. 'To
be married to a man I have only just met, and little
choice in the matter, it is a wonder that I did not fall
into a permanent swoon.'

'It is a woman's lot,' said Bernardo sententiously. He
hesitated. 'It is best so. For you to be married, I mean.
He wanted you, and none else has ever done so. I cannot
keep you, and if anything happened to me. . .' And his
voice tailed off.

'And now I am a Manfredini, and the Lady of Astra,' said Bianca. 'I suppose that there are worse fates.'

'Not exactly a Manfredini,' said Bernardo miserably. 'I thought I ought to tell you.'

'Not exactly a Manfredini? And what do you mean by that, brother?' Bianca's voice was hollow.

'Oh, there are many Manfredinis,' said Bernardo, avoiding her eyes. 'And I suppose he is one—of sorts, that is. He is the bastard, you see. His father is strange, does not acknowledge his bastards. But Piero calls himself Manfredini all the same. I had thought him his legitimate brother, but he told me no, while we were at play. I would not have you think that he deceived me.'

'No, *you* preferred to deceive *me*,' retorted Bianca bitterly. 'And that, I suppose, is why he wanted me. An unacknowledged bastard might find it difficult to marry a noblewoman, but now I have given him a rank of sorts. Only the unwanted Lady of San Giorgio would be allowed to him by her ne'er-do-well brother. I thank you, Bernardo.'

'He will be a great man, you see,' insisted Bernardo desperately. 'His reputation is already high, and will grow, and he but twenty-three. You will be a duchess, yet.'

'And a fine duchess I shall make!' said Bianca furiously. 'They will be fighting to paint my portrait so that the world may see what a freak the Lord Piero married to make himself noble. You should have told me, brother.'

'Oh, I knew how you would go on if I did,' he said. 'But it is for the best, truly.'

Now all seemed plain to the desolate Bianca. Unaware that Piero had already been offered noblewomen of higher rank and greater wealth than herself, she thought that she had found the key to this strange marriage, the explanation of the wager and the haste. But how had he known that he would win his game of dice with her brother?

She remembered the typically swift movement of his hand to toy with the dice when Bernardo had told her of her fate. He had changed the dice over for loaded ones, when at play, in order to win, and, having won, had changed them back again! Yes, that was it. Oh, when it suited her, she would let him know that she understood by what trickery she had become his wife.

And what a perfidious treacherous monster he was, after all. What peasant girl had spawned him after pleasing her lord, and how had he come to be what he was? By double-dealing, that was for sure. But no matter; God, through Father Luca, had blessed their marriage, and between them all she was his wife, and would be leaving within the hour. But she would be wary of him now.

Bernardo saw her face, winced, and put out an arm to embrace her. His first embrace in many long years. Bianca shrugged him off. 'No, brother. You sold me to him knowingly, and it is I must keep the bargain, not you.' She moved away from him. She would not cry, she would not. Last night and this morning she had thought him kind—and he could well afford to be, could he not? She lifted her head proudly. 'I give you leave to go, Lord Bernardo. I must be ready to accompany my lord. Tell Agneta to be ready.'

'Ah, but there is that, too,' said Bernardo. 'She is not to go with you. He does not wish it. Only he and his lieutenant will travel with you. He says you will have waiting women enough now that you are his wife, and she is old.'

Bianca's face grew whiter still. 'N-not take Agneta?' she stammered. 'I know that she is a great nuisance and a gossip, but she has looked after me since our mother died having me. He cannot have ordered that.'

'He can and did,' said Bernardo. 'And he is your lord now, and I cannot countermand his orders. She is to pack your bags and then bid you farewell, as we all must.' He looked uneasily at his sister. 'You are not to cry. I forbid you. And I think that it is better so. She has bullied you cruelly.'

'Well, you *would* think it better so, wouldn't you, having arranged it with him?' said Bianca with her usual perfect logic and in her usual nagging voice. It seemed that she would leave San Giorgio as she had lived in it— in the role of a shrew, badly dressed, and now without even a woman to accompany her. 'What did Agneta say when you told her this?'

'A lot,' said Bernardo ruefully. 'Cursed him, and then me, though why I should be cursed is beyond my wits. It was his decision, not mine.'

'Oh!' exclaimed Bianca, stamping her foot. 'You cannot be as stupid as you pretend to be. It is all your fault that I am married to him, and the whole tower knows it—and, by now, all San Giorgio as well.'

'So they do,' said Bernardo, goaded, 'and they all think that you are impossibly lucky, and wonder why such a flower of chivalry as he is should wish to marry a plain nag such as you are. Fall on your knees, sister, and thank the Lord God. You do not appreciate your own good fortune.'

What Bianca might have replied to these home-truths was never to be known, for Piero returned, dressed to leave, looked from one to the other, and said to Bernardo, 'You have told her, then?'

'Yes,' said Bianca, before Bernardo could answer, 'and why you could not have told me is beyond my wits. Unless, of course, you are ashamed.'

'Ashamed?' Piero gave a short laugh. He was as splendidly accoutred as usual, which seemed to make everything worse than it already was. 'Why should I be ashamed? I cannot be taking elderly trots into a soldiers' camp—she would set the whole *condotta* at one another's throats. No, my plans are quite different, and you shall know them in time. You must break your fast, make your farewells, for I wish no delay in setting out. I trust you are ready?'

Goaded, Bianca glared at him. 'My farewells? It is all one to me whether I go or stay. Either Bernardo rules me, or you do. At least you appear to know what you are doing, which Bernardo never does, so I suppose that I may be regarded as having gained by marrying you. But I would have liked Agneta to come with me, scold though she is.'

All the pleasant harmony they had shared in bed had vanished. Piero said coldly, 'No. I am sorry, but no. Now, run and eat your breakfast, and when you have finished your brother will escort you to the courtyard for us to make a formal farewell. Come, you are the Lady of Astra now, and must behave as a noble lady should. Your first lesson in your new life begins now.' He bowed to her. 'I await you, wife.'

CHAPTER FIVE

'Now, lady,' said Piero to Bianca when they were about to leave the tower. 'You must make your proper farewells to the townsfolk. You will smile, will you not? They must think you happy.'

'Then they will think wrong; but I was San Giorgio's lady, and I will not disappoint them.'

And the streets, as well as the courtyard, were crowded with those she had known, to say goodbye. Raimondo came forward to greet her, bowing low, saying, 'God save you, lady. May he give you a good journey home, a long life, a happy marriage, and many sons.'

Well, the last bit seemed to sum up her worth in the world, thought Bianca, but she was touched by the concern on his face, and the echoing murmurings of his staff. Agneta embroidered matters by hurling herself at Bianca and howling, 'The monster—he will not let me come with you. God save you, little lady, and give you many fine sons, although he does not deserve them.'

Through all the hubbub Lodovico sat on his fine horse with a face like stone, and it was Piero who threw her into the saddle, to ride sideways, something she hated, preferring to ride in the old-fashioned manner for women—like the men, and in boy's garments.

Bernardo was smiling, happy to have her off his hands at last and married to someone rich and powerful. He walked up to her. 'I see that you are a true lady at last, correctly mounted and obeying your lord. Continue to do so and all will be well. May God's blessings go with you, sister.'

All in all, it seemed to be God's morning, rather than hers—a blasphemous thought which she tried to suppress, but somehow being married had not changed her, or, if it had, had made her the more internally rebellious, not less.

She gave one last look around before Piero said gently, 'Come,' and then they were leaving her childhood behind, riding through the tower gateway, the crowded streets, finally through the Porte Maggiore into the open country beyond. Then San Giorgio was suddenly behind her, and her new owner was riding first before her, and then beside her, Lodovico shadowing her, as well as his master, their packhorse, loaded, behind them.

They rode on and upwards beyond the land she knew, and once, as they turned, she had a last glimpse of her old home, lying far behind them, tiny and perfect in the distance, like a small town in a painting, and it was difficult to believe that people lived there, that its streets pullulated with life. And then it was gone, and her world was Piero's, and his decisions hers.

Towards midday they slowed down—their mounts were tired, and the packhorse Lodovico was in charge of was heavily laden. They picked their way along a forest path, after turning off the road north, although road was a dignified name for the track built by the Tuscans who had lived here long ago.

Bianca looked eagerly about her, wondering what their destination was, as they slowed down even more and finally stopped in a wide clearing in the scrub which had succeeded the forest. There was a large hut there, and, beyond it, a pool of clear water, shaded by stands of trees—a pretty and idyllic spot.

Piero stopped, dismounted, waved a hand at Lodovico, who also dismounted, and then helped her down. Her legs were weary, and she sat down on a small bank, gazing about her.

Lodovico walked over to where Piero was busy unstrapping one of the packs on the spare horse.

'A word with you, boy,' he said, his voice high and angry, his manner astonishing Bianca—it was not at all that of a subordinate addressing his captain; and perhaps Piero thought so too, for he turned to Lodovico, saying,

'Must you? Ah, yes, I see that you must.'

'Yes,' said Lodovico, voice harsher still. 'A reckoning, we must have a reckoning, you and I. You lied to me. You promised me that you would not touch her. You gave me your worthless word. But Agneta showed us all the brute evidence of what you did. This for a drunken coward who violates girl children!' And without warning he struck Piero hard in the face.

Piero, taken off balance, staggered and fell to the ground. A fury of rage consumed Bianca at the sight of him on his hands and knees. She hurled herself at Lodovico, beating him about the body with her small fists.

'Oh, you villain! You wrong him. He never touched me.'

'But the sheet, the blood. So much of it. . .'

'His, not mine,' shrieked Bianca. 'He cut himself on the arm last night and stained the sheet so as not to shame me before San Giorgio, and then he slept on the floor. Oh, you have hurt him, and he was so kind to me last night. So kind.'

A sudden understanding overwhelmed her. She ran over to where Piero, still on his knees, was watching them. Of course, he had been kind, both last night and this morning.

'Oh, lord, let me help you.' She turned her angry face on Lodovico again. 'You don't understand. He is the only person in the whole wide world who has been kind to me. Ever.'

'Well, don't make too much of it,' said Piero from the ground. 'I am seldom kind to anybody, as Lodovico will tell you, and I doubt whether I shall be kind to you again.'

'I don't care. You were kind last night,' she replied,

and she began to cry, great gulping sobs, although whether they were for herself or Piero she hardly knew.

Lodovico helped her up, and then put out a hand to Piero, who took it, and rose himself. 'The child speaks the truth?' he asked in a low voice.

'No,' said Piero, 'she lies to save me. I deserved the blow.'

'Oh, I do not know which of you is the worse,' panted Bianca, 'you for striking him without warning, or he for lying. You may send for a wise woman when we reach the next town, and she will certify me virgin. Are you all mad in the world outside San Giorgio? How could you let him strike you, and go unpunished? You are his lord and his master.'

'No,' said Piero, then hesitated. 'You are my wife and must know the truth. He is my uncle, my mother's brother. He taught me arms, cared for me when the world rejected me. Without him I would not be leading a *condotta*, be a noted captain. He has the right to strike me—no one else has it, without danger of death, that is. I owe him everything I am.'

'And what is that?' said Bianca bitterly. 'Something to be proud of?'

'No,' said Piero, 'but better than I was. I thank you for defending me, wife, but do not care for me overmuch. Lodovico is right. I am not worth it.'

'Well, I know nothing of that,' said Bianca sturdily, 'but I would not have a man mishandled who does not deserve it. He may be all you say, but he should ask your pardon for striking you, and you should ask God's for miscalling yourself and me.'

Both men smiled, and, 'I am sorry for the blow,' Lodovico said. 'Whatever the truth, the child does not fear you. I would not have you break your vows to me; you have never done so before.'

'Break my vows!' said Piero. 'I have broken so many that you may consider you struck me for those.' He paused. 'And now you have brought the lady the clothes I commanded?'

'I did, although I am not happy about that, either.'

'Nor I,' said Piero, 'but I am not taking a woman of mine into a mercenary's camp where I, against all custom, have followed the English habit and do not allow my *condotta* to harbour women of any kind. And you well know that I cannot spare the men or the time to take her to my villa outside Florence or my estate at Astra. She may be my wife, but I cannot be seen to allow myself what I do not allow my men. Unpack what you have commandeered and hand the clothing to her.' He looked at Bianca. 'You may use the wood-cutter's hut to change yourself. The wood-cutter is long dead, and none lives near here now.'

'Change myself?' said Bianca. 'Whatever can you mean, lord?' and then, as Lodovico handed to her the clothing and other accoutrements of a page, flushed scarlet. 'I am to be a boy, lord? But why?'

'Safer so,' replied Piero. 'Fortunately you have the form and figure of a boy still, if an undermuscled one. My last page tired of following my banner, and decided to be a merchant's son again. His name was Dino. You may be Dino—easy for me to remember, and you must learn to answer to it.'

He considered her closely. 'I am sure that for the moment none will think you a girl child. You will live in my tent, and I shall protect you as much as possible.' He smiled. 'With your spirit I think that you may even like the life.'

'Oh, famous!' said Bianca acidly. 'You marry me, which makes me a woman, and then you unsex me to make me a man. What next? Is this truly necessary, lord?'

'Truly,' said Piero, 'given that I needed you away from San Giorgio. I had no intention of leaving you there. I would not ask you else. Even Lodovico agrees with me, although he is not happy about the whole affair. It will not be for long, I promise you, and after that you may be my wife again and a woman.'

There was no arguing with him. There was always something about the way he spoke and acted which compelled obedience. She had seen it with Agneta and the other servants, and with Lodovico. Even when Lodovico had struck him, he had retained his control over his uncle. She picked up the clothes and walked to the hut, where she stripped off the ugly gown in which Agneta had dressed her so long ago—was it really only that morning?—and began to put on her page's garb.

There was a little pair of man's underpants—a mutande—a fine linen shirt, and a doublet of blue and silver, rather like the one Piero had worn to marry her in; a pair of blue hose, which had to be laced to the shirt, and something which resembled the underpants to be worn to cover her non-existent male parts decently. Over all this was a kind of quilted tabard or tunic, without sides, again in blue and silver, with grey fur running along the hem and round the neck; a leather belt with a metal buckle, a hanging purse on it, and a small dagger with an elaborate handle. Finally, a pair of boots, a trifle large, but of the finest leather, completed her outfit.

Nothing had been forgotten; there was even a conical hat with a piece of jewellery, embellished with a tiny sapphire, pinned to it. Later Bianca was to discover that she had also been given a miniature breastplate, and a metal gorget to be worn round the neck. Nothing fitted quite perfectly, but well enough. After all, pages were not supposed to be glasses of fashion, but utilitarian things. There was also a quarterstaff, with a metal knob and point at the end, which would rest in a harness beside her saddle.

Last of all she put on a long cloak with a fine clasp at the neck. She walked outside, feeling rather foolish in all this strange finery, for everything was of a much better stuff than anything she had ever worn before, to discover that Piero and Lodovico had changed out of their courtier's clothing into the working clothes of the soldiers they were. Piero still managed to look impossibly hand-some in his worn leather hacketon or jerkin, hammered steel belt, coarse linen shirt and serviceable boots.

They had also removed the lady's saddle from her horse, and replaced it with a man's. Both Piero and Lodovico stared at her as she strode forward, trying to pretend that she was a boy, instinctively copying the swagger of the pages at San Giorgio. Piero began to laugh.

'Do I look so strange?' she asked, nettled. '*I* did not choose to wear such garb.'

'Not strange. You make a splendid boy,' said Piero gravely, 'handsome even. But your hair, it must be shorn.'

Bianca let out a wail. 'Oh, no! It is my only good point, or so Agneta says. Cruel to lose it.'

Piero was severe at this. 'Agneta is quite wrong, as appeared usual with her,' he said. 'And I cannot have a page with hair down to his waist,' he added reasonably. 'Think of the comment it would occasion. I have my reputation to think of!'

He dived into his pack and came up with a small pair of shears. Did he carry everything he might need? thought Bianca, and as though he caught her internal question he said, 'One should be prepared for all even-tualities, wife. Come here, and we will make a charming little Dino of you. Pretty, but not too much so.'

Pretty! He was mocking her again, Bianca thought resentfully, but allowed him to throw a small silk towel about her shoulders and cut her abundant tresses. She watched them fall to the ground, the tears not far away, as he turned her to and fro, and used the cruel scissors until her curls sprang neatly about her face.

He stepped back to admire his work, and nodded approvingly. 'There, that will do. Now remember. Your name is Dino, and you will not think of yourself as Bianca. When I give you an order, or if anyone else does, you will jump to it. That is correct, is it not, Lodovico?'

'True,' said Lodovico, who had reverted to his usual silent self. 'A page is expected to be obedient, not to argue. No tantrums, lady, no nagging. Unruly pages have a hard time of it.'

'I might have known there would be drawbacks to being a boy,' grumbled Bianca, 'even though I have always wanted to be one. I thought that they were allowed to run free, unlike girls, but from what you say I see that I was wrong.'

'Very wrong,' said Piero, the secret smile on his lips again. 'It is girls who have the best of it, as you will soon find out. Boys, especially pages, are expected to work hard. You must take care of my horse, clean its furniture, as well as my armour; lay out and see to my clothes, keep my boots in good repair, and serve me my food and drink as and when I wish, and clean up after me. Beside all this you will be expected to learn how to use a quarterstaff, a sword and a dagger, wind and use a crossbow, a longbow, and shoot with them, too. Then you will be trained to be part of a three-man lance— that is, you will hold the horses of the men fighting with the lance, which takes two to wield it, and, although you will be at the rear of the battle, when the enemy breaks, you will ride forward on your own horse, with their horses, and pursue the enemy with them.

'So, of course, will you be expected to be able to control and school a warhorse. Your days will be full, indeed, with so much to do. On the other hand, you will not be asked to scrub floors—that should be a comfort to you.'

Bianca listened to this solemn recital of her duties in horror. 'If I am expected to do all that at once, when do I eat and sleep, lord? If that is to be my life, I shall grow smaller with effort, not larger.'

'Oh, no,' said Piero decidedly. 'On the contrary; exercise will make you grow, especially as I shall take every opportunity to see you properly fed for the first time in your life. We shall begin now, I promise you. See, Lodovico has started to unpack our food. Your first duty is to assist him, and your second is to eat as much as possible—and drink a little of the good wine he has brought along in that skin, as well.'

So he was—unpacking the food, that was—and so she did—eat and drink as she had never done before, wolfishly tearing at the food, for the ride had given her an appetite. They sat beneath the trees, and Lodovico handed out sliced meat and bread, and cheese and fruit. The wine was good, and she drank it from the skin, copying the two men.

'Not too much,' said Piero approvingly, as the red liquid ran down her throat. His face, as he watched her attack her food with such energy, had lost its usual impassivity; he was openly smiling at her.

Bianca looked at him, her mouth full. 'I amuse you, lord?'

'A good appetite always pleases me.'

'I know I am not ladylike, but, now that I am a page, I may eat as they do. I have been so hungry all my life. Pages do not need to be dainty in your *condotta*, do they, lord?'

'Have no fear of that,' said Piero. 'Pages are many things, but never dainty.'

'Well, that is a relief for me,' said Bianca frankly. 'I have never managed to be dainty yet, and Agneta was always grumbling about my bad habits. She would have fits if she could see me dressed like this and eating so greedily.'

'So now you see why she could not accompany you. I hope that your masquerade may not be for long, but I must return to the *condotta* without delay. I have been away quite long enough. You will be careful to remain a page at all times, will you not? If you are troubled about anything, for the life will be strange and harsh, you must

seek my help or Lodovico's, although I must say I hope
that that will not be necessary.'

'I understand you, lord,' said Bianca, licking her
fingers carefully—no point in wasting good food even if
there was going to be plenty of it in future. 'But I cannot
think that I shall be a very useful page. I may be the
same size as a boy, but I do not possess a boy's strength.'

'No, but we shall tell everyone that you are a very
young boy, and raw at that. That you must not be
schooled overmuch until you have grown—and by then,
God willing, you will be gone, and will be my lady
again.'

There was one good thing about him, thought Bianca,
after the meal was over, and they lay sleepily in the sun,
for they must give their horses—which she had helped
Lodovico to feed—time to recover: he did not talk down,
or condescend to her. Would he always treat her so? Or
would he, when she wore women's clothing again, speak
to her as though she were a fool, as men usually did to
women—except when they were trying to make them
sleep with them that was, thinking of Bernardo's treatment of Giulietta and her predecessors. Oh, she did hope
not. Father Luca had said, often and often, that her
understanding was good, and more than a woman
needed. Perhaps it would help her now that she was to
be Piero's page, even if only for a short time.

'You had best begin your duties now, Dino,' said
Piero, the half-smile still on his lips. 'It is your duty to
tidy up after meals, and also to hand me more drink, if I
need it. I do need it, and you may serve it to me in the
metal cup you will find in my saddle-bags.'

Bianca—no, I am Dino, must think of myself as Dino,
she told herself—decided that he was not joking, found
the cup, took the skin from Lodovico and poured her
lord a good measure. She did all this using the page's
trot, the half-run all good pages employed, and which
would be her hallmark as long as she wore boy's
clothing. She handed the cup to her lord.

'On one knee as you serve it,' he said gravely, and watched her do as she was bidden, before he took the cup from her. In doing so their hands touched, and again that sudden shock of pleasure ran through Dino. She thought that Piero felt it, too, for his eyes widened a little, and the smile he gave her was lop-sided and questioning, one eyebrow raised.

'You learn rapidly, Dino,' was all he said.

'At your pleasure, lord,' she replied, as she had heard the pages speak to Bernardo. Sitting there, his expression faintly mocking, he was even more impossible than ever. How could anyone be so much in control of himself as Piero de' Manfredini was? Dino wondered. Even when Lodovico had struck him, and he had been helpless on the ground, he had somehow retained control of himself. Had he been taught that? Or was it an integral part of him, as her fiery temper was part of her? Would she ever find out, or was he to remain always a mystery?

'And now you must go to the pond and clean the cup and the knives,' he said, 'and finally pack all into the bags. Lodovico will show you what to do.'

Both men watched her trot down to the water. Lodovico said, 'I misjudged you once, boy, and would not do so again. Do not be too hard on the little one. She has a brave spirit, but she is far from home and friends.'

Something moved in Piero's now impassive face. Some emotion was repressed. 'It will not help her for me to be too kind,' he said. 'She must survive among the pages. My protection can only stretch a little way.'

'And this is necessary?'

'You know it is.'

'I know that you could have left her in San Giorgio and claimed her later.'

'Left her to what?' said Piero drily. 'To have her brave spirit destroyed by the fools around her? She is best away from them. You know that.'

'And you are God, of course,' said Lodovico, 'to dispose of men and girl children as you please.'

Both Piero's eyebrows climbed haughtily. 'You presume on our relationship at times,' he said. 'And now that she is my wife I must protect her, as her brother did not, and would not have done, else he would not have virtually sold her to me in such a careless fashion.'

Lodovico smiled a little sourly at that. 'And who got the best bargain, nephew, he or you?'

'Why, I did,' said Piero coolly. 'I have a wife who will do me honour when she grows up at last, and will be a beauty besides.'

It was the turn of Lodovico's eyebrows to climb. He said sardonically, 'You tell fortunes, too?' but fell silent as Dino returned to drop to her knees beside the pack he had opened, and begin to replace what they had not eaten, and the utensils they had used. Her dark head was bent over her task and the slender fingers moved to and fro as she finally relaced the pack and handed it to Lodovico, who said, 'No, Dino, you must keep it with you now. I will show you how to fasten it to your horse furniture.'

Helping her, he asked, head bent towards her, the stone face a little kind, 'It will not trouble you to ride astride?'

'Oh, no,' said Dino, face eager. 'I always preferred doing that to using a lady's saddle. But Bernardo said that the Lady of San Giorgio must try to be a lady, and for the last year he has made me ride like one—which I do not enjoy at all.'

She was so quick and eager to learn, now trotting beside Lodovico to finish her duties, now tidying up and removing the last traces of their meal, that Piero, despite himself, caught his breath a little. Oh, I have the right of it. I know that I see true. She is a bright spirit, and one day will be a wife to bring me honour, perhaps—who knows?—a wife to love—if I can bring myself to love anyone, that is.

By late afternoon, however, even Dino's spirit was a little daunted and she had begun to droop in the saddle.

She was not accustomed to lengthy physical exercise, as
the two men were, but she was determined not to
complain. She had often wished to be a boy, and now
was one; it was humiliating to behave so weakly on the
very first afternoon. Pride and her will pulled her erect
in the saddle again.

Just as she was beginning to feel that even this would
not be sufficient to keep her going, the path suddenly
began to lead downwards, and she saw, far below them,
tents, pavilions, banners and pennants, and heard, even
at that distance, the noise of a camp of men, a noise
which she had never heard before, but which was
unmistakable. A noise which she would learn to live
with, and finally ignore, so that quiet seemed strange
when she encountered it again.

She sat up even straighter, determined to shame
neither herself nor her lord. Piero looked across at her,
and said quietly, 'Bravo, Dino. We are here at last, and
you have not complained once. A good start to your new
career. I need hardly tell you that that is my *condotta*
camped below us, before Trani, and they will be expecting me, I hope.'

They passed sentries, who saluted them, their captain
bowing low to Piero, who acknowledged them with a
brief lift of his hand. The flags, which flew everywhere,
bore falcons on them.

They rode through lines of tents, some large, some
small, past straw huts in which the lesser men-at-arms
lived, past smithies, where blacksmiths clanged their
hammers on their anvils, making, repairing and improving armour, and shoeing horses. There was even a
spacious area set on one side, near the stables, covered
in straw, which Dino wondered at, later to discover it
was where the pages and the horses were schooled. Fires,
with tripods carrying braziers to cook food, were everywhere, and men.

They were men of all shapes and sizes, wearing
different clothing and accoutrement, but all with the

falcon on them. They stared, but not too hard, at their captain and his lieutenant as they rode up. He had acquired a page, but that did not interest them.

Dino saw many pages, wearing similar clothing to herself. Some were large, some as small as she. Piero had told her, before they set out from the clearing where they had changed, that many pages were noble, learning the trade of arms, as landless younger sons, while others were peasants who sought to better themselves. 'I was a page once,' he had said.

They finally entered a kind of square where the largest tents of all were pitched. One—Piero's—was particularly large and splendid. In the middle of the square were rude tables and benches. Pinned to one table, by a dagger, was a large square of parchment. A man sat on a bench, examining it, other men standing about behind him; they all looked up at the sound of their coming, and, on seeing who it was, the sitting man jumped to his feet and made a rough salute, as did all the other men, who straightened themselves up, losing the unmilitary slouch they had adopted before Piero's arrival.

'You are back betimes, lord,' said the man who had been seated.

'Yes.' Piero dismounted then shouted to Dino, 'Take the reins of my horse, boy,' and then to the man who had greeted him, 'My journey was a fruitless one, as I expected.'

The man to whom he spoke was dressed like Piero, and was nearly as tall as he was. He wore a falcon on his tabard, over half-armour, and was red-haired in a handsome, rather ordinary way. Perhaps everyone looked rather ordinary, once you had seen Piero, was Dino's conclusion. He reminded her of a hundred men-at-arms, and his idle gaze swung over her, and then away.

'I see you brought back a page, if nothing else.'

'Yes—Dino,' said Piero, looking down at her. 'Make your salute to Captain Han Van Eyck, Dino. He is my second in command, and will probably run you around, too. Otherwise, San Giorgio was a waste of time. Its ruler is a drunken clod without money or lands, and proposed a deal by which the Medici would fund him to raise troops for me! By which you may learn his lack of understanding of the world of politics and war. The *condotta* is in good order, I trust, and ready to regroup?'

Van Eyck, who looked as though he thought that Piero's acquiring a page was a waste of time, replied, 'Yes, but there will be more trouble and delays, I fear. I had the Florentine Commissary, Bruschini, here yesterday. He has arrived with a company which he says is run by Alberic Carpacci, but I suspect that he has funded it, and that Carpacci is a figurehead. Thus he tries to bite us twice. He complains that Trani is too difficult to attack, that somehow the siege is failing.' He gestured in the direction of the town which lay before them, hidden by its walls. 'He says that they should long ago have run out of food and still they do not surrender. He talks of a frontal attack.'

Piero went quite still. 'How very helpful of him,' he said, his voice steel, 'to tell us what we already know. But a frontal attack! Not with my *condotta*. He may sacrifice his own with pleasure.'

Van Eyck began to laugh. 'Aye. I told him that you'd say that. He said that Florence paid you, that he was here to oversee the way you spent their money, and he would have his dues.'

'Did he, indeed? And what dues are these? Let him read my contract before he asks the impossible. I, and no one else, control any company before Trani, whether hired by Florence or Bruschini or the Lord God Almighty. Moreover I warned the *signoria* when they hired me that to take Trani would prove long and difficult, and that being so they might think twice before attempting it. They said then that they were prepared for me to take as long as was necessary to reduce it, and paid me accordingly. We haggled for a week over the contract's terms, and if Messer Bruschini does not like them he must blame his masters in Florence, not me. Now, I see that you have the map I asked you to prepare before I left, but before I examine it I need to go to my pavilion. Lodovico, take Dino and the horses to their stables, and then report back to me. Han, in five minutes come to me with the map, and before we regroup tomorrow I'll think this matter of Trani through. There are more ways of cracking a nut then smashing both nut and crackers to pieces.'

He is as sharp with everyone as he is with me, thought Dino, which is a relief. She let Lodovico lead her through the encampment to the stables, and, tired though she was, fed and watered her horse and Piero's, Lodovico helping her with her new duties, and showing her what to do.

Back at Piero's pavilion her final duty was to prepare Piero's bed for the night, and find a palliasse for herself to sleep on, in one corner. This meant trotting to the quartermaster in charge of stores, and then a visit to a cook to arrange food for herself and Piero and Lodovico.

Han and Piero talked at a table inside Piero's pavilion, seated in great chairs even more magnificent than Bernardo's. Everyone who came in—and Piero sent for several captains and lieutenants—obeyed him without question, although he often stopped to ask their opinion of what he proposed, and sometimes adopted it, but there was never any doubt that here he was supreme.

Later, she helped to serve a meal to the small council of war. She gathered that Piero was rearranging the company around Trani—he was sure that somehow they must be smuggling food into the town, although how, and where, no one knew.

'The trouble is,' he said to Lodovico, while Dino helped him out of his half-armour and his clothes, 'no company is large enough to police all the land around Trani, and the thinner we spread ourselves, the more dangerous our situation if they should try a sortie out of

the walls. Not that I think *that* likely, but who would
have thought it likely that they would withstand us so
long? Bruschini does have a point there, and even though
I warned the *signoria* of the difficulties before us I think
that they expected miracles from me, and at the moment
they are in short supply. Dino,' he said, without changing his tone, 'you look tired unto death. I give you
permission to go to bed at once. I will be my own page
tonight.'

Dino had carried out her duties manfully, but her
head was drooping however hard she tried to hold it up.
'Do not look distressed, my page,' he said. 'You have
much to do in the morning. Your real duties begin then,
and you will feel better after an early night. You have
had a long day.'

'And then,' said Naldo, Van Eyck's page, to Dino as she
sat cleaning Piero's harness. 'What did the Lord Captain
say to you then?'

'Why, that he wanted a page and that I would do.'
Dino breathed on the bright metal, and polished it with
the cloth which Lodovico had given her on her first
morning with the *condotta*. Since then, they had upped
sticks, as Naldo said, and moved to another position
outside Trani, before the great gates, so that the inhabi-
tants could see that the Golden Falcon himself considered them his prey.

Naldo was Dino's friend among the pages. He was
smaller than the rest, clumsier, incompetent, and was a
target for Tavio, the pages' lieutenant. Tavio was large,
nasty and aggrieved. He didn't like Dino because he had
hoped to become de' Manfredini's page himself, and felt
that he had been passed over.

He bullied Naldo a lot, but not Dino—or at least not
so much—because he was a clever bully who didn't wish
to annoy the lord more than he thought wise. The lord
had said that Dino was raw and should not be pushed
too hard, at first. Watching Dino, Tavio had decided

that the lord was wrong, for once. Dino was a cunning
little bastard, with too much spirit for a novice page,
needed to be put down a little, rather than cosseted; he
even protected Naldo, helped him as though it were
Naldo who was the newcomer. Dino had a high temper,
too, and a nasty tongue. Well, if for some reason he had
to go careful with Dino until he was ordered otherwise,
he could get back at him by persecuting Naldo the
harder. Then Dino might do something which would
allow him to rightfully punish the pretty little bastard.

Dino, unaware of all these curdling passions about
her, was seated with Naldo in the early morning sun,
doing the first of her day's duties. In a little while, she
was, with the others, to be put through her paces by the
sergeant of the pages—an old man, kept only to train
them in the military arts of which he had once been a
master.

Dino had expected to dislike this part of her work, but
found that some of it was strangely exhilarating, some
difficult, and some repulsive. She liked learning to use
the page's sword, a miniature of Piero's great broadsword. Not that they used a real sword in practice, only
a wooden one, made heavy with lead so that they could
learn to understand its true weight. But the thought, as
she swung it around her head and dodged and panted,
and finally hit Naldo with it hard, that in a real fight she
would have killed him made her feel sick, and later made
her stay her arm, so that the sergeant swore at her, using
words she did not understand, although in the rough life
of the camp she soon came to know them, and occasionally to use them, to Piero's secret amusement.

Piero had come to watch them that morning, and she
threw him an agonised glance, as the sergeant finally
roared, 'I'll have no girlish milksops in my troop. When
you see an opening, boy, strike, and strike hard! No
hanging back.'

And then it was Naldo's turn for rebuke. 'And, Naldo,
if you can let a novice teach you lessons after all this

time. . .' And more dreadful oaths followed, Dino listening, fascinated, and Naldo blinking back the tears.

'Let me teach the new boy, Sergeant,' shouted Tavio, 'I can show him what's what, you may be sure,' only to be sworn at in his turn.

'Be silent, impudence! He is not ready for you yet.'

Piero turned away, the long mouth twitching. He had been worried about Dino's survival among the pages, but he had seen the fiery way in which she had squared up to Tavio when he had made his challenge, and later had said to her, 'You will be careful, my page. It is not for you to try to fight Tavio. He has almost achieved his man's strength, will soon be a man-at-arms, which is why I have not made him my page—I would soon lose him.'

'Well, I certainly don't want to fight him, in any way,' returned Dino frankly. 'He is far too strong for me, as are most of the ones who are my true age. But the smaller ones, like Naldo, I am on equal terms with. I don't think that they guess that I am older, or a girl.'

Piero was astonished at how worried he was at the thought of Dino coming to harm, not only because she was his wife, but because something inside him trembled at the mere idea of her being hurt. 'You will not be here long, I hope,' he said, 'and you must try not to be too much involved with them. I will think up duties for you inside my pavilion.'

'But not too many, lord,' said Dino cheekily, smiling up at Piero in a way which made his heart lurch again. Surely he could not be falling in love with the child? It was pity he felt for her after all, he told himself sternly. Love did not exist—it was something one felt briefly when sexually engaged with a woman, it had no part in his real life. Eventually they would mate, and she would bear children for him. Meantime she was here, and must not be injured.

Dino knew little of how Piero was beginning to feel. She knew that her own feelings for him were changing now that she was so much with him, but the difficulties and pleasures of living among the pages engrossed her, too. She was remembering this last conversation with him, and the strange way he had looked at her at the end of it, while she cleaned his harness and chatted with Naldo, peaceful after preparing their respective masters for the day.

She was happy because they were to school horses again later that morning. Yesterday it had been quarter-staff training and she liked that less than sword practice. As with the sword she was skilful with her little staff, having the good co-ordination of hand and eye which served her well on a horse, too, but, even more than with the wooden sword, she hated to hit anyone hard, even in play, and Tavio and the sergeant had both noticed this. More oaths and reprimands followed from the sergeant, with further comment from Tavio.

'Couldn't knock the wings off a fly, let alone knock Naldo's head off,' he scorned, Naldo being her opponent again, seeing that they were much the same size. Tavio had jeered this at her as she jumped out of Naldo's clumsy way for the twentieth time, and still had not battered him with her staff as she should have done.

She had leaned on it breathlessly at the end, gazing fiercely on her tormentor. Tavio reminded her too much of Enzo, the page who had tried to force her on the battlements one morning. She shuddered at the thought of what Tavio might do to her if he discovered that she was a girl, and said sharply to him, 'God give me another few inches of height and a little more strength, and I'd soon show *you* what I could do with a quarter-staff, that's for sure. Poor Naldo's been battered by every page in the camp. Why should I add to the number? It's plain that I can defeat him, without me addling his brains for him further. I've no wish to render him witless.'

'The lord said a priest had the raising of you,' had said Tavio nastily, 'and that is plain to see. Such care for others and such unmanly modesty.' He was referring to Dino's delicacy; his refusal to relieve himself publicly, and play in the other pages' games when they did; his refusal to join in the dreadful boasting about women, which all the pages indulged in to show their manliness.

'So long as I do my duties, to you and to my lord and Taddeo, the sergeant,' she had said, 'what matter if a priest, or a *madame* in a brothel had trained me?'

Tavio had raised his fist at her. 'That's right,' she had said, dodging away from him and pulling a face. 'Who's the brave lad, then, who only beats the small pages and dodges the large ones?'

She was saved from mishandling by Facetti, Tavio's captain, appearing, and bellowing for Tavio to assist him with his armour. He had unwillingly taken Tavio on when his own lad had graduated to man-at-arms.

'You'll go too far one of these days, Dino,' had been Naldo's admiring comment. 'Your tongue is nearly as nasty as the Lord Piero's. Did you learn it from him?'

'Well, not from Father Luca, that's for sure,' had said Dino, with a grin. 'And I doubt whether the Lord Piero got his from the religious, either.'

Naldo had begun to laugh at that. 'You don't know his history, then? Only met him when he came to San Giorgio, did you?'

'What history?' she had said, interested. Useful to know something more of Piero de' Manfredini; it might help to explain him.

'Why, that he was Manfredini's bastard, son of the Marquis of Alessio, and was shoved into a monastery to be got rid of when he was a little lad—the Marquis is of the old school, too proud to acknowledge bastards. And then the monks booted him out when he was fifteen for slipping out at night and enjoying himself with the girls and women in the neighbouring town—even pleasured himself at the house there, they say. He can have any woman he wants, rumour says. Merely by looking at her. God grant that I may be like him when I am a man,' said Naldo wistfully. 'Imagine how the feathers flew when the monks found out what he was doing. And then that uncle of his, who had been a man-at-arms, took him off to the wars and trained him, and before anyone could turn round he had his own troop, and then a *condotta*. Even the greatest captains are afraid of him, and they say that he is Florence's favourite, which is why Bruschini hates him.'

'How do you know all this?' she had answered, fascinated by this career of original sin at such an early age.

'How he started, you mean? Oh, everyone knows that. And about Bruschini? Why, Tavio was listening when the lord and Van Eyck and Facetti talked with Bruschini and Carpacci. The Florentine said that he had a good idea—that the Lord Piero's *condotta* should raise a frontal attack to take Trani. Whereon the Lord Piero said, "Why, I have a better, Messer Bruschini: that we should use yours, instead." Tavio said that the Florentine was like to expire of a syncope. He called the Lord Piero an ignorant young pup, and the Lord Piero said, "Better that than being an ignorant old dog." '

They had both laughed heartily until the sergeant had appeared to round them up to work with crossbows. None of them liked winding the bows up, but they all enjoyed using them to fire at targets, and Dino found that she was good at that, possessing a true eye.

The harness was clean at last, and her thoughts returned to the present. Always, when she worked, she found herself thinking and thinking. About the past, the present, and Piero. What Naldo had told her, the day before, had given her an insight into him and his character. Nobody loved him, she thought suddenly. We are alike in that, if nothing else. Bernardo certainly never cared for me; and Agneta—well, she might have loved me, but she showed it in strange ways. She heard Taddeo shouting, and jumped up eagerly. The horses! It was quite her favourite exercise, and she always looked forward to it. How she had resented Bernardo's orders that she was to be a lady, and ride a horse like an old woman. Now she could ride bareback and enjoy herself to her heart's content, and be praised for doing it, too. She ran forward to join the others.

CHAPTER SIX

'LODOVICO.' Piero spoke from the table in his pavilion. He was leaning forward, chin propped on hand, staring unseeingly at the map which he had drawn from memory in San Giorgio, and modified from the one which Han Van Eyck had made for him while he had been away.

'Captain?' replied Lodovico stiffly.

'I must see Bruschini today; I cannot put it off, or he will be striding round here, bellowing orders. This afternoon, perhaps. Tell Dino when he comes back to put out my half-armour—wearing that should remind Bruschini that he is a clerk, however much he pretends that he is a military leader. He needs to have that rubbed in.'

'Is it wise to antagonise him quite so much?' queried Lodovico.

'Wise?' said Piero, as though he did not know what the word meant. 'It depends where wisdom resides. But if I give way at all, then farewell, leadership, and I might as well hand him my *condotta* to slaughter—for sure, slaughtered it would be if he were given his head.'

He had sat down after Lodovico had gone, and his expression was by no means as confident as the one he usually wore in public. Trani was beginning to turn into a mountain to be climbed. It had never been a molehill, but he thought that it should have fallen by now. Every day which passed without surrender made the campaign costlier, and annoyed his paymasters. Never mind that he had warned them of the difficulties ahead; that would count for nothing if he could not hand them victory— and soon, particularly with Bruschini dripping poison in everyone's ears.

He rose, and began to make his way to Facetti's tent.

Van Eyck had ridden out to the perimeter of the camp and beyond to check for convoys which might be supplying Trani secretly.

He only walked for a little way, men-at-arms staring at him as he passed. He was not usually alone, but he had deliberately left Lodovico behind to guard Dino a little, to see that she did not wander far from the pavilion when the morning's training was over. He heard the noise of shouting and cheering coming from the arena where the horses and pages were schooled.

Curiosity overcame him, as well as his determination to oversee as much as possible, as often as he could, what went on in the camp. His habit of appearing suddenly kept his men on their toes, and even though they cursed him for his ubiquity the more thoughtful were aware that his success was founded on his tireless leadership in everything to do with his *condotta*. Not for him the pride of those *condottieri* who left the mechanics of running the company solely to their subordinates.

Lodovico, there before him, doubtless to watch over Dino, without Dino knowing that he was doing it, arms folded, was leaning against the blacksmith's hut, where others, too, had assembled to watch Taddeo school the pages in horsemanship. They were riding in a huge circle, Taddeo in the middle, waving a stick, and shouting orders. Piero's whole body stiffened, he said, 'Ah, God, no,' and made to stride forward to stop the training, only for Lodovico's arm to shoot out to stop him.

Riding bareback, at the front of the circling line, on his big black warhorse, Attila, was Dino, face alight with joy. She was controlling the horse with only a headstall. Taddeo, his stick pointed in her direction, was shouting orders at her. 'Left, lad, left a little, use the foot gently, gently; that's it. Sweet Jesu, you are an example to them all.'

Piero did not hear him. Saw only Dino doing something dangerous. A great surge of protectiveness swept over him—something he had only felt once before, when she had entered her brother's room to find that he had won her.

'She cannot. . .' he began and started forward again, only to be stopped again by Lodovico.

'There is no she,' said Lodovico. 'You have willed it otherwise. And you must pay the price. You cannot make a favourite of your page, you for whom discipline is everything. Besides, she is safe on the horse, and even if she were not there is nothing, in honesty, that you could do for her. Watch.'

Taddeo continued to shout his orders. Dino stopped the great horse, and with gentle movements of her arms and legs put him through his paces while she held him in a standing position. One leg raised, and then dropped, he began a standing trot.

'*Per Dio*,' one of the watching men shouted, 'put the lad in for the Palio at Siena, Taddeo, and I'll bet a year's pay on him. He talks to the horse, and the horse to him.'

It was true. Dino, sitting there, was filled with an ecstatic happiness which she had never known before. She had always ridden, and ridden well, but this kind of discipline was new, and she and the horse were one. She suddenly saw Piero, face white, and flashed him a blazing smile. All the hard work of the past weeks was nothing. It had given her this. It was as though she were an extension of Taddeo, as well as the horse, and when he called she obeyed.

Behind her the other boys were performing clumsy imitations of her skill, and the sergeant swore at them for their lack of grace. With the quarterstaff and the sword she could only compete with the little boys, but here she was supreme, Diana, goddess of the hunt in boy's clothes. Her happiness overflowed when she saw Piero watching her, and could not imagine why he, who usually showed so little emotion, should look so worried.

The moment Taddeo released them, she flung herself

off the horse, and, holding the reins, ran towards him, to the amusement of the men around him.

'You saw me, lord? And Attila? He is a marvel. Does exactly what he is told. Taddeo thinks that I do it, but it is Attila who wills it.'

'*Per Dio*,' said Piero, amusement on his face, unable to prevent himself from responding to her pleasure. 'I have a likely page who expects his lord to applaud his exploits, instead of the other way round!'

Dino clapped her hands over her mouth. Bowed. 'Oh, Lord Piero, I forgot the honour due to you.' She then went on one knee, and bent her head as she had been taught. 'I am yours to command. Command me.'

The laughter from the soldiers around them grew. Piero put a hand on the dark head bowed before him. 'Get up, boy. Go to my quarters immediately. I need to change out of this finery——' he was dressed in splendid scarlet '——put out my working armour. You know where to find it?'

'Of course, lord. I fly like the wind.' And she gave him a smile so sunnily impudent that it unexpectedly wrung his heart, so full was it of unadulterated happiness. She ran off, shouting as she went. 'I will see you later, Naldo; my lord needs me *at once*, and I must go.'

Guffaws followed her. 'And where did you find that cheeky sparrow, lord?' said one bold man-at-arms.

Piero took no offence. 'Why, in the priest's parlour, where else?' He was as amused as they were. The Lady of San Giorgio had found her spiritual home in the corps of pages in a *condotta* camped outside a town that would not be taken.

Dino, almost bursting with happiness, was reverently laying out Piero's clothes when he re-entered his pavilion, closing the flaps behind him. For the first time in her short life she had an aim and a purpose, was not being tugged and pulled by others, was suddenly finding that she had skills and abilities which she had not known she possessed.

She was humming gently as she worked, and did not hear Piero enter. He stood and watched her, overcome by some of the strangest sensations he had ever felt. His wife, and not his wife—a boy who was a girl; Dino, who was Bianca. He saw, too, something else, something which echoed Dino's own thoughts. He saw that all her fire and passion, which had been wasted in San Giorgio, which had dwindled there through lack of opportunity into wilfulness and naughtiness, were translated here, through opportunity, into action and accomplishment. Saw, too, that she had the mind and spirit, if not the body, of a brave and gifted man, and he, by his idle and selfish whim, had given her the possibility of fulfilment beyond anything she could ever have hoped for.

And when she became a woman, what then? Was it not his duty to see that, wife to him though she might be, what she had learned should not be lost, but should be used to turn her into a fit partner of whom not only might he be proud, but would also make her a superb mother for his children, and an ornament to his name?

Oh, and more than that he suddenly knew that he could hardly wait for her to be a woman, that the last weeks of having her with him, being looked after by her, had created in him a desire for more than mere companionship, that he had put himself into temptation. And, worse than that, or perhaps better—who knew?— he was beginning to feel something for her which he had never felt for any woman, and he was fearful that that sensation was love.

Dino suddenly sensed his presence, hidden though he was, behind her.

'Lord? All is ready for you, lord,' and she proudly indicated the result of her work. Everything was carefully laid out, the armour polished and shining.

Piero moved forward until he reached her, and said gently, 'Look at me, little one.'

Dino raised her head, 'Lord?'

'You must not put yourself in danger, Bianca.' To his surprise, he was thinking of her as a woman.

'Dino, lord, my name is Dino,' she said quickly. 'And how may I avoid danger? I am your page, lord.'

'Do not be reckless,' he said softly. 'Be a little of a coward.'

Her bright face darkened. 'I could not be so, lord. Naldo is a little of a coward, and he is not happy.'

'I cannot protect you too much,' he said, and took her hand. It was stained and grubby. He turned it over, saw the calluses which hard work was giving her, saw suddenly that the last few weeks of good food had filled out her face, given her a good colour, and that Dino the page was a handsome boy.

Dino looked up at him. She could have sworn that impossibly perfect Piero had a worried expression on his face. How could that be?

'Lord,' she ventured, 'if any come in, they will think it passing strange that you hold your page's hand so tenderly.'

He lifted it and kissed it before he let it go.

'You are a better schemer than I am, madam wife.'

Dino unconsciously stroked her hand where he had held it. The strange sensations she felt whenever he touched her were growing stronger and stronger. Today she felt odder than ever. Moths had invaded her body, and she was suddenly enormously conscious of it, as though his eyes could pierce her clothing, and see straight through to Bernardo's filleted herring. Only, she was not quite so filleted these days. Yesterday, when Piero and Lodovico were absent, she had a meagre strip-wash in the pavilion, and when she had removed her shirt she had discovered that she was no longer completely flat. Her breasts had grown into two little buds, buds which felt quite tender, and had not been there last week. She was grateful for her padded doublet because she suspected that once such growth had begun it would not stop. Perhaps perfect Piero was right again.

Good food and exercise were beginning to change her. Suppose her courses began? That would be inconvenient, to say the least. She also had the strangest desire to be even more impudent with him than she had been in San Giorgio—almost as though she wanted to provoke him into the knowledge that she was with him, and was his wife.

To his last protestation about her duplicity being greater than his, she could not help responding cheekily, 'Oh, that would be difficult, lord,' and her whole face was innocently naughty. 'I am assured that the Captain de' Manfredini, the Lord of Astra, is the biggest trickster in all Italy.'

'You deserve a blow for that, my page,' said Piero softly, but neither his voice nor his manner were reproving—loving rather.

They were closer together than they had been since they had shared the bed at San Giorgio. I may have no chest—or only a little one—and still no hips, thought Dino, and I wear a boy's clothes; but can it be that these strange feelings which are beginning to overwhelm me are quite womanly, and not at all proper for the lord's page to entertain? How strange to think that I may be falling in love with impossibly perfect Piero, whom I was so sure I detested?

Her heart had begun to hammer, and she felt as though she were about to melt inside. She again wanted to put out a hand to touch and stroke him, a desire much stronger than the one which she had felt at San Giorgio. What would he think? He could not possibly want her to do such a thing. It was plain that he had no such thoughts for *her*.

Her eyes met his, and, as once before, she felt that she was about to drown in them. She put out both her hands, blindly, almost imploring him—to do, what?

'No,' said Piero, stepping back. 'You are my page here, not my wife. And you are still not a woman, for I trust you to tell me when you are. You are quite right to

remind me that to be too intimate with you would not
be at all the thing, would cause great scandal, particularly if I am seen embracing a boy as pretty as you are.'

'Oh, now I know that you are teasing me, lord,' said
Dino confidently, as the strange tension between them
broke. 'I was long ago reconciled to my lack of looks,
and what an advantage that is now that I am pretending
to be a boy. Shall I unlace your shirt and points? I am
not a page unless I carry out all my duties.'

'No,' said Piero, thinking that his strength of mind
only stretched so far, and to have Dino unlacing his
points in such a vital place. . .! 'You can cease chattering
and fetch me some more wine. I have a great thirst.'

Which is another lie, he thought, but I have to send
her away before I forget myself. She is still only a child,
and does not know what life and love are. But she is
beginning to change. Between good food and happiness
she is less and less like the Lord Bernardo's plain sister,
and temptation is beginning to wear a woman's face.

If the day she had schooled the horse so well was a
happy one for the page Dino, what was the next day
like? It started out well. She had put Piero into his war
gear, for he was going on a tour of all the camps,
including Carpacci's, to see that his orders were being
carried out. Her steel cap had arrived, which the
armourer had specially made for her; he had measured
her head the previous week, and Piero had put it on her
himself, there in the privacy of the pavilion, and if his
hand had lingered, stroking the black curls which
emerged from beneath it, as he settled it on her head,
she ignored that in her excitement.

She didn't really want to be a warrior, to take part in
a proper battle, but, all the same, wearing it for a few
moments had given her the same feeling of pride which
all the male pages had when they first wore full armour.
Like wearing one's knightly spurs for the first time, it
was a badge of honour.

Piero had stood back to look at her, and had given her one of his rare, true smiles. Piero's smiles were usually subtle, slightly mocking things, showing a knowledge and understanding of life beyond his years that was almost frightening. 'My child warrior,' he called her, and told her that she would wear it at his command. Child again. Well, that showed what he thought of her, but never mind. The armourer was also modifying the little breastplate she had been given; it was too broad, and the plates for her arms too long.

She wanted to giggle a little at her transformation, but after his one smile Piero's face was as serious as it had become over the last fortnight. He was, she thought, troubled that the campaign was going on so long, the siege showing no sign of breaking, and expenses rising each day. And if the campaign failed—which was always possible—she had heard him tell Han and Lodovico that Bruschini would see that all the blame was his.

She was thinking about this, and was trying to remember something Bernardo had once told her about Trani, long ago when she had been a little girl, and he a hopeful youth, before drink and his own inadequacies had made a bitter drunkard of him, when she heard Taddeo calling for her.

What he wanted her for was not the excitement of the riding school, nor even to practise with sword, quarterstaff or bow, but instead to carry out some of the necessary dirty work of the camp. The novice pages were to carry buckets of swill and waste to throw into the great trench of ordure outside the camp, which was periodically filled in at one end, and then enlarged at the other. She made a face, but she had no choice; she had to take the bad with the good, as Agneta had been fond of saying. She could hardly have thought that one day her charge would be carting about great buckets of filth—but there it was.

Carrying the second nasty bucket, she had another fit of the internal giggles, wondering what Taddeo would say if he knew that she was the late Lady of San Giorgio, and the present Lady of Astra, and was reduced to heaving ordure about. At least, she thought, even impossibly perfect Piero cannot think that this is dangerous work, which, as she later acknowledged, just went to show how useless it was to make such comments on life, they usually being as ill-informed as this one turned out to be.

She was staggering along, sweating gently, when she saw Naldo emerge from a tent, and then, on seeing her, begin to bolt back inside again. She put the bucket down, grateful for any excuse to stop work, and called to him. He did not reappear, or answer her. Exasperated, she called again. 'What are you playing at, Naldo? Come out. I know you are there.'

This time he came out, slowly and unwillingly, and she saw him properly for the first time, and gasped as she did. One of his eyes was closed shut, and there were great bruises on his face, and he was limping slightly. She threw up her hands, shocked. 'Naldo! Who did that to you? Tavio?'

He nodded a yes. Speech was obviously painful, and then when she said, 'Why?' turned his head away. The intuition which Father Luca had told her was hers as a woman, although she had noted that Piero possessed it, too, worked on her, and she said suddenly, fiercely, the Lady of San Giorgio again, 'It was because of me, wasn't it, Naldo? Wasn't it? Answer me, at once.'

Her lordly manner, her unthinking dominance, worked on him; it provoked an answer, a grudging yes.

'What did he say? I'm sure that he must have said something to cause you to fight him.'

'He said——' and Naldo gulped '—that you were so pretty that it was no wonder the Lord Piero kept you in his tent. . .that it was likely that you were the lord's. . . that you were more than the lord's page.'

The scalding rage which had sometimes overcome Dino when she had been Bianca ran through her now.

Oh, she knew what vile thing Tavio was hinting at—shameful, shameful to speak so of Piero.

'And you denied it, so he beat you?'

His nodded, unwilling yes, and the hesitating qualification which followed, 'It is not true, is it, Dino?' fuelled her rage. She was suddenly almost beside herself. And strangely it was not herself she cared for, but Piero, to have that snivelling peasant Tavio badmouth him. . .!

'To say that of my lord, and then to treat you so for proclaiming the truth! He knows that you are no match for him. He beat you for his wicked pleasure. Oh, I will. . . I will. . .' Rage made her speechless. She bent down, picked up the bucket of ordure and staggered away with it, not in the direction of the trench, but into the heart of the camp, Naldo following.

'Dino, what are you doing? Where are you going?'

She made him no answer. Consumed with a rage far beyond anything she had ever known, a sign of her growing maturity, she struggled on, saw Tavio and the other pages before Taddeo's tent, waiting for their orders, Piero and some of his lesser captains at a little distance away. As she had sometimes experienced when with Piero, the world had become sharp and clear, its focus centred on Tavio, who, as she neared him, filled that world. There was nothing else in it but him, and her desire to revenge herself on him for his vile accusations about her lord.

Tavio saw her coming, thrust his hands into his belt and began to laugh at the spectacle they presented. She approached, carrying the bucket, with Naldo running behind her, suddenly fearful, for he knew what she was about to do, and implored her to stop.

'So Naldo is begging you for your favours now, Dino. Doesn't the lord satisfy you that you require the knight of the bruised countenance, too?'

'Scum, you are scum!' shrieked Dino. 'And scum deserves scum. Take that!' And on the last repetition of the word 'scum' she up-ended the bucket of ordure over the laughing Tavio, so that his jeering and mocking face disappeared, lost in filth.

There was a moment's shocked silence at this gross act of indiscipline, before Tavio, face and hair dripping, filth running down his clothing, launched himself at her. She was pinned beneath him on the ground. She bit his chin—never mind the filth—to make him let go. He gave a fearsome roar, and then they were rolling over and over. He was striking at her, she was shrieking, clawing at him, trying to bite him again, pulling at his hair.

Men came running, another bucket—of water this time—was emptied over them, and they were torn apart, still spitting at one another, and trying to fight free of their captors.

Dino found herself lifted up, then shaken, and someone was shouting her name. The rage which had sustained her in her unequal battle with Tavio fled as suddenly as it had come, leaving her weak and shaking. It was Piero who was holding her. The world righted itself. She saw that Van Eyck had Tavio pinned against the wall of the blacksmith's hut. He was still shouting incomprehensible abuse at her; was still beside himself at the humiliation put upon him.

'Sweet Lord in Heaven, Dino. Have you run mad? Are you trying to kill or be killed? What could possess you to behave so?'

'I *will* kill him,' she panted, the rage suddenly on her again. 'Taddeo may give me a sword, a true one, and I will cut out the tongue that said. . .' And then she stopped. She could not tell Piero what Tavio had said of them; he would kill him, and the scandal it would create. . . She shuddered. And her own masquerade might be revealed. . .and that would never do. It would hurt Piero's reputation too much.

'That said. . .?' repeated Piero grimly. 'What did he say that started this misbehaviour? You know that you will receive a beating for such an unprovoked attack on your lieutenant, Dino. You do understand that?'

'Nothing, lord, he said nothing,' she replied wildly. 'It was between the two of us, Tavio and me only.'

'Nothing? The Lord God give me grace,' said Piero sharply, wrenched out of his usual imperturbability for once. 'Nothing, you say. You go screeching and brawling and throwing filth about the camp, and have the impudence to tell me that it was a private fight?'

He put her down, but still held her—by the same ear, she noted ruefully, that he had held her with on their first meeting at San Giorgio. He called over to Van Eyck, who still held Tavio. 'In the name of all the devils in Gehenna, what is his explanation for this?'

'He has none,' said Van Eyck, grinning. Pages seldom provided the camp with such entertainment, usually being quiet and meek in the presence of their superiors, however badly they behaved in their absence. 'Only that your page deserves a thrashing for a wanton and unprovoked attack, although I doubt that the attack was unprovoked, for such a little fellow to attack such a big one so fiercely.'

'Well, whatever the cause of this unseemly brawl, we all appear to agree that Dino deserves a thrashing, and I shall see that he gets one,' said Piero, exasperated. 'But I must say that he usually has a good reason for his naughtiness.'

'I am not naughty,' said Dino, swallowing tears. 'And you may thrash me if you will, but I do not deserve it.'

'I shall do nothing until you go to my tent and change your clothes so that you do not look and smell like a sewer. Facetti shall deal with Tavio when he comes back from his duties, and you will do as I tell you, immediately, without further argument. Go!' And his voice on the last few words was the trumpet which led his men, and expected instant obedience. A voice he had never used to her before.

He stood still, watching the small valiant figure trudge

back to his pavilion, dripping water at every step. He saw Naldo watching, face white beneath its bruises, eyes fearful at the commotion he had unwittingly caused. Piero said to him, 'How got you that face, boy?' and then stopped, remembering that it was the camp's joke that small Dino defended larger Naldo.

He whirled on Tavio, still pinned negligently down by Van Eyck, and pointed to Naldo. 'Did you do that, boy?' he demanded and, as Tavio gazed on him white-faced, without answering, used his commanding voice again. 'Answer me, or I promise you I'll roast you over a slow fire if that is what it needs to make you talk.'

Tavio nodded a mute yes.

'Why?' And as Tavio and Naldo stared at him dumbly, both now white with fear of him, neither wishing to tell him the unpalatable truth of what Tavio had said to start off the whole brouhaha, he roared at them, 'Are you all run mad in the camp today? Answer me, or I'll flay the lot of you.'

'He—he said that he did not like my face, and would use his fists to improve it,' stammered Naldo, hoping that Tavio would have the wit to support such a barefaced lie, and enable them both to escape further questioning. He thought that, given another minute, Piero's hard eyes would force the truth from him.

'And that's the truth?' asked Piero of Tavio. And again, to Naldo, 'That is why Dino threw ordure over him—to avenge his treatment of you?'

Naldo, mute in his turn, nodded assent.

'So,' said Piero, looking fiercely at both pages, and at Dino turning, desolate, into his pavilion, 'the truth at last—or is it?' And then, with a flash of the intuition which he unknowingly shared with his unacknowledged wife, he said, 'I do not believe a word of it, but I suppose it will have to do. Han, see that Facetti punishes Tavio for bullying. Discipline must be stern, but I will not have my men indulging in senseless cruelty. I will deal with Dino. We cannot have ordure flung round the camp, and, Naldo, you had better learn to defend yourself. Shameful to rely on a little one to defend you.'

With that, he wheeled away, to return to his pavilion and deal with naughty Dino. The good God alone knew what had got into her to behave in such an outrageous fashion!

Piero de' Nobody, or Piero de' Manfredini, as he called himself in defiance of the father who had rejected him, and was now so called by the world, had known ever since his mother had died suddenly in childbirth, when he was seven, that if he did not look after himself no one else would. He had used the power of his will, fuelled by his intellect, his athleticism, his good looks and charm, to dominate and control those around him for as long as he could remember.

Thrust into a monastery by his father as a boy, to get rid of an unwanted by-blow kept only since his birth to please his mistress, now dead, Piero had cold-bloodedly plotted his way out of it when he was fifteen, had joined his mother's brother, Lodovico, and become a page in the *condotta* in which Lodovico was a sergeant. At eighteen he was already in control of a troop, which, because he disobeyed foolish orders, he had rescued from a hopeless position, taking over the command of the fool who had nearly killed them all, when the fool was fortunately killed himself, and had won a small victory. This brought him to the notice of the *condottiero* Gambini, whom he served, who praised him for his ability, promoted him, and continued to promote him, until, at twenty, he was Gambini's trusted lieutenant. Gambini, childless, had made him his heir, and when he was killed in a minor skirmish Piero inherited not only his *condotta*, but also the lordship of Astra. After that, he had embarked on a meteoric career, which had brought him fame, further fortune, and a reputation now known across all Italy, making Dino's description of him as impossibly perfect Piero a just one.

He had rescued Bianca from her brother almost as a

joke, amused by the child's fiery spirit, taking her as a
wife who would owe *him*, rather than marry someone
who, by bringing him wealth and power, would also
bring him unwanted ties, relations, and policies which
would bind him when he wished to remain free, as well
as a family who would claim him as part of them—as he
had told Lodovico, when saying that he did not want a
rich and powerful wife.

Instead he had found that the landless and powerless
child had brought him something else—he was faced,
for the first time, with a will and intellect equal to his
own, even if in a woman's body, but quite untried, and
now, with independence, eager for life and experience.
His amusement at her was tinged with admiration as
well as exasperation. When he had so lightly made her
his page, he had offered her freedom, and he had not
anticipated the problems she would bring him. The fiery
spirit was free to range, and now he must contain it
without hurting her, or the fragile relationship which
was beginning to grow between them.

He entered the pavilion to find her washed and newly
dressed, standing by his table, no signs of shame or
distress or repentance about her. Instead, she stared
steadily at him as he said, almost ruefully, 'What am I
going to do with you, Dino? You are continually setting
the camp into an uproar. I really ought to thrash you,
but tell me, how does a man thrash a scrap like you,
who is his wife into the bargain?'

Dino lifted her head proudly. 'I am not your wife here.
I am Dino. I do not regret what I did, and I would do it
again. You may beat me if you will, and I shall cry. I
have been beaten before, often and often, so you must
not let that distress you, lord. You must do your duty.'

Piero's emotions were so mixed that he hardly knew
what to say or do—a rare thing for him. He took her
chin, and tipped her face towards him. She did not drop
her eyes, her expression remained defiant.

'Listen to me, Dino. I know that none of you told me

the true reason why you hurled ordure over Tavio, and I neither know nor care what that reason was. I cannot have you throwing ordure about the camp. I understand that you partly did it to protect Naldo, and I will not have that, either. You do him no favour. If he is truly a coward I do not want him in my *condotta*, and the sooner he is smoked out the better.'

As Dino began to answer him, he raised his voice again, towards its battle note. 'No, do not answer me, boy. I have had enough insolence from you for one day. You wish to be treated as a boy, as a page, and so you shall be. You need to be disciplined, that is certain; a fiery spirit must be ruled, must not rule the one who possesses it. So listen!' And on the last word his voice was fully that of the commander in battle exhorting himself and his men. He lowered it a little. She had shivered at the sound, but her will was still unbroken, and she thought, as she met his eyes, I will not let him frighten me, no, I will not. I was defending his honour, but oh, I cannot tell him, and I must bite the steel, and take what comes.

She heard him, and felt him—the hand that held her chin was his, as she was his, but he was hers, too, and she must never forget that. It was plain that he knew that both these things were true, and that in some fashion they were tied together by something which transcended love, but which she dimly understood might come to be love.

His voice had changed—not to the one which he normally used to her, but more serious, almost with a plea in it. 'Now, as to Tavio, he may be an unpleasant foul-mouthed bully, but he is not a coward. He went for you when you provoked him, despite my presence, and Taddeo has just told me that he has the heart and guts to be a good soldier—as I believe that you would be, were you truly a boy. I shall also be compelled to give you at least two blows, for I do not wish either of us to be complete liars. For the rest I will spare you. Your

body is too tender for overmuch punishment, and I have
neither the heart nor the will to hurt you. I am sorry to
strike you at all, but your conduct leaves me no alternative. I cannot spare you what I would not spare my true
page.' He hesitated, then asked, 'You promise to behave
yourself in future?'

'I can't, lord,' faltered Dino, 'if it means that my good
behaviour conflicts with my honour.'

'Your honour?' roared Piero. 'Your honour required
you to throw filth over Tavio? Body of God, Dino, do
not toy with me.'

'You made me, Dino,' said his wife. 'It was your will,
not mine, and you must live with what you have done,'
and that was a daring thing to say to him. She caught
her lower lip with her teeth anxiously, as his brow grew
thunderous. And then he began to laugh.

'My fault,' he said. 'I should have left you scrubbing
the floors in San Giorgio if I had wanted a quiet life.
Come, Dino, accept your punishment. I shall try not to
strike you too hard.' He had a sudden terrible wish to
take her into his arms, and kiss her troubled face. God
alone knew what had been said, or done to her, to make
her behave as she had. Something which had roused her
to act. And when he struck her, as he must for his
honour, and hers, the two blows were as gentle as he
could make them, mere tokens of his displeasure, and
truly disturbed him more than they disturbed her.

'You cheated,' said Dino reproachfully. 'You did not
hurt me at all. I told you that I was used to being
thrashed.'

And that thought distressed him, even though, exasperated, he seized her, lifted her off her feet, and shook
her. '*Per Dio*, Dino, you would annoy a saint, never mind
an all too human *condottiero*. You are more of a nuisance
to me than a whole troop of mutinous men-at-arms. Go
and finish carrying ordure for Taddeo—and try not to
throw any more about. And if you remind me once more
that it was by my choice that you became a page, I shall

really give you the beating which you richly deserve. Now, be off with you—and not another word,' as Dino opened her mouth again.

Scuttling along, carrying yet another disgusting bucketful, Dino cursed Piero fiercely and internally, and when Taddeo finally took pity on her, bearing in mind the thrashing which she had received from her lord, she limped artistically away to find the pond which lay beyond the camp, in order to check what had now been said by several: that Dino, the page, was a pretty child.

But it was still the same old Bianca reflected back at her which she saw there. Big eyes, and if the cheeks were no longer thin, and the hair curled even more extravagantly, there was nothing pretty about her which she could see. She walked disconsolately back, because she had been hopeful that, after all, the Lord God had transformed her into something amazing. What could they all be thinking about, to tell such lies? Tavio's idea of beauty must be twisted. She saw Naldo coming towards her. He had watched her go to the pond, waited for her to return.

'I wanted to thank you, Dino, for standing up for me. I hope that the lord didn't overdo the beating.'

'He was as you might expect,' she answered, thinking, I am becoming as devious in my speech as Piero often is. She hesitated, then asked, 'Would you say that I was pretty, Naldo?'

'Well,' said Naldo judiciously, 'I'm hardly the right person to ask. I like women big, round and blonde, like my mamma, I suppose,' and he sketched a woman's shape in the air. 'Not little and dark, with big eyes, and a graceful walk.' He looked at Dino doubtfully. 'Yes. Yes, you are pretty. But, mind you, I'd have said that it was Tavio who fancied you, if the truth were known, and was jealous of the Lord Captain. Which is stupid— everyone knows for a fact that the lord likes great armfuls, like the redhead in the mountains, and that woman he had in Florence. Not shrimps like you.'

The news that impossibly perfect Piero liked them huge and bosomy had the most extraordinary effect on Dino. First she felt quite hollow, as though someone had punched her, hard, in the stomach, and then she was overwhelmed with red rage.

So! He liked them big and blowsy, did he? Well, he could pleasure them one by one, in rows, all the way from Florence to Milan for all she cared, and charge good money to watchers, too. It was nothing to Bianca di San Giorgio what he did.

Which wasn't true, any of it. She was either Dino, Piero's page, or Bianca de' Manfredini, the Lady of Astra, Piero's wife, and either way she cared dreadfully. Yes, she did, she did. Oh, damn him, and all men, and Naldo into the bargain.

'Well, it's a good thing you don't fancy me,' she said cuttingly to him. 'For I'm sure I don't fancy you, or Tavio, or the Lord Captain, either. You may all go and pleasure half Italy, men and women both, for all I care.' And she flounced off in a typically feminine way, which would have told Naldo what she truly was, had he not been blinking deliriously at her, remembering the big blonde woman who had made a man of him in Florence.

'And to think I found myself in all that trouble for defending his honour,' she muttered to herself, the limp not all assumed, for carrying buckets had been cruel work. 'Oh, I hate you, Piero de' Manfredini.'

And, oh, dear, what a lie that was.

CHAPTER SEVEN

DINO would have been completely happy, posing as a boy, enjoying her freedom, no longer that unconsidered thing, a girl or a woman, had it not been for Tavio. After her dispute with him, and the punishment which they had both received, he was no longer openly antagonistic to her, or to Naldo, but made her life hard in little insidious ways.

Naldo had said that he thought Tavio fancied her, and whether that was true or not he contrived, by pushing and pinching and tweaking her, by seeing that she always had the dirty unwanted tasks, to make her life difficult. She thought that Taddeo knew what Tavio was doing, but she would not complain to him—oh, no, she would look after herself, she would find a way of getting back at him that would not be obvious but would teach him a much needed lesson, and a week after she had thrown the ordure over him she found an opportunity.

Taddeo was teaching them the secret tricks of overcoming a man without using a weapon, and what he said was also important—how a little man could safely attack a larger one. That morning he placed them in a circle around him, and said that he would show them what they could do with a belt, or even a lady's scarf. He demonstrated what he meant by using one of the larger boys, who was told to walk along whistling. Taddeo, holding a scarf, the ends in each of his hands, crept up behind him, flung the scarf round the boy's neck, quickly and quietly, and then pulled, but not too hard. 'I don't want to throttle you, or kill you,' he explained, as the boy choked and struggled. 'Now, let us all practise that. In pairs. First one half, and then the other.'

Tavio, as lieutenant, drew straws to make up the pairs, and contrived, Dino was bitterly sure, that he and Dino were paired together. 'Good,' he said. 'You're such a dwarf, you'll need my help. I'll go first, and show you how it's done.'

Taddeo heard him, and said sharply, 'No, let Dino go first. I'll help him, if necessary.' He handed out scarves to them all, and Dino took hers, well aware of the ugly scowl on Tavio's face. After Taddeo had spoken, he had leaned forward and said, beneath his breath, 'Just you wait, Dino. I'll pay you back for covering me in filth, you see.'

She held the scarf as Taddeo had shown them, and watched Tavio walk away from her. She knew in her heart of hearts that when it was his turn he was going to hurt her and badly, and blame it on his lack of control. If he did, they might start to strip her, and if they did they would discover her true sex at once, because the little buds were growing day by day, and, seeing them, no one would now think that she was anything but a girl.

Piero might beat her again, Taddeo would roar, and she would be in dreadful trouble, but there was only one way to stop Tavio, and she would take it. Unseen by the pages who were the victims, Taddeo lowered his stick, and Dino leapt on Tavio from behind, and without actually killing him flung the scarf around his neck and pulled on it with all her strength, so that he, alone of the pages, fell to the ground, taking her with him, still holding the ends of the scarf, and still pulling.

Taddeo was on her, heaving her away, while Tavio, down on his hands and knees, face purple, neck bruised, was coughing and choking, finally falling prone, his training over for the day. As once before pandemonium reigned. 'Our Lady forgive me,' she babbled. 'I am not very strong, so I thought that I would have to pull hard.

I overdid it, I did not mean to choke him.' She fell to her hands and knees beside Tavio. 'Oh, forgive me, I did not mean to hurt you,' she cried when all the time she was filled with elation that, whatever else, Tavio would not be breaking *her* neck today. Tomorrow must take care of itself.

'Stand back, you little scorpion,' roared Taddeo, while the other pages helped Tavio up, many of them secretly pleased that their tormentor had been laid low, and by Dino, of all people. 'Go to your lord's tent,' said Taddeo, once he was satisfied that Tavio was not permanently harmed, although bruised, and only able to croak. 'He must decide what to do with you.' Taddeo's gaze on her was sharp. He knew that Tavio had been persecuting Dino, but so long as Dino stood there wailing and apologising there was little he could do or say.

Again, as once before, she walked back to the pavilion. Piero was out, but she knew that Taddeo would report to him, and what then? She was not sorry that she had hurt Tavio, thought of her bruised arms, and Naldo's delighted face at the sight of Tavio moaning and thrashing on the ground. At least she had that to comfort her. She did wonder, though, what Piero would say and do to her when he heard of her latest naughtiness—as he would think it—but that could not be helped either. She had a right to defend herself: he had made her a page, so he could not really complain when she behaved like one. She would not be trampled on like poor persecuted Naldo—no indeed.

When Piero finally arrived, she could see by his face that Taddeo had already reported to him. He came over to where she sat mending one of his doublets with careful, tiny stitches not at all like the poor work she had always done for Agneta.

'I must speak with you, page,' he said severely.

'Lord?' said Dino, looking up from her task, and pretending that she could not imagine what he was about to say.

'I thought that when I reprimanded you last week for throwing ordure about that you understood you were to behave yourself. Now Taddeo tells me that you have nearly throttled Tavio to death in your exercises, and he thinks that you might have done so wilfully. Hardly the act of a page attempting to please his lord and his sergeant. Stand up when I speak to you, boy!'

Dino looked up, mischief written on her face, put down her sewing and jumped smartly to her feet.

'Lord, you told me not to throw ordure about. You said nothing about throttling Tavio.'

There was an awful silence. Piero sighed. 'Tell me, Dino, why, when in general you are a good hardworking page, the best I have ever had, you are also quite the naughtiest: I hear daily of your tricks. This is beyond a trick.'

'I am not naughty, lord,' replied Dino spiritedly, 'but when I see the need to defend myself, or my honour, then I must act.'

Piero sighed again, 'And your honour told you to throttle Tavio. Why?'

She nodded vigorously at the first sentence, but could not answer the second, without betraying either what Tavio had said of them, or the mean assaults he was making on her.

'What,' said Piero, 'if my honour told me to punish you for defending yours?' He did not tell her that Taddeo had informed him, a little hesitantly, that he thought that Tavio had been privately bullying Dino, and that Dino had used the exercise to get his own back. He watched her reaction, the speed with which she answered him.

'Oh, that is easy,' she said cheerfully. 'You must do your duty, that is plain, as I must do mine.'

Piero was silent, but amusement shone on his face at the sight and sound of her impudence, her unbreakable spirit. Watching him, Dino was daring again. 'Lord,' she said pertly, 'have you done with me? I must remind you that you are keeping me from my work. I have not yet finished this task, and your helmet still requires burnishing in time for your visit to the Lord Bruschini.'

'No matter,' said Piero, 'I shall not be wearing it when I speak to him.'

'Yes, lord. I understand that. But I shall be required to hold it behind you, and if it is dull all the world will think that I have failed in my duty, when it is really your fault for keeping me from it.'

Piero put out a hand, and took Dino by the ear, but gently.

'Tell me, Dino, my page, how it comes about that when I begin by reprimanding you I always end being reprimanded *by* you? Another lesson in prevarication from Father Luca? I must remind you that we have not yet dealt with the matter of your throttling Tavio.'

'Father Luca never taught me to prevaricate. He would have regarded it as sinful. As for Tavio, an accident merely. I miscalculated my own strength, thought that I was weaker than I was.'

'I only know that after a few weeks of having you for a page I am a great deal weaker than I was, and taking Trani is made no easier for me when I am constantly called on to control you.'

'I'm truly repentant, lord, and promise to do better in future. All this good food I am eating is to blame, you see. I am no longer Bernardo's poor weak filleted herring.'

She smiled up at him as she said this, and she had no idea how truly charming, how naughtily pretty she had come to look. She took her husband's breath away. The wave of desire which he had felt for her in the bed at San Giorgio broke over him again. Continence, with the knowledge that this desirable child, with her wit and spirit, was his, was again almost too much for his resolution.

Dear God, he thought, I cannot keep her in my tent. She is safe neither in nor out of it. In, and I shall be tempted to take her, out, and she is in physical danger because of her bold spirit. I never knew what I was doing when I took her away from San Giorgio and put her in boy's clothes.

Something of the passion which had begun to rage in him reached Dino. The smile on her face trembled. He had put out his hands to hold her by the shoulders, his eyes glittered, and some instinct told her that he was roused and ready to take her. 'Lord?' she said, as once before, and this time he ignored her, and began to pull her towards him until they were closer than they had ever been.

'Captain?' It was Lodovico in the pavilion-opening. His eyes, not yet adjusted from the light outside, did not see them for a brief moment, and by then they were apart. Lodovico's voice had brought Piero back to sanity, and he had released Dino. Dino hardly knew whether she was glad or sorry for the interruption. 'Lord,' said Lodovico, now seeing only Piero by the table, Dino picking up his helmet and beginning to polish it vigorously, 'I came to remind you that you are shortly due to see Bruschini—a tactical mistake to be late, I think.'

'Oh, indeed,' said Piero drily. 'I can recite beforehand what he will say when I talk with him, but we must go through it all again, I suppose. Dino, you may leave the helmet. I will go to him on my own, without captains or pages. Pity to waste everyone's time as well as mine.'

Which was not the true reason why he did not want her or anyone else with him. He needed to be away from everyone, to restore the cold, uninvolved Piero he had always been before he took himself a wife.

The camp at night, when darkness fell, was paradoxically a bright place. Cooking fires burned everywhere. Flambeaux were set up on poles. Talk, laughter, and occasionally the music of a lute, sounded in the warm dark. Piero, returning to his tent, found Dino laying the table for their evening meal, carefully putting out his knife, fork, and spoon. She looked up shyly as he came in, but did not speak. He watched her, and it occurred to him that, as at the tower, she was always busy. When not performing her page's tasks, she found others in caring for him and for Lodovico, who also lived in the tent.

Presently, she looked up at him, under the dark fringe of her lashes. 'Lord,' she said.

'Yes, my page.'

'Lord, I have been thinking. You were right to tell me not to protect Naldo overmuch. Right to say that he must learn to protect himself. I was wrong there—I acknowledge it. But——'

'Oh,' interrupted Piero, his wry smile on his long mouth. 'But. There is always a but in such sentences, Dino. What is your but? I am agog to hear it.'

'Why, lord, it is this. Where a matter concerns my honour, then I must take steps to repair it. You understand?'

'That your honour required you first to throw filth over Tavio, and then to throttle him. I take your word for it, but I must say that you are requiring me to swallow a camel.'

Dino's gravity was shattered by this. She began to laugh, and said primly, 'Father Luca would not approve of your making fun of the Bible. Swallow a camel, indeed. No, lord, but you take my point?'

'Once again that if your honour requires it you will do as you please—fling filth about, try to murder Tavio. What will it require you to do next?'

'Oh, I had to use the only weapons I had to hand. I am not strong enough to fight Tavio as another boy might.'

'I understand that, too, my page. You know we could carry on this conversation until the night passes and the bell rings for Prime, and neither of us would be any the wiser at the end. Let us discuss supper instead.'

'By all means.' Dino skipped across to the tent flap.

'Lodovico has something good for us tonight. A chicken, he says. The Lord God knows where he got it.'

'I doubt that the Lord God has much to do with Lodovico stealing chickens,' remarked Piero. 'Between you both, I am served by a fine set of rogues.'

'You know the old saying, lord,' remarked Dino cheekily, helping Lodovico to carry in and serve the food, 'like master, like man.'

'I know that sooner or later Page Dino will earn a beating for his impudence, either from me or from someone else,' remarked Piero, eating the chicken with relish. 'And in the meantime we sit before Trani and the siege fails, and the Florentines will put the blame on me and my reputation will be in tatters, and I shall be unable to beat, feed, or pay pages.'

Dino ate with her usual dreadful gusto. One thing about impossibly perfect Piero—he understood eating, and how good it was. She watched him, the candlelight softening the harsher planes of his face, the aureole around his head making him look more than ever like one of the beautiful saints painted on the walls of every church in Tuscany.

'The townsfolk in Trani feed, too,' she said thoughtfully. 'I wonder. . .' And then fell silent.

'You wonder, page. Tell your lord what you wonder.' He filled her cup with the good red wine, and passed it over to her. 'Drink up. It will make a woman of you.'

'You know that there is a secret passageway into San Giorgio?'

'Some secret,' said Piero, inelegantly for once, mouth full of chicken. 'All the world knows of it.'

'Ah, but,' said Dino, 'Bernardo used to say that there was another town which possessed a truly secret passage, which he knew of and visited. Only the lord's family knew of it. I have been thinking. I am sure that he said it was Trani.'

Both men looked at her. Piero put his wine down. 'Your brother said that? True, the world does not know of it. Let us suppose that he is speaking true. Let us further suppose that food is coming through it, then. . .'

'That would explain the siege's failure, if they are being supplied from outside; but we have guards around the town.' Lodovico was grave.

'Oh, that,' said Piero. 'Think of the miles of country, and how hard it is for us to police it, not knowing where a secret way in might be. Particularly if the trail begins well away from the town, one might as well suppose that, if anything. And where would the food come from? We have cut Trani off from all its normal sources of supply. . .or have we?'

Both men were staring at one another, Dino forgotten. Piero said, his subtle smile on his face again, 'Bandelli, of course. The ineffable Agostino, the bandit king. My old master. Who else in these parts? He has sent a token force to help us, and takes our pay. Think how it would amuse him to supply Trani with food. The longer the siege goes on, the richer the rogue grows.'

'This is all supposition,' said Lodovico, watching his nephew. 'We have no proof, no evidence to offer to enable us to act.'

Piero rose to his feet and began to pace about. He was completely the warlord, face hard and manner dominant. 'It is not supposition that by all the laws of war and logic Trani should have fallen through hunger weeks ago—and has not. No reflections on God or Father Luca, Dino, but there are no miracles today.' He struck his hands together. 'By God's blood, I know that I am right. Who else would have the nerve to do this but Bandelli? He owes me, and he shall pay me, and if I am right there is only one way to find out.'

'Find the passage?' queried Dino, fascinated by the change in Piero.

'Not a chance in all these square miles of wood and scrub and mountain. No, I must visit friend Agostino and turn the screws on him.'

'Take the *condotta*?' asked Lodovico, still sceptical.

'No. Not at all. We must not seem to threaten. Only you, myself, and Dino will go. None shall know we are absent. I will have the grippe, an infectious one. You and Dino will nurse me. None shall come near our pavilion. Van Eyck will see to that. Infection, even of the leader, must not spread. He alone will know that we have gone—and why.'

'And if we do not come back? This is a brute chance.'

Piero propped himself against the table. 'Why suppose that? Bandelli owes me. And if we do not return, Van Eyck takes over. I only know that we are lost if Trani is not taken, and soon. Pay and reputation gone. We shall be beggars in Italy.'

'I say you risk Bandelli cutting our throats,' Lodovico asserted.

'I think not. But it is a chance we must take.'

'You would bet our lives on it? Dino's life?'

'I cannot leave her behind. You know that, Lodovico, and your common sense should tell you why.'

They all stared at one another. Lodovico made a sign with his big hand, and said, 'No, this is madness. I still say that you have no proof of anything.'

'Madness?' Piero struck his hands together again. 'No,' he said firmly. 'No, believe me. I know this as I have known such things before.'

'Guesswork,' said Lodovico. 'To risk your life on. I do not say ours, but that, too.'

'No, not guesswork,' said Piero slowly. 'It is the logic of the situation. There must be a secret way in; there is no way in which Trani could have stored such quantities of food beforehand to withstand a siege so long. We can see them, and they are not starving. They laugh at us. And none but Bandelli can be supplying them. All other sources have been stopped.' And as Lodovico shook his head in reply Dino saw that impossibly perfect Piero was going, really going, to lose his temper for once, really lose it—no pretence, all his perfection cracked.

'By God, Uncle mine! If I had not known when to act

and why, to trust those things which I know, but of which I have not been told, I should still be wearing my knees out in a monastery, and you would still be a peasant in a hut. Trust me, and you will have a lordship of your own, but otherwise Trani will ruin us both.'

'But the little one. It is her life you will be gambling with.'

'Ah, the little one.' Piero wheeled around, and dropped to his knees beside Dino. 'The little one, who holds the secret in her head—or does she?' He took Dino by the chin again with his big hand—but oh, so gently, his touch a caress—put the other hand on her left shoulder and said, 'Look at me, sparrow, and think carefully—our lives may depend upon it.' And as she looked at him, drawn by his icy blue eyes, drowning in them again, he spoke to her in the language of love, not in the voice of the master. 'Thy brother, my dove, my little wife; was it of Trani he spoke to thee? Consider thy answer well, and tell thy lord what thou truly knowest.'

For a moment she was looking at Piero, her face held firm by his hand, and then she was a child again on the battlements at San Giorgio, at the top of the tower, looking out over the chequerboard of the countryside below them. Bernardo was saying, 'I know a secret.' He was tall and gangling, not soft and fat as he now was, and he spoke to her of Trani. Yes, it was Trani. 'And you are not to tell, Bianca. Our father would be grieved if you told. This is a secret for lords only.'

She had nodded solemnly at him. He had been her hero then, she remembered, the beloved big brother, not the unpleasant bully which disappointment and drink had made of him. The vision faded, and it was Piero— but who was he, this stranger, who compelled her so?— at whom she was looking.

'Yes, it was Trani,' she whispered. 'I remember now.'

'Thou knowest no more? He did not tell thee where the passage was, my dove, my life?'

She shook her head. He released her gently, and she

blinked at him as he took his eyes away. 'No matter,' he said, and stood up, hooking his thumbs in his belt of hammered silver—he was still in his splendid clothes. 'That settles it,' he said, 'beyond a doubt. The child remembers.' For Dino had spoken, as he held her, in the voice of the little girl she had been when Bernardo had told her of Trani's secret entrance, something which his father had said would be of use to him as San Giorgio's lord.

'So,' continued Piero, beginning to pull off his fine clothes, 'fetch me my war gear, Dino. And, Lodovico, in a moment you may bring Van Eyck to me. We must risk all on this throw, or the dice will be against us forever.'

Well, you could see that Van Eyck thought that Piero had run mad, thought Dino, but once Piero had made up his mind they could all save their breath—he was so lucid that it was like arguing with the Lord God; and so there were the three of them, with Van Eyck wailing behind them, as Agneta had once done. 'One day, my captain, you will take a risk too many,' as they rode out in secret.

It was nothing like so long and hard a journey as the one from San Giorgio to Trani, Dino found. And finally, when the rough track they had followed ended, they found themselves on something uncommonly like a real road, which led to the small settlement and the large castle which was Bandelli's eyrie, as Piero called it, when they had stopped once to eat. 'A good soldier always eats when he may,' he had said, 'since he never knows when he might have the chance to do so again.'

The castle—for it was far bigger than Bernardo's tower—dominated the whole countryside. Bandelli was more of a bandit than a nobleman or a *condottiero*, Piero said, for, although he had claims to be noble, they were quite spurious. He preyed on those around him, and on those distant, and in a land famous for its treachery Bandelli's name was a byword.

'But he owes me, and there are other things which tie us,' Piero had told her on another of their brief rests.

'And will he betray us?' she had asked.

'I think not,' said Piero. 'My instinct says no, and it is seldom wrong. Moreover——' and he laughed '—I kshall offer him the kind of inducement he will not care to ignore. I have never known Bandelli refuse a payday yet.'

The sentries at the massive gateway recognised Piero and waved him through. It was plain that both Piero and Lodovico were known and welcome. Bandelli met them in the outer courtyard, and he fascinated Dino because he was so much what she had expected—and so unlike Piero. He was short and squat, as broad as he was high.

He embraced Piero, giving him a fierce bear hug, then held him off, and swore at him. '*Per Bacco*, bigger than ever. Wait until Maddalena sees you!' And he gave Piero a grotesque wink. He had red hair, Dino saw, and she remembered with a pang what Naldo had said of Piero having a red-haired woman in the mountains.

She did not have long to wait, before a positive giantess with streaming red-gold curls to her waist, dressed like a booby in a fair, thought Dino acidly, hurled herself at Piero. Well, if he liked great armfuls, this was an armful and a half, and no mistake, and apparently Piero thought so, too. And then he was laughing—a little ruefully, although Dino was not aware of this, and he held the woman off, with Bandelli booming, 'Later, later, you can have him all to yourself later. You have not come here for nothing but dalliance, I'll be bound, have you, Pierino? Old Bandelli knows you better than that.'

And he laughed, a deep booming laugh, clutching at his great belly. He might be short, thought Dino, fascinated by him, but everything about him was massive.

The shrewd eyes saw her intent stare, and he suddenly

took in the small page, large Lodovico, and nothing else. 'No *condotta* behind you, then. No coming here to bully your old master?'

Piero raised both hands, open palms towards Bandelli. 'Oh, Agostino, you sadden me. I come in friendship, as always. Only my body servant and my shadow with me. See how I trust you.'

'But Manfredini, the Golden Falcon, always wants something,' roared Bandelli. 'Don't forget that it was I who first taught you, boy, and I taught you well, Lord of Astra, and like many pupils you think to best your teacher. Trani goes badly for you, does it? And you need Agostino's help?' And his laughter redoubled, but the old eyes were hard, very hard.

'I do not seek to deceive you,' said Piero, who now had his hand in Maddalena's, and was swinging it lightly. 'I come with a business proposition for you. One that I am sure you will welcome. Could I say fairer than that, old friend, old teacher?'

'La, la,' said Bandelli. 'More of that later. Food and drink first, eh? Fun before business, and then the business goes better. You still like your vittles, Pierino mine?'

There was no point in arguing with him. He led them further in, roaring, 'Business tomorrow,' and he was the one with something to sell, and they were the suppliants—Dino knew that as well as Piero did. A steward came towards them, carrying his wand of office, and began organising matters. Their horses were led away, Piero disappeared with Bandelli, Maddalena still holding his hand, and once, just before she lost sight of them, she saw a surreptitious kiss exchanged behind Bandelli's back. Oh. . .by all the devils. . .need he advertise his bad taste so plainly. . .?

She and Lodovico were taken through the guard-room into a cell in the rock wall; it was quite large, with a big bed in it, and a servant followed them in carrying two palliasses, and a candle, the light from the slit in the wall being poor. The bed, of course, was for Piero, he being the lord. They were trapped here, Dino understood; there was no way out without Bandelli's permission. They were flies to his spider.

She went over to the slit, and saw the land far beneath them, the road which they had followed disappearing into the trees. How had she arrived here, married and not married, to the enigmatic man who was her master? She whose confines had been limited to San Giorgio's tower? How had she been acquired by a man whom she half loved, half feared, the more so because she was beginning to read him?

Dino understood, too, that she had a talent for reading people, that she had used it unknowingly in San Giorgio, and that it had sometimes made life uncomfortable for her there, and that she was now beginning to use it knowingly to protect herself in the world outside. What was Maddalena to Bandelli—his sister, perhaps? And, more importantly, what was she to Piero? But she knew, she knew. She was Piero's red-haired mistress—there was no doubt that Naldo had been dismally right about that, and all the more surprising, then, that he had made such a small brown sparrow as herself his wife.

Lodovico was as silent as she. They unpacked the saddle-bags and he fetched water, and they washed their faces and hands in an earthenware basin. A page the size of Dino, but with a snub comic face, put his head around the door. 'The lord bids you to his table. All share with us, master and man alike.'

To her surprise, Dino found that this was true. She trailed Lodovico into a vast echoing hall with a long table down its middle. She and Lodovico sat at one end, Piero was in the centre, seated between Bandelli and Maddalena, who was feeding him titbits, and generally making an unseemly fuss of him—as though he were her great baby, she thought crossly. Even more annoying, Piero did not seem to mind, but drooled over her, the ninny! And, although Dino's mouth watered at the sight of all the beautiful food, the spectacle of Piero so publicly enjoying his blowsy armful soured her pleasure a little. And Maddalena was old, she saw—old enough to be his mother, perhaps? No, that was unfair, a lie; but she was much older than Piero, at any rate.

She caught Maddalena looking at her and Lodovico, face assessing. She leaned over, spoke into Piero's ear, and he looked at them, said something, and they both laughed together. Oh, amusing, are we? was Dino's bitter reaction to this. Have I come all this way to provide entertainment for a bandit's fat sister, and a bedmate for impossibly perfect Piero, who really cannot be so perfect if his taste in women is so poor?

The emotions which were tearing her apart, as she sat there silent, were plain to Lodovico sitting beside her, if to no one else. He pushed slices of bread over, and said gently, into her ear, 'Do not worry, little one. He has his duty to perform.'

'How lucky for him, then,' she could not prevent herself from replying, 'that it entails such obvious bodily delights. We are not all so fortunate, I fear.'

'True,' said Lodovico, 'and some of us have to learn patience, and the art of concealing our feelings. It would be as well to remember that Piero is a master of deception, and it is never wise to take anything he does at face value.'

'Including marrying me, and making me his page?'

'That, too,' said Lodovico, looking around. 'Now forget all this. You are merely your lord's page, and you must not attract attention.'

She would have liked to say, 'But I am his wife, he married me, and when he did I could not have cared if he had bedded a thousand women, and not me, and now I care quite dreadfully, and pray nightly to the Lord God to make me a woman soon,' but knew it was best to take Lodovico's advice and enjoy the good food and wine—particularly as the meal lasted far into the evening, and included the performance of a group of tumblers, as well as the tricks of a pair of jugglers.

Dino was entranced by the entertainment, such sophistications never having been part of her life at San Giorgio. Not only Lodovico watched her innocently smiling face. Piero, looking down the table, saw his child-wife, eyes shining, lips parted in delight, her whole body trembling with joy, the picture of happiness, the danger of their mission forgotten. He had forgotten, too, what a child she really was, and that he had no business to bring her here, and put her at risk.

Later, she and Lodovico repaired to their room, and she awoke in the night to see the great bed empty, and it remained so.

When she awoke again, in the early light of the morning, she knew he had spent the night with Maddalena, and, forlornly, she wept silently into her pillow, Piero's flat-chested wife—not so flat now, but lying in her lonely bed, her lord and husband sporting with another woman. She slept a little after that, and awoke to find him in the room, fully dressed, speaking to Lodovico. He looked over his shoulder at her as she stirred. 'You slept well, then?' She could see that he had not, and her answer to him was a lie.

'Yes, very well.' Disguise them though he might, the marks of weariness were on his face.

Piero sat down on his unused bed, looked at Dino, sighed, and thought of the conversation which he had had with Maddalena in the small hours. They had just finished their lovemaking, and she had lain, satisfied in his arms, pleasured so thoroughly that she had known that it was a long time since he had been with a woman. There had been a hunger about him, and for all her own enjoyment she thought that he had not been truly satisfied.

'You are more yourself than usual, Pierino,' she had said to him, looking up into his eyes.

'And what does that mean?' he had said, rolling away from her.

'That your body is with me, as skilled as ever, but

your mind and heart are not. Hardly flattering, but then I grow old. Is it your page you are thinking of?'

'You know that I do not favour boys,' he had answered, a little roughly.

'Oh, but he is not a boy, is he? Although you call him one. Why is your page a girl dressed as a boy, Pierino?'

He had started at this. 'Is it so plain, then?'

'No,' Maddalena had replied. 'She makes a brave boy. But I saw your interest in him, which is not usual with you, and looked closely. She is flat-chested, has no hips, and is not yet a woman, but she will be a beauty, as I suppose you know. What is she to you?'

Piero had looked at her. 'You made a man of me when I was a boy, and helped me to cheat the monks so that I might escape their prison. Can I trust you?'

'With your life—and hers,' Maddalena had said. 'My brother might sell you—though I do not think so—but I never would. It is goodbye for us this time, is it not? For you and me, I mean.'

'Yes,' he had said. 'She is my wife, unbedded as yet, you see.'

'Your wife?' Maddalena had begun to laugh. 'No, I will not ask you how or why. And it is plain that she is unbedded. Come, give me another kiss, and pleasure me until day breaks. If this is to be our last night together, we must celebrate it.'

Well, if Agostino owed him, he owed Maddalena, and he must now start the day having betrayed his wife, and wearied himself into the bargain, by thanking his long-time mistress, who had been generous enough to wish him well, when at last he had left her.

'You are to come with me,' he said to Dino, 'when I talk to Bandelli. But you must say nothing unless I ask you to. You understand me, Dino? I know that Lodovico will not speak; he rarely does so even when I command him.'

'Yes,' said Dino, 'yes, lord. But you will allow me to say before we leave that you are not buttoned and tied correctly, and that this will reflect on your page's ability to prepare you for the day. The world will not know that you dressed yourself in a hurry, and will think me remiss if I do not repair your deficiencies.'

'The world would not believe how severely my page bullies me,' said Piero, noting that even Lodovico was amused at Dino's impudence. 'But, yes, you may remedy what is wrong.'

And he stood to allow Dino to fuss about him, rebuckle his belt, pull out the cords of his shirt to retie them, saying pertly, 'Were you so tired from your night's exertions, lord, that you are so little yourself this morning?'

'And you, my page, are so much yourself,' remarked Piero, looking at the nimble fingers restoring his appearance, 'that you are in danger of having your ears boxed for impertinence.'

'A poor thing,' responded Dino, 'for the servant to be reprimanded for wanting his lord to make a brave show when such a show is important.'

Piero caught her active hand after it had smoothed him into elegance again, and kissed it. 'Your tongue,' he said, 'is even longer and clacks more than it did in San Giorgio. Being a page has not taught you humility.'

'On the contrary,' she said, recovering her hand, and trying not to show him how strongly the touch of his lips had affected her. She fell to her knees, and began to relace his right boot. 'It has taught me that a humble page is in danger of being permanently crushed. Look at poor Naldo.'

'I prefer to look at cheeky Dino!' replied her lord. 'At least you have made me appear as fine as a maypole in spring. I thank you, Dino, and if it requires an impudent tongue to make me splendid, so be it.'

'Oh, the splendour is all yours,' said Dino, looking up at him as he laughed down at her, thinking with a pang that she had seldom seen anyone so handsome, even with the marks of a night's sleeplessness on him. 'Your page is lucky that he has such remarkable material to work on.'

Even Lodovico laughed out loud at this final piece of cheek, delivered with such panache, and they walked into Agostino's presence with such careless ease that he smiled at them in admiration.

'Bright as a day in spring, my Lord of Astra,' he said. 'I see that Maddalena has not overtired you. A pity, that. I could do with the edge off you.'

Piero bowed, said, 'I always need an edge to deal with you, Agostino. Particularly when I need a favour from you.'

'Sit, sit,' roared Bandelli, 'and bring wine—send your page to help mine to look after us.'

Dino was not best pleased at this. She did not want to miss the fun of the bargaining, but when she came back, carefully carrying a tray of goblets—fine things, if rather battered—the preliminaries were still being gone through.

'So, Trani goes badly for you,' remarked Bandelli when they had all begun to drink—all but Dino, who was excused by her lord. 'Not so clever as you thought you were, my Falcon?' He slapped his thigh, and the little eyes were shrewd on Piero.

'Not so clever as some,' remarked Piero, idly admiring his wine. 'I only boast one paymaster—Florence; you, I think, may claim three.'

'Three?' replied Bandelli, grinning. 'Two I might manage, at a pinch, but three? Your powers of calculation are not usually so faulty, Pierino.'

'I only talk hypothetically, mind,' said Piero.

'Hypo. . . Such words!' said Bandelli. 'But then, you were nearly a monk, Pierino. Explain, explain, I am an ignorant old man.'

Piero allowed himself a graceful splutter into his wine at this sally. 'Oh, Agostino, if only all of us were as ignorant.'

'You flatter a poor old man,' sighed Bandelli.

'Poor?' said Piero, raising his eyebrows. 'With three paymasters?'

'Paymasters? What paymasters?' queried Bandelli, his eyebrows disappearing into his hair.

Piero held up his left hand, and began to count fingers on it with his right. 'Item,' he said, 'one set of ducats from Florence for providing several troops to help take Trani.'

'True,' agreed Bandelli, 'and that counts for one in any books I keep, not more.'

'Oh, my books tell a different tale,' said Piero, putting his right hand out to take a great draught of wine and looking sideways at Bandelli, before he returned to his count. 'Now Trani holds out as you well know. You taunted me with it, did you not? And no wonder.' He ticked off another finger. 'Item, how much is Giacomo Uberti, tyrant of Trani, paying you to supply him with food by a secret route, my old friend?'

'Oh, you slander me, boy, you slander me,' roared Bandelli delightedly. 'But what a slander!'

'Indeed,' said Piero, watching him. 'Paid by both sides—a fine thing, that; I must remember it.'

'So you say, boy, so you say. You credit me with your own low cunning.'

'But oh, my father by adoption, who taught me? And now a further item. . .' And Piero paused dramatically.

'Item? How can there be a further item? Two already,' said Bandelli. 'At least, that is what *you* claim—though, mark me, *I* said nothing—why is your page grinning, Pierino? He has a cheeky face.'

'My page, grinning?' said Piero solemnly, turning to look at a suddenly scarlet Dino. 'Are you grinning, Dino? If so, kindly tell Agostino and me what you are grinning at.'

'L-lord, I do not like to say,' she stammered.

'Come, boy,' roared Bandelli, joyfully. 'He who grins must tell. You were quick enough to show us your pleasure, lad. Now be equally quick to tell us what you showed your pleasure at.'

'Why,' she gulped, and then threw caution to the winds, 'I could not tell which was the greater fox—you, or my lord.'

'And?' prompted Bandelli, winking at Piero.

'And, lord?' said Dino desperately.

'Yes, there must be an and to that,' was Bandelli's bellowed answer. 'And which of us is the greater fox, hey? Tell us true, boy, tell us true.' And the old eyes were hard on her.

'Why,' she said, since needs must, 'there is nothing to choose between you.'

Bandelli threw his head back, and shouted approval. 'By God, Piero. We may be a pair of foxes, but your page makes a splendid cub. Wine, wine, for Messer Page, here. No, I'll brook no denial, lad,' he said as Dino shook her head. 'You shall drink with us for that.'

Dino looked pleadingly at her lord, who shook his head back at her and said, 'You must learn not to talk with your face, my page. You must drink up.'

He and Lodovico watched as Bandelli made Dino drain his goblet straight away—one swallow, no heel-taps, was his demand. 'You shall drink level with us, boy.'

'Lord?' asked Dino, desperation written on her face.

'You must please your host, my page,' was all he said.

'So,' continued Bandelli, handing Dino another brimming goblet, doing the honours himself, 'your third item, my fine young fox. Three is my lucky number—will it be so again?'

'Why, I think that a really bushy-tailed old fox might earn himself a third payday, by selling the whereabouts of the secret passage into Trani to yet another party. For sure Trani's tyrant asked you to supply him with food—but I doubt that he had the wits to specifically ask you not to say anything about a secret passage, or, if you said nothing, that you might allow an interested *condotti-ero* to accompany your men.'

Bandelli put a finger against his nose, and said to Dino admiringly, 'Pay attention to your lord, boy. They taught him to chop logic at his monastery, and he has never forgotten it.'

'Dino the page has a nice line in logic-chopping himself,' said Piero slyly. 'He hardly needs teaching.'

'Has he, indeed? Small, but choice, is he?' said Bandelli approvingly. 'And I like your third item, my Lord of Astra, particularly if the pay for it is commensurate with the treachery it might require to do as you suggest.'

'You may be sure of that,' said Piero. 'Treachery rarely comes cheaply in my experience. But I would need your solemn assurance that there would be no fourth item, selling me to yet another party in my turn,' added Piero with a grin. 'Need I remind you that Maddalena would take it ill if anything untoward happened to me through you? You would not like to see her grieving.'

'No, nor hear her, either,' said Bandelli, lying back in his chair. 'My life would not be worth living in such a case. All I ask of you is that you go in with my men, but come out on your own—I must not seem to sell Uberti too obviously—and that none knows of this transaction but yourself.'

'A little difficult that—seeing that I needed Van Eyck to cover for me while I came here. But be sure he will not talk—he is Lodovico's double for that.'

'So, Pierino, we are agreed?' asked Bandelli and, as he waited for Piero to answer, he suddenly bellowed at Dino, 'What say you to that, page? Do you agree?'

'If my lord——' began Dino.

'No, lad. I asked you, not him.'

'Why, Messer Agostino,' said Dino, throwing the laughing Piero an agonised look, and stumbling over her words, for the drink was beginning to overcome her, 'it seems a fair bargain to me. No fourth item, and my lord to see that your men are not involved.'

'And you, page. Do you go into Trani with your lord——?'

'No,' interrupted Piero. 'I shall go in alone, dressed like one of your men, and an idiot, to boot, hired for his brute strength. Dino and Lodovico shall wait for me outside, and either we all return or, if I do not, they will return without me, and I trust you to see them back to the *condotta*.'

Lodovico, silent until now, began to protest, but Piero put his hand up. 'I have decided,' he said. 'You knew before we came here what I proposed to do.'

'Your page is quiet,' said Bandelli, grinning wolfishly at Dino, who had fallen asleep in her chair, face scarlet with drink. 'Only sleep can stay his tongue and keep his face straight. You have a likely lad there, Pierino.'

A sleepless night and alcohol had felled Dino. She had watched the two foxes snapping and dancing around each other with great delight, had drunk almost absent-mindedly, and was paying the price.

'Yes,' said Piero, looking fondly at his overset wife. 'It is a bargain, then?'

'Remains only the price,' said Bandelli. 'Take Lodovico and your page away, and then return for us to haggle in private. I want no witnesses to what we decide, and nor, I think, do you.'

Piero nodded, bent down and scooped Dino up, and, Lodovico following, carried her back to their room, to lay her down on the great bed, and when Lodovico would have stayed with her said, 'Go and eat, Lodovico. I will join you later after I have seen Dino settled.'

He sat on the edge of the bed, loosened Dino's collar, and, smiling, brushed the black curls back from her face. He bent to kiss her, but as he did so she surfaced for a moment, said, 'Lord?' questioningly, and then put out a hand to grasp Piero's, opening her eyes to stammer, 'D-did I say right, lord?' and then sank back into sleep.

'Very right,' breathed Piero; he closed his own eyes then opened them to lean forward and kiss his wife on her scarlet cheek.

'Lord?' she said again, but did not wake for an answer.

CHAPTER EIGHT

BIANCA awoke in a room which was quite strange to her, and for a moment she was the Lady of San Giorgio, bewildered by her attire and her circumstances. Sitting up, her memory returned. Piero—and Bandelli—and the wine she had drunk! By rights she should have a bad head, be moaning and wailing as Bernardo did after 'a night of it', which was his phrase for over-indulgence. But apart from an odd feeling of disorientation, and a slight difficulty in remembering that she was Piero's wife, and Dino the page, she felt remarkably well.

She remembered nothing of the morning's conference after Bandelli had asked her her opinion of his and Piero's agreement, had no idea how she came to be in the big bed. She supposed Lodovico had put her there.

She swung her legs over the side of the bed, found that she could walk, and wandered out to find Piero and Lodovico. It was about noon, she thought, or a little later. Men-at-arms stared at her. She discovered that she had a great thirst, and perhaps the other pangs she felt were hunger. A page might be welcome in the kitchens. She trotted along, revelling, as always, in the freedom of being of boy, nobody wailing along behind you, no one saying, You must not go there, do that—ah, *Dio*, you should not have heard *that*! Well, there was nothing now which she had not heard, and for the life of her she could not understand what the fuss was all about. Men were men, and women were women, they had bodies and appetites, and if men were noisy, loud, rude and smelly, didn't trouble too much about washing—all excepting Piero, who managed to be spotlessly sweet and clean at all times—were gross in their conversation and did some things which were unspeakable, which made her shudder, then that was how the world wagged. It was useless to think otherwise.

Of course, when she was a woman again, or rather became one, then she supposed that she would have to pretend that the world was really like the one most women pretended it to be. For, behind all the veneer which women put upon life, she was suddenly sure that they really knew the truth of it all the time. Else why did the Agnetas carry on so? And, too, she now knew why girls were so carefully guarded. To protect them, to keep them spotless for the man they were going to marry— never mind that he had probably enjoyed dozens of women, as Piero had done—his wife would have to be a virgin.

And all that out of too much wine, she thought, amused, as she neared the kitchens. *In vino veritas*—when drunk the truth comes out. Was that what the old saying which Father Luca had taught her meant? It hadn't made Bernardo wise, that was for sure. He ought to be the Archmage himself, so much had he drunk over the years. Perhaps, *in Dino, truth* should be her motto!

Smiling to herself at her absurd thoughts, she almost ran into Maddalena, the red-haired widow, the mistress of Astra's lord, who came through one of the doors into the hall, and hailed her.

'Ha, Messer Page. A word with you.'

She did not really want to talk to Blowsabella, as she had irreverently nicknamed Maddalena, but there was no help for it. She gave a perfunctory bow, which had Maddalena grinning at her insolence.

'Yes, lady?' Dino asked, and her voice was hardly respectful.

'Yes, lady,' mimicked Maddalena then shot out a brawny arm to grasp Dino's chin, and lift her face. She must have learned *that* from Piero, thought Dino resentfully.

'Come, let me look at the page who so occupies his lord's thoughts.' Near to, Maddalena's age was visible, and the coming ruin of what had been an astonishing beauty was plain for all to see. She must have been in her prime when Piero had been a lad at the monastery.

'Lady,' said Dino defiantly, raising her dark eyes to look into Maddalena's green ones. Oh, I shall never be as lovely as you were, she thought desolately. No wonder *he* still favours you.

Maddalena thought quite otherwise. A pang of pure jealousy shot through her. Oh, the child will be astonishing, and soon. Such great dark eyes, such a pure complexion, and her hair! She put a woman's form on Dino, lengthened the hair, softened the cheeks, saw the rounded bosom, the swelling hips; there was no need to foresee anything for the kissable mouth—that was already perfect.

How strong was her lost lover's will, for she knew that she had lost Piero, that he had not laid hands on this delightful child already, immature though she was. It was foolish to be jealous—she had been lucky to keep him so long; only his kindness and gratitude for the past brought him to her bed at all, these days—she knew that, and knew that their long liaison was finally over. Agostino had told her after the morning's meeting that Pierino had a page whose brains matched his own. She was not sure whether her brother had seen that the page was a girl, or whether, knowing, he had said nothing—he could not possibly have guessed that the page was Pierino's untouched wife.

'You are pleased to serve your lord?' she said.

'Yes,' said Dino and, speaking, knew that Maddalena was aware of who and what she was. She shivered.

Maddalena smiled painfully. 'Fear not,' she said. 'Your secret is safe with me. You are ready to serve him—in every way?'

'When he wills it,' replied Dino steadily.

'Oh, I know him well,' said Maddalena. 'He will not require anything of you until he and you are ready. You understand me, page?'

'I think so, lady.'

'Never forget that he is a hard man,' said Maddalena softly. 'Life and circumstance have made him so. But he is never wanton, either in love or cruelty.'

'I must believe that,' said Dino steadily.

'And you love him?' Pain tore at Maddalena's heart as she spoke.

The truth was wrenched from Dino. The truth she had hardly dared to confess to herself. The truth, that unconsciously she had known since the first moment she had seen him on the stairs at San Giorgio—Piero had been right about that when speaking to Lodovico before his marriage.

'Yes,' she admitted and, saying the word, she was suddenly engulfed in one vast blush. The unacknowledged passion which she felt for him, had felt on their wedding night, overcame her. She burned for him, and the thought that last night he had enjoyed the woman before her made her feel almost ill.

Maddalena remained rock-steady, knew something of what Piero's page was suffering, and said simply, 'Good,' and dropped the hand which held Dino's chin at last. 'Being the best, he deserves only the best, although the Lord God rewards us as He wills, not as we will. You understand that, too?'

'Man proposes, God disposes,' said Dino stolidly. 'I have known that all my life.'

'Indeed,' said Maddalena. 'That is good. We understand each other well, and the world a little. You were looking for food when I stopped you.'

'Always,' said Dino, with a little laugh, and then, hesitantly, 'I am always hungry these days.'

'Good again,' said Maddalena. 'Food will make you grow. The kitchens are through that door. Bid the servants there feed you in the name of the lady Maddalena. God go with you, Lady of Astra, and with him.'

So she could not hate Maddalena, after all. The older

woman loved Piero, there was no doubt, and had loved him when Dino had been a little girl stumbling around San Giorgio. And she had unlocked Dino's innermost thoughts. Made her acknowledge the truth of her feelings about her lord; and whether that was a good thing, Dino did not know, but it was the truth, and Father Luca had always said that above all we must strive for the truth, and not deny it.

It seemed to be Dino's morning for revelations, and she was pondering on them as she entered the kitchen, to find Lodovico eating at the table there. He greeted her. 'Awake again, I see. I was coming to fetch you to eat. We leave soon, for Trani. Your lord and Bandelli have made their bargain, and we join today's convoy. Piero's luck held again. We arrived pat upon the hour— we might have had to delay a week.'

'And the Lord Captain—he will come to eat with us?'

Lodovico smiled a strange smile. 'He ate with Bandelli while you slept, and now he is preparing himself for the journey, and his entry to Trani.'

You had to admit one thing, Dino thought, cramming bread and cheese into her mouth, and declining further wine with a shudder; life with Piero de' Manfredini was never dull. Hardly had they arrived at Bandelli's castle but they were off again; it was so unlike life in San Giorgio, where one unchanging day had followed another.

Lodovico read her thoughts a little, and said, 'The Falcon roves at will, and is tireless. Does that frighten you?'

'No,' she said, and knew that she was telling the truth.

But, later, fear was what she felt. Some of Bandelli's men-at-arms were to accompany the convoy, suitably disguised, and were to join it some miles from the castle. She had expected to see Piero among them, similarly garbed, when they all assembled in the courtyard. There was a wagon with them, with some provender from Bandelli's own stores, and two men were to ride on it.

One was a sturdy fellow, the marks of the martial trade plain on him, the other was a shambling figure, ill-dressed, grimy, a patch over one eye, and a dragging leg.

She looked around for Piero, at the men on horseback, at the mules, and at the wagon, and the two peasants tending it.

'Where is he?' she asked.

'Can you not see him?' said Lodovico.

'One of the men on horseback?' she said tentatively, although none looked like Piero.

'No,' said Lodovico, 'look again.'

She looked harder this time, realising that she had been looking for a tall blond man, and there was none to be seen. Some of the men were mocking the shambling peasant, who was now quite near to her. Her hands flew to her mouth as he reached out to catch her by the belt. 'Your blessing, Messer Page, on our errand,' he mumbled, and then winked at her with his good eye.

'No,' she said.

'Yes,' said Piero, letting go of her belt. 'I must be well disguised. The Lord of Astra is known to the world. You will do as Lodovico tells you, will you not, Dino? Promise me. I trust you.'

'I trust you,' she said fiercely, 'to come back to us.'

He gave her a slightly lop-sided smile. 'Why, my dove, I do believe you care a little.'

'Come back,' she said. 'For Lodovico.'

'Not for my page?' he said, grinning.

'A little,' said Dino, thinking, I could not bear it if anything happens to him, but I will not say so to the man who slept with Maddalena last night.

'A little. Well, that will have to do.' He saw her trembling mouth, her eyes which gave the lie to her careless words, and said gently, '*Addio*, my page.'

'And *addio*, to you, lord,' she said, watching him ride out, unrecognisable, before she, too, mounted her horse to ride off with Lodovico, to wait long hours for him after they had parted in the early evening, Piero and Bandelli's men joining the convoy of food which would leave for Trani early next morning. She and Lodovico had rested in what shade they could find, after a night which they had spent in the open.

The day had been hot, unduly so, and she was glad to drink from the skin of water which she and Lodovico had packed at Bandelli's eyrie.

Lodovico had been as silent as ever during the day, but, as usual, was careful of her comfort. Had he always lived for others? she wondered. Did he have no life of his own? She was grateful for his silence as the long day passed. They had camped away from the road, and earlier had heard the noise of the returning convoy passing below them after delivering its supplies to Trani. They knew that Piero would not be with them, but they had expected him to arrive not long after. They were wrong. The hours slipped by, and still he did not appear.

Dino said nothing. She was fearful that she might wail, cry out, beat her breast, and somehow it seemed important that she retain her self-control. He would have expected it, she knew. She remembered his last words to her: she must obey Lodovico—who said nothing, occasionally rising to look out over the miles of scrub below them on the mountainside. Somewhere in the distance was Trani. This trail, itself secret, leaving the road a little way below them, led to the hidden route in and out of Trani itself on the side which was away from Piero's encamped *condotta*, they had discovered from Bandelli's information.

Finally, as the light changed from blue to orange in hue, and she sat there, twisting her hands together, her eyes hurting from the effort of peering into the distance, her ears betraying her, for she heard him coming again and again—only for it to be an illusion—she began to lose hope.

Lodovico, who had walked some distance higher up the side of the mountain, came back to say, 'No sign, no sign of anything, human or animal.' He saw her anguished eyes, brilliant with unshed tears, staring at him.

'You care for him, then?'

Dino nodded. 'Yes,' she said, hardly able to speak. 'He does not care for me.'

'I think that you are wrong,' said Piero's uncle. 'He cares for you, I am sure, though I grant that he may not love you as a man loves a woman—but I would not bet on that, either. He is a good man, if a severe one,' he said, echoing what Maddalena had said to her earlier. 'But he is a true man, and love often begins with liking, and God knows, he likes you. I have seldom seen him so easy with anyone.'

'Oh, love might come, if he returns,' said Dino passionately, 'but that is by no means certain.'

'Have faith,' Lodovico told her. 'Piero is a great one for surviving.' But he, too, was anxious, and later he said, 'It will be dark soon. Trust me, Dino, I am going to look for him. I will not desert you, but who knows what might happen in this wilderness? If I do not return by morning, you must go back to Bandelli's eyrie. Do you think that you could find your way?'

She nodded. 'Yes, but I hope—oh, I do so hope that when I return there will be three of us. I don't want to go back without you.' She hesitated, and then threw her arms about Piero's uncle. 'I could not bear it if anything happened to either of you. No one has ever been so careful of me before as you and he have been.'

Lodovico stood quite still, holding her. 'You are the daughter I had, but who died, as did my wife and son, long ago, before you were born. You and Piero are my children now, and I share your feelings, *carissima*.' It was the first time that he had ever displayed any real emotion—to her, or even to Piero, but later, after he had walked away, she thought about it, and knew that he spoke the truth. He behaved to Piero and herself as a stern but loving father would. And she grieved for his poor wife and children, dead long ago, by what he said, and wondered how they had died.

He had been brave, and survived, and so would she, if Piero had died in Trani. . . And she began to shiver, although the day was hot, and the shivering would not stop. Only, just when her teeth had begun to chatter, and the slow tears to run, unwilled, down her cheeks, she could hear noises below her, and Lodovico calling in the distance.

The dreadful shivering stopped, as she willed herself to be brave. Her husband must not find her in this condition; he would be ashamed of her. She did not run down to Lodovico; she guessed, correctly, that he had called to reassure her that Piero was still alive, and she could hear their stumbling progress, which told her that, though Piero still lived, something was wrong.

She ran to their saddle-bags, fetched out the water-bottle, and food, thought again, and pulled out bandages and dressings, made from strips of old linen, carefully washed and cut, ready for use in the field. There was a small skin of wine, and she put that out, too, and a bag of simples, which Lodovico had shown her one day, back at the camp, and told her what they were for. There was willow bark, which, infused, caused pain to go away, or be reduced, he said. She looked dubiously at everything, pulled a blanket from her horse, and waited, until finally they appeared, Lodovico helping Piero, who was bent nearly double, feet dragging, not in pretence, as at Bandelli's, but through real hurt, and when he looked at her his face was swollen and bruised, and there was blood upon him.

He gave her a faint version of his usual mocking smile, said painfully, 'I told you I would return, my page,' and then, letting go the reins of his will, which had brought him from Trani, despite his hurts, closed his eyes and let his whole unconscious weight fall upon Lodovico, who gently laid him down on the blanket which his child-wife's forethought had placed ready for him.

Dino's relief that Piero was alive and was with them again was succeeded by distress at the condition he was in. She watched, hands pressed to her mouth, as Lodovico examined him, spoke to him, heard Piero's muttered answers, and noted feverishly that sometimes he did not answer at all.

Presently Lodovico raised his head, laid his nephew gently down again, and said, 'You must help me, Dino. There is a cave in the rocks behind us. I'll carry Piero there, and you must bring along the packs.'

'Carry him,' said Dino and then watched Lodovico hoist Piero over one shoulder, head and arms dangling; he was helpless and only half conscious. Nausea threatened to overcome her. She swallowed it down, did as Lodovico had bidden her: picked up the packs, the bandages and simples, then trotted after him into the cave to find that Piero was now sitting, half propped up against the cave wall.

'How hurt is he?' she asked, and tried to keep her voice steady; it would be useless to add a hysterical girl to Lodovico's problems.

'Neither dead, dying, nor like to be,' said Lodovico, brief as usual. 'Beaten, stunned and exhausted. Running a fever. Bad enough, but he could be worse. Much worse.'

'Praise the Lord God that he has returned at all,' said Dino fervently, going on her knees, and beginning to follow Lodovico's terse instructions to ease the patient's hurts, only to find Piero opening one swollen eye, and muttering,

'Try praising me, Dino. The Lord God didn't seem to be about today.' He had evidently heard her last comment, and was still sardonic Piero de' Manfredini, brought low though he was.

Well, she must trust Lodovico, and if Piero could make dreadful jokes then perhaps all was not lost, but she could see by the way he held his body, and how his head twisted and his hands clenched as they handled him, light though they were, how much he was in pain.

'A rib—or ribs—broken, I think,' said Lodovico. 'Hurts you to breathe? Nod, if you can't speak,' he added, and his hands were on Piero's body. Piero stifled an exclamation, and nodded.

She was sponging his face, wiping away the blood with a piece of the linen, wetted now, which she had prepared earlier. The bruises were plain upon it, and his split lip made talking difficult. Once his eyes closed, his head drooped, and when he lifted it he looked at her as though he did not know her. He shuddered away when she put the wet cloth on his face again, clutched at Lodovico and cried out in a muffled voice, 'No.'

'What happened?' asked Dino. 'Has he told you?'

'A little. Not long before he was ready to leave he was set upon by youths, for sport—an idiot is always fair game. Luckily some soldiers saved him from being killed. He made his way here as best he could. On his hands and knees mostly, judging by the state he's in.'

Impossibly perfect Piero seemed to have disappeared; but had he? How many would have used their will to return at all? She had admired, if resented, the haughty being who had changed her life so dramatically, but this broken man brought out all the compassion and pity which were an essential part of her, but never before expressed. It had little to do with love for him, although love was part of it; it was more a response to the fact that he was human, after all, could bleed and suffer, and need to be succoured, could put out a hand to take hers once, and press it in gratitude, even though he hardly knew who she was.

She filled a metal cup with water and handed it to Lodovico, who put it to Piero's lips. He drank a little, but suddenly, in the middle of a swallow, his head drooped, and he fell sideways, this time into a deeper unconsciousness than before, his head on Lodovico's arms, face white, with great blue bruises and smudges on it.

'Oh,' wailed Dino, all her hard-won self-control gone, 'you said he would not die.'

'Nor has he, nor will he,' said Lodovico briskly. 'The effort of drinking was too much for him. God is kind, and for the moment he does not suffer. Look you, little one, he seems in a bad way, but that is partly exhaustion. He will be better tomorrow, providing only that his fever remains light.'

Dino knew it was best not to ask herself whether Lodovico was telling the truth, or merely reassuring himself and her—best to be practical, to think how to help him. 'He will need watching over,' she said, brisk in her turn. 'You will have to care for him in the day, when he is awake; I have not the strength. So, you will sleep tonight, and I will nurse him. Besides, you must be strong for tomorrow.'

The little face turned up to Lodovico was so earnest and loving that he blinked a little and swallowed.

'As you wish,' he said, and began to lay out two blankets, and to prepare for the night. 'I will care for him now, but later it will be your turn. You must promise me that if he falls into a natural sleep you, too, will rest. You also need your strength for tomorrow.'

But when her turn came Piero was very far from a natural sleep. He was restless, spoke to those who were not there, was once in a battle, began to shout, until she put a loving hand on his lips. After that he was a lad in the monastery again—streams of Latin prayers, resentment at his lot there, flowed from his lips. He tossed and turned, rolling his head on the improvised pillow Lodovico had provided for him.

Troubled and distressed at his distress, Dino bit her lip, saw that Lodovico was sound asleep, moved from her sitting position to wriggle into the bed with Piero, beneath the blankets—Lodovico had said that he must not be cold—and, to comfort him, took him into her arms.

He did not have Piero's usual clean smell of soap and freshly laundered linen, and spotless healthy man, but the sour smell of sweat and sickness—he had vomited at least once on his journey to them. He had the male harshness of the uncared-for soldiers and pages she had known at San Giorgio. But none of that mattered at all; it only caused a great wave of love and tenderness to surge over her for impossibly perfect Piero, now no longer perfect.

Piero in his semi-delirium had no idea of who shared his bed. He was back in his childhood again, reliving events long gone, memories of loss and pain which would be always with him. He gave a great sigh, said in a low voice, almost like a little boy's, 'Mamma, where are you, Mamma?' and then loudly, 'No, I do not believe you,' and he was weeping and clutching at her.

Piero was in a large room, gloomy, with candles burning round a strange box, before an altar. He was shouting, running from the tower's chapel, a child, seven years old, looking for what he had lost, back in the past, in the place where he and his mother had lived, where his father often visited them.

It was his mother whom he had lost, and he ran along a corridor and then up some stairs, into a room full of light. Lodovico was there—a young Lodovico—and a tall man, who had his back to him, turned as he burst in. But not his mother—no, she was not there!

He saw the tall man fully at last, and it was himself! How could it be the himself he saw in the mirror? How could he be a child, and also the man he had become? Some part of him knew that it was his father, and when he ran to him his father pushed him away. Grief and guilt tore through him. Grief that his mother was dead, guilt and grief that he was so like his rejecting father.

And then all that he knew was that he wanted his

mother, not this father who had come to take him away from everything he had known and loved.

Someone was comforting him, someone soft and warm, and in his dazed state he thought that it was his mother. 'Oh, God be praised, Mamma, I thought that I had lost thee,' he whispered, and he burrowed his head into Dino's breast for comfort.

'Hush,' she said, 'hush,' understanding that he was lost in his past, and needed comfort. 'Thy mother is with thee—sleep, my child,' she murmured, and clutched impossibly perfect Piero to her poor, not-so-flat bosom, and comforted him with her stroking hands and her gentle voice until, secure in his 'mother's' arms again— the arms of the child he had taken for a wife, half in pity, half in jest—he slept at last.

Lodovico awoke in the early light to see Dino propped up against the cave wall, the sleeping Piero in her arms. He took one look at her white face, felt Piero's forehead, found it cool, thanked the Lord God for his mercy, and gently lifted him away from her. Piero stirred, but fell immediately back into sleep.

'Come, little one,' said Lodovico, putting his nephew into a comfortable position, then helping Dino out of his bed, and making her lie down, too, his own blanket over her. 'His fever has broken, he is sleeping naturally, and you must rest, or you will be ill yourself.'

'Yes,' said Dino gratefully; she was stiff from her uncomfortable night, and from holding herself still, so that Piero might sleep. 'I did not wish to disturb him.'

'He will sleep until it is fully light,' said Lodovico, 'and I will watch over him until he wakes.'

He watched over both of them, Dino sleeping the sleep of exhaustion, and Piero the sleep of healing. He looked down at Piero's wife, and thought that day by day she was changing and maturing—the wilful child was becoming a responsible woman. And even in her tiredness he could see that she was rapidly turning into the

beauty Piero had said she would become. He did not
think that she knew or understood either of these two
things, and he was beginning to wonder if Piero truly
deserved her, then thought, almost as though Piero had
whispered in his ear, 'But it is the discipline she has
undergone, the good food and the care she has received
from so many which have transformed her.' Yes, he
thought, she owes what she is to Piero's intervention,
and he is proved right again. He sighed, began to fetch
food from his pack, and prepare it, making an infusion
from the willow bark which Dino had put out for him,
ready for Piero to drink when he awoke.

He returned from his last journey to the nearby
stream, to find Piero painfully pulling himself into a
sitting position. He stopped when he saw Lodovico, and
spoke, although it was plain that he found speaking
difficult.

'How long?' he asked, as brief as Lodovico.

'Oh, one night only,' replied Lodovico. 'You were
lucky. Drink this to ease yourself.'

'Lucky to be alive,' said Piero, looking across at Dino.
'It was good of you to keep watch over me last night and
let the little one sleep.'

'Not I,' said Lodovico. 'You must thank your wife.
She held you in her arms all night and comforted you. I
persuaded her to lie down and rest barely an hour ago.'

'I thought,' said Piero slowly, 'I dreamed, rather. . .
that I was a child again.' He moved restlessly under
Lodovico's ministering hand, as he rubbed salve into his
wounds.

'So you were,' said Lodovico, gently. 'Her child for a
time. And now, what happened? Were you set on
immediately you entered Trani, or had you time to
inspect it? Have you remembered what you saw—or has
the blow to the head taken your memory away?'

'No,' said Piero almost bitterly. 'My memory is as
usual. I sometimes wish it were not. Every blow is
engraved upon it, as well as a map of Trani's streets,

von Steinach's dispositions, and the whereabouts of the guard house, the stores and the armoury.' He winced. 'Yes, and I know how best to take Trani, too, and when Dino awakes we must return to the *condotta* at all speed.'

'No,' said Lodovico. 'You are hardly fit.'

'Yes,' insisted Piero quite fiercely. 'I must. I don't trust Bruschini, he doesn't trust me. Every day we delay makes it more likely he will discover my absence, and adds to the count against me for not taking Trani before now. The sooner I am with my *condotta* again, the better. It needs me. Good though Van Eyck is, he will not be able to stand against Bruschini. Even I have found it difficult.' There was an almost unconscious arrogance in the way he spoke, but Lodovico knew that he said true.

'And Bandelli?'

'To be paid when we take Trani—as I am sure that we shall. And even if by some mischance we don't, he shall still be paid. It is a debt of honour.'

'I still say that you are not fit.'

'We must start, and if I fail on the way we can always rest. I shall not rest here, knowing what I know—of Trani and Bruschini both.'

There was no arguing with him. He put out a hand for Lodovico to help him up. Both were silent, and both startled, when Dino gave a great cry, and then sat up.

'I dreamed,' she panted, looking at them both. 'I do not know what I dreamed. Only, that there was danger for us all. . .' She looked again at Piero, on his feet, and thought with a pang, Dear Lord, impossibly perfect Piero is back with us again! For, hurt though he was, the arrogant set of his face and his body told her so. The lost boy whom she had comforted in the night had disappeared. He was her child no longer.

But the look he turned on her was kind and loving although it seemed quite clear that he had no memory of what had passed in the night, nor did she wish to remind him.

'Are you rested enough to ride back to the *condotta*, my

page?' said Piero gravely, and then, almost formal, 'Lodovico told me that you watched over me last night. I thank you.'

Oh, why did she feel that she wanted to cry as he spoke so coolly to her, she who had held him in her arms all night, who had felt his lips on her cheek when he had thought in his fever that his mother embraced him? Now she was simply his page, the wife who was no wife. Almost, last night, she had felt herself to be a woman, and for the first time, holding his hard man's body to her heart, she had felt a genuine passion.

Oh, dear Lord God, she prayed silently, grant that I may become a woman soon, so that my lord may desire me, as I now desire him.

But none of this showed, for she was determined that it would not, and when Lodovico had helped Piero on to his horse she mounted her own, and, tired though she was, prepared herself mentally for the journey back to Trani.

They had left the camp under the cover of darkness, but no such considerations moved them on the way back. The journey was shorter, and by the early afternoon they were past the first gaping sentries, who had heard that their captain was ill, and were astonished to see him ride in with Lodovico and Dino on foam-flecked horses.

Only his will, constantly exercised over the last twenty-four hours, kept him in the saddle at all, Dino knew, and when one of the sentries would have stayed them—the Lord God knew why—Lodovico bellowed at them, 'Way, make way for the Falcon,' and they were thundering down towards Piero's pavilion, men running towards them, but Van Eyck, surprisingly, was not among their number.

A junior captain, a young man Piero trusted, came up, saluting Piero, saying hoarsely, 'Thank the Lord God that you are back. The Florentine grew suspicious. . .'

Piero said fiercely, 'Help me down, man,' which he did, gazing at his lord's ravaged face, and, once down, holding on to Lodovico's arm as the world swayed around him, Piero ordered, 'Make your report, man, and quickly.'

'Bruschini grew suspicious. Came here yesterday, caused your tent to be entered, found that you were gone. Accused you of treachery, said that you had sold yourself to Trani for extra pay, and was tricking him and Florence. He took Van Eyck to his headquarters for questioning, and today is demanding that your *condotta* mount a frontal attack on Trani as evidence of good faith. Van Eyck holds out, they say, but for how long? The Florentine is like to hang him out of hand for helping what he says is your treachery.'

'My treachery?' Piero laughed shortly and mirthlessly. 'Given everything, that is a joke to share with my friends—if I have any left, that is.' He swayed, steadied himself, and gave orders to Lodovico. 'You will ride to Bruschini's headquarters at once, tell him that I am back, and will be with him shortly. Dino, you will help me to order myself a little. I cannot go to him as I am.'

'No,' began Dino and Lodovico together. 'You are not fit——'

'*Per Dio*,' roared Piero at them. 'Am I your captain or your slave, that my minions can defy me? Lodovico, ride to Bruschini at once, before that benighted fool gives an order that will destroy my *condotta*, and Dino, dismount immediately, and help me to prepare to see Bruschini. The blue, lad, the blue, and quick about it. I want as few signs of weakness when I face him as is possible at short notice.'

His voice was enough to make an army quail, and Dino thought ruefully that the lost boy of the previous night had indeed disappeared. Wordless, for nothing would move him, she assisted him into his finest cloth- ing, bathed his face, and poured him a great draught of wine, which he drank, shuddering, but which restored some colour to his ashen cheeks, so that the bruises stood less plain upon them.

He threw her his blue houppelande, said, 'Carry that for me to put on before we enter his lair, and no argument,' and his voice rose again. Pain and anxiety rode his shoulders.

'Your servant, lord,' she thought it politic to reply.

'Body of God, you would do well to remember that,' he shouted at her; for the present she was his page, nothing else. His anger at the Florentine mounted with every moment of his preparation. The speed with which he had tried to take over his *condotta*, to misuse it in a frontal attack, which he knew its captain had rejected so often, the conviction that from the beginning Bruschini had meant to destroy him, was strong in him.

The young captain and Tavio—a Tavio who was worried, and had neither time nor inclination to bait the newly returned Dino—helped him on to his horse. Teeth gritted, he held himself erect, and tried to move easily— he would give no signs of weakness to allow Bruschini an advantage. They set off, the young captain before him, Tavio and Dino following.

'The Lord Captain is injured?' Tavio had whispered to Dino, to hear her curt answer,

'Yes, but not seriously.'

Curious eyes followed their progress until they reached Bruschini's lines, where some jeered at them, but not too loudly. Men-at-arms ran forward, but the young captain waved them back,

'Make way, make way for the Lord Piero, Count of Astra, who comes to see Messer Bruschini,' he shouted, deliberately giving the Florentine no honorary title as Piero had instructed. And the lack of troops with them was deliberate, too. A risk, as with Bandelli, to disarm suspicion, which might mean death for them all, but Piero was a risk-taker, and before he had left he had briefly seen Facetti, and told him what to do if he and Van Eyck were murdered.

'But that, I am sure, is something Bruschini will not do once I have spoken. And Florence does not sanction murder,' he had said.

Dino prayed for all their sakes that his judgement was as acute as ever, not blurred by his injuries.

And then they were before Bruschini's headquarters—which had been a barn—their horses were being led away, and, as with Bandelli, they were flies before a spider.

Light streamed in through the open door, and candles were burning in great sconces. Heat met them as they entered, and Dino was fearful for her lord. Before her, he walked as erect and easily as if yesterday had never happened, but at what cost? The Florentine, Van Eyck and other officers were standing around a table in the centre. Lodovico was there, being held by guards. His face lightened as he saw them. Piero took in the scene with one furious glare.

'Splendour of God!' His voice was as imperious and cutting as he could make it, but not overloud—the voice of a man in total control of himself. 'Is this necessary? Are you determined to destroy my *condotta* and my officers by any means, and for any reason?'

'So you are here,' said Bruschini. Dino had never been so close to him before. He was a big man, richly dressed, but, soft, was not, and never had been, an athlete, was in his middle forties, and had the pursed, self-satisfied face of a man who had found success easy, who had never, unlike Piero, had to struggle to make his way upwards. Now he was bidding for power in Florence, and, as a commissary, and a man who had proved better than a noted *condottiero* in the trade of war, would have carved himself an irresistible power base. To do so he only needed to destroy Piero's reputation, or even the man himself.

'I see a man who lied, who claimed an illness. What have you been doing, Lord of Astra? Selling yourself to Trani? Or were you sold already, that you have delayed and delayed, turned that which was easy to that which was difficult? Can you give me any reason why you should not face trial and judgement? You and your tool here——' and he waved a hand at Van Eyck '—who has steadily refused me a proper account of your doings, who is your accomplice in everything including your treachery.'

'For a man who claims learning,' said Piero, 'your leaps in logic do you little credit——'

Bruschini broke in angrily, 'Pah, I know treachery when I smell it.'

'Do you, indeed? Then your sense of smell is deficient—which does not surprise me.' Piero was at his most easy and most mocking, thumbs hooked into his hammered silver belt. He certainly did his page credit this morning, was Dino's reaction, through her fear. 'Now, my idea of treachery,' he continued, 'is when a commissary persists in trying to order his captain to carry out a frontal attack, which even Dino, my page here, would tell you is the strategy of a mooncalf. And since, whatever you are, you are not a mooncalf—what does that make *you*?'

Bruschini began to splutter, but Piero interrupted him, waving a graceful hand, the sapphire on his finger catching the light from the candles. 'No, do not answer me. I have no wish to learn the workings of the sewer you call a mind. Let me tell you what I propose to do, since I am still the captain of these forces—read my contract, Messer Bruschini; there is no word in it that gives you any power over me, or allows you to arrest and harm my officers. On the contrary, I have a mind to hang *you*, for interfering with my legitimate conduct of this campaign. No, you will listen to me. Yesterday, I was in Trani—not invited in, by no means. I entered through the secret passageway by which they have been supplied—and that is why they have held out for so long, not because of moonshine about my good faith. I now know how to take Trani, and in short order. I will lead a troop into it, through the passageway. A surprise attack should occupy them, while some of my men open the gates to you. You, Carpacci, will, with Van Eyck's men, mount the frontal attack this witling has long wanted, but it will be on a town being destroyed in two directions. This will be done at dawn tomorrow, while the townsfolk and soldiers are sleeping—thinking themselves secure. My troops and myself will move into position this evening to enter by the passageway at first light.'

'You were in Trani yesterday?' said Bruschini, refusing to give way easily. 'I do not believe you.'

'Oh, believe me, believe me,' said Piero. He turned to the table, where ink, a reed pen and parchment stood. 'Allow me,' he said, and bent to write, and the wince he gave as he did so was missed by everyone except Dino. Before them all he drew the map of Trani, speaking as he did so, describing it, indicating where the key points stood, the entry for his troops, and how, when and where Carpacci and Van Eyck should attack.

For a moment there was silence, then all the soldiers in the barn began to talk together, even Carpacci excited at the prospect of a sudden easy victory where before had been a long-drawn-out stalemate.

Still Bruschini would not give way. 'How do we know that this is not a trick? That you went in at all? You could have had this map in your head at the beginning of the campaign, to use when you were ready with your treachery.'

Dino could not contain herself; she forgot that pages were silent, invisible things.

'A trick?' she said, her voice a squeak until she cleared it. 'Not in Trani! Oh, what a calamitous lie that is! Not only did my lord go into Trani, but Messer Lodovico and I awaited his return all day yesterday. And he went in disguised and gained a grievous hurt, but still insisted that we ride here today, so that the campaign might be won and speedily. Shame on you, shame.'

Piero had moved to stop her at the beginning of this outburst, but halted, as her patent honesty, and real indignation, not only informed every word she uttered, but were enough to convince everyone in the barn that what she said was the truth.

'The page tells true, Lord Captain?' asked Van Eyck, who had remained silent until then. 'You are injured?'

'The lad exaggerates,' said Piero evenly. 'I suffered only a little.'

'More than a little,' said Lodovico, speaking at last. 'He should not be on his feet.'

'Nothing to that,' said Piero roughly. 'You should not have spoken, my page, and shall be reprimanded for it. But the truth has many voices, and chose you to tell it this time. So, you are all satisfied. We proceed as I said.'

He had the room with him, and Bruschini could not hold out against them, particularly when his own nominee, Carpacci, was as enthusiastic as the rest, saying to him loudly, 'Why, I told you I could not believe Manfredini to be a traitor. His word is as sound as any in Italy.'

And so they took Trani.

And Dino, part of the reserve force which was led by Lodovico, was glad that the victory was won without overmuch bloodshed, thinking of all those whom she had come to know in the weeks outside Trani's walls.

And later, riding into the town by Lodovico's side, leading Piero's spare horse, she knew as she saw him, his great helm off—looking like Mars, the God of War, in a painting she had once seen—receiving the rites of honourable surrender from von Steinach and a disappointed Uberti, that her heart was irrevocably given to him, whether he loved her or no. She knew that her life was so bound up with his that all that mattered to her was his survival. What she would have done if he had been killed, she could not think, for Piero was now her world.

CHAPTER NINE

BRUSCHINI was not best pleased at the Falcon's victory, Dino could tell, and by the eye he cast on her at the ceremonies of surrender he was not best pleased with the cheeky page who had turned the tide at the meeting before the battle.

But what of that? Piero had not reprimanded her for speaking out at the Council of War. After the brief storming of Trani, and his subsequent disposition of his forces and the beginning of the haggling over ransom, and the sending of messengers to Florence telling of victory, he had, at the end of the day, allowed himself to collapse and her to tend him.

His collapse only came when they were private together, in a room in Trani's citadel, once occupied by the *castellano*. He had refused to allow her to send for Lodovico, who was engaged in arranging the billeting of Piero's main army in the town itself, saying faintly, 'I want no nannying, from anyone. You are my wife, and you may help me; otherwise, nothing.'

Lying on his bed, face grey with mingled weariness and pain, he had allowed her to undress him, and once, looking up at her, had said hoarsely, 'You know that you should not have spoken in the Council yesterday, wife.'

Wife. He had called her wife, for the second time that evening, and had he not been exhausted, almost to death, she would have rallied him, would have said, 'I am Dino here, not wife,' but, instead, replied simply, 'Yes, husband, I know that. But Father Luca always told me, "*Magna est veritas, prevelabit*"—"Great is truth, and it shall prevail", and so I spoke, for truth would not speak of itself—I was its chosen instrument.'

172

This was said with Dinoesque style and cheek, so that Piero laughed, a little painfully, had put up an arm to pull her down to him, kissed her on the brow, and said, 'Father Luca is at fault again, I see, but glad I am that you were naughty Dino and not my obedient wife, although when you were ever obedient I cannot think. I could never have foreseen that what you said would ring so true that none could gainsay us, and so Bruschini was forced to yield.'

Us, he had said us, for the first time, and surely, as he held her to him, he could feel how much his touch affected her. But she must not make too much of what he had said, for he let her go, and she stood up, saying briskly, to hide her longing for him, her desire to climb into the bed with him, to comfort him, perhaps for him to. . . No, no. He did not want it. . . 'Naughty Dino would be truly naughty if he did not persuade you to stop talking and rest. It will be another long day tomorrow. Now drink this.' And she handed him an infusion of willow bark.

'Two bullies to run me ragged,' he said drowsily, his exertions and the willow beginning to work on him. 'An uncle, and now a wife. A wise man would not carry such furniture around with him to distract him from his duty.' But he put out a hand to press hers before he turned his head on the pillow and slept. She had to be content with that, and the watching of him, until Lodovico came in and shooed her to bed.

By the time they finally rode into Florence, all the church bells ringing to greet them, and the citizens in the streets cheering them, and the *signoria*—the town council—standing outside the oratory in the district of Orsanmichele, to greet the victors, with an official orator standing there, reading out their exploits, and finally putting a laurel wreath on Piero's head, as he stood by his horse, he was fully recovered again. Impossibly perfect Piero was back, and all that he said and did in the hours of his triumph was graceful and correct, his appearance impeccable.

On the night of the day after their return there was to be a great feast, but before that Piero and his immediate train repaired to his villa on the outskirts of the city, which a grateful Florence had given to the Falcon for his earlier exploits, which was now awaiting his arrival, and where they were to live for a time. Dino was still in her page's clothes, but would wear them for the last time, Piero had told her, when they rode to the villa, and after that she would be a woman again. For good, he hoped.

Dino had never seen or heard of a villa before, and gazed in wonder at the buildings which dotted the hills around Florence. Some were like miniature castles or towers, with fortifications, and battlements, as though their owners were ready to fight mimic wars in them. They had been built in the peace which had followed Florence's ascendancy as a commercial capital, and noblemen and merchants withdrew to them to live the country life, away from the bustle of the town with its narrow and winding streets that were filled with life.

Piero's villa was not like a fortress at all, but was one of the newer ones, built—although Dino did not know this—in imitation of a Roman villa. It stood in its own grounds, and she found its white and pink walls, with delicate brown decorations, glowing in the sun, beautiful in the extreme, surrounded as it was by trees and flowers and statuary, with fountains playing on flat lawns. Everything she saw was as unlike brutish San Giorgio as it could be.

Servants ran to meet them, and took away their horses and their retainers, leaving herself and Piero and Lodovico on a paved forecourt before great double doors, through which a grave steward, carrying a wand of office, came to greet them, saying, 'Welcome, Lord of Astra, welcome, and enter. You have a visitor already, lord.'

'A visitor?' Piero paused in mid-stride.

'Yes, lord. I was compelled to admit him, although you were not as yet here to receive him.' He hesitated. 'I could not argue with him, lord. He said that he was the Marquis of Alassio and your father. He insisted that I admit him.'

'Did he, indeed?' Piero's voice was as cold as Dino had ever heard it, and she watched Lodovico look hard at him as he spoke again. 'And where did you put this insistent Marquis who made such an extravagant claim?'

'In the garden-room, at the back. He said that he would await your arrival.'

Piero shrugged. Dino wondered what he was like. Piero had never spoken of him, nor his uncle, either. 'You wish me to accompany you, lord?'

Her husband turned, and gave her a wolfish smile. 'Yes, my page. You are still my page. Why not? And you, too, Lodovico; I need protection. You may both protect me. Lead on, Ricardo. We will all see the noble Marquis.' His tone was so savagely satirical that it made her tremble. At the same time she was filled with an intense curiosity. She remembered the rumours she had heard: that Piero was Manfredini's bastard, and had been abandoned by him as a child.

They walked through the beautiful house, as lovely inside as it was outside, and the garden-room was the finest thing of all. One wall had a series of delicate archways pierced in it, opening on to a flower-filled quadrangle, with a fountain playing in the middle. The floor was a mosaic, showing a boar being killed by a blonde woman holding a spear. There was a long stone bench at one end, and a man was seated there, chin propped on his hand, looking down.

Dino saw with surprise that he was admiring a small pool filled with goldfish. Shrubs in terracotta urns stood around it. The man rose to greet them as they entered, Piero leading, Lodovico to one side, and Dino trotting behind, aware of her travel-stained appearance, her lack of a recent bath, and her own masquerade as a boy, which seemed strange and odd before this impassive man.

For his appearance was a shock. He was so like Piero as he would be when grown old. The blond hair was fading into silver, the face was harsher, and even more mocking. He was neither so tall nor so broad as his son, but he held himself with the same superb arrogance, and was dressed with the same careful magnificence in a doublet and houppelande of blue and silver.

'Ah,' he said. 'The victor of Trani. Welcome.'

'Yes?' said Piero, his face stone. 'And to what do I owe the honour?' But his voice said that it was no honour at all.

'Come, may not a man greet his son when he has performed with such bravery, and won such a signal victory? All the world knew that Trani could not fall. But it fell.'

'His son?' said Piero. 'Nature made you my father, nothing else. But neither I, nor the law, acknowledge you.'

His manner could not have been more indifferent. He gave nothing, offered nothing, and if the magnificent figure before him gave no quarter, neither did he.

'No?' drawled the Marquis. 'But I hear that my son took his unwanted father's advice and ennobled himself by marriage. Bernardo di San Giorgio has informed me that you have wed his plain shrew of a sister. I congratulate you on the marriage, but not on your choice of a wife. What have you done with the lady? Your steward informs me that she is not here, and she has, I see, not arrived with you.'

'No?' Piero was smiling, almost feeling behind him Dino's seething rage at this description of her. Plain shrew, indeed! 'You think not?'

'I see your perpetual shadow—as who could not?—and your grinning page, but no lady.'

'Ah, my grinning page!' Piero, laughing openly, now swung towards Dino. 'Are you grinning *again*, Dino? I thought that Bandelli had cured you of that—but, yes, I see that you are. I am sure that you are willing to share the jest with us. You are seldom slow to speak.'

'Indeed, lord,' said Dino, showing her teeth, and glaring at Piero's father—one more rude man to be put down, and a pleasure it would be, too. 'I am only too happy to entertain you. I see where you acquired your vicious tongue, Lord Piero. You learned it from your father. I shall seek to emulate you both as a good servant should. Your manners may be execrable, but your impudence is beyond reproach.'

'You hear, Father,' said Piero, swinging back towards him, 'a page of quality. Choice in his judgements, as Agostino Bandelli was quick to see. Tell me, page, what you thought of my marriage. The lord my father would be interested to hear your opinion of that, I am sure.'

'You encourage your servants to be insolent,' said the Marquis, eyes hard, brows raised, staring coldly at Dino. 'Most unlike you. But, yes, boy. What did you think of your lord's marriage?'

'I, lord? Why, it is not for me to judge when impossible perfection, which I see that Lord Piero also inherits from you, along with his wicked tongue, chooses to stoop to San Giorgio's flat-chested lady. Such perfection occasionally falters, or perhaps my lord was tired of blowsy armfuls in his bed. Who can say?'

There was a moment's stunned silence, and then Piero threw back his golden head with a crack of laughter. 'Blowsy armfuls, indeed! You wrong Maddalena. And that, Father, should dispose of any reservations you might have had about my choice of a wife. Such an ability to speak her mind so plainly and in so few words should commend her to such a master of unpleasantness as yourself. May I present to you my page, Dino, who is also my wife, Bianca, late the Lady of San Giorgio. Bianca, you may curtsy and apologise to the Lord Marquis that you were compelled for your own safety to abandon your skirts.'

If he had hoped to distress or wrongfoot his father in any way, he had failed, and so had she, thought Dino. For the handsome old man before her put out a hand to lift her, as she sketched a curtsy, took her own grubby paw, the paw of a hardworking page, and kissed the back of it gravely, looking closely at her as he did so.

'I think,' he said, 'that report may have lied a little. The tongue is sharp, true—but as for the rest——' And he shook his head. 'Blonde is the colour all admire, but black, my dear, as I see now that I look more carefully, carries its own beauty, too. And you, my Lord of Astra——' and he turned abruptly to his son '—if you thought to demean either of us, you failed.'

Piero was as cool as ever. 'I demean you, or my wife? Oh, you mistake. I would not dare. I know the quality of both of you. I would as lief try to demean the Grand Porte or the Lord God. And now, I think, you will allow the lady Bianca to retire in order to resume her proper self. Her housekeeper and her maid await her. You may leave us, lady, Lodovico will attend you.'

Bianca stared at both men. So alike, despite the difference in their ages. 'My proper self?' she said. 'Pray, what is that, my lords? I leave you to discuss the matter.' And she swept out, head held high. The Lord God damn the pair of them. Let them both dance in Messer Dante's Hells, and sup with the Devil at the end of it. She would not be a plaything between them—no, never.

'And that,' said the Marquis, watching her go, amusement and admiration mixed on his face, and echoing his son's earlier words, even down to their mocking inflexions, 'should dispose of any notion that your lady is one with whom anyone might safely take liberties.'

Which was exactly what Bianca herself—for Bianca she was now allowed to call herself again—was thinking as she left the room to find Piero's housekeeper, unwanted tears pricking behind her eyes. San Giorgio's plain shrew of a sister, indeed. What a horrible old man, and no wonder Piero was as he was, with such a sire.

She thought angrily of the pair of them, facing one another like two spitting cats, and the thought amused her enough to quell her tears.

'So,' continued the Marquis, 'you are pleased to disown me, Ser, and before your new wife, too.'

'Disown *you*?' said Piero. 'You disowned *me* long ago, when my mother died, and you consigned me to the monastery, and left me there. I recall no visit, no care for your son then.'

'And if I said that I was wrong to do so?'

'Wrong?' repeated Piero, raising his brows. 'You were not wrong. I thank you, my lord. I may have lost a father, but I gained much else. What I learned at the monastery was of more value to me than if I had been a pet at your debauched court. And what I owe to Lodovico Orso and to Agostino Bandelli makes either of them my true father—not you.' But he had never looked more like his true father, and that true father knew it. He smiled wryly.

'And did you choose San Giorgio's sister to spite me for telling you to mend your birth with a splendid marriage? Deliberately to choose one as little splendid as you could?'

'I see you do not know me at all,' said his son, and smiled. 'And had I done so, why, I chose better than I knew.'

'And I bred better than I knew,' said his father, and for once sincerity rang in his voice. 'I wish I could say that my legitimate get could match you in any way, for looks, intelligence, or achievement.'

'As I dare swear you are kind enough to tell them every day,' said Piero, with good-humoured savagery. 'I take it that you came to inspect my wife? You have seen her. You may leave.'

'You are a hard man, Messer Piero, beware.'

'Why, who made me so, but you? I thank you for it. And pity your favoured sons.' He bowed. 'I must join my wife, my lord Marquis. She is a brave child, but I have brought her to a strange place, and hurt her into the bargain.'

'And you will be kinder to her than you are to me,' said his father, the note of sincerity in his voice again, joined with a bitter regret.

'And what is that to you? But yes; after all, she has never abandoned me. On the contrary, she has been consistently brave and true.'

'I deserve all that you say,' admitted his father simply. 'I hope that you may never feel as I feel today.'

'Oh, indeed,' said Piero, laughing again, eyes contemptuous. 'You destroyed my softer feelings for me long ago, but if I have a son, legitimate or otherwise, I shall not abandon him to others.'

There was nothing more to say. They were too alike, as Bianca had seen, and the older man had done the younger one a grievous wrong. He made one last attempt at reconciliation. 'I am here on a diplomatic mission,' he said. 'Your brother Michele is with me. He wishes to know you.' He paused. 'He admires what he has heard of you. Not for my sake, but your own, a little—and his—if you meet him, do not reject him. He, at least, did you no wrong.'

Piero's eyes widened a little at the request. 'No wrong?' he said. 'He is my age, I understand, almost exactly. Was he abandoned to a monastery? No, I will not reject him, for it was I who had good fortune, not he.'

Well, he had given way a little, but only a little, and nothing to *him*. Piero watched his father walk, straight-backed, from the room, and was astonished to find unwanted tears in his eyes, and did not know for whom, or what, he wept.

Lodovico had followed her, Bianca found, and it was he who took her to the waiting housekeeper, and the little maid who stood beside her. The housekeeper was a tall blonde woman, in her late thirties, buxom, and had once been a beauty, that was plain. Her face was calm and her manner to Bianca was impersonally kind.

The room she was taken to was to be Bianca's own, and had a door into the master bedroom, which was Piero's. Indeed, her own could only be reached through Piero's, where a big bed, of carved wood, with beautiful embroidered curtains, standing on a dais, dominated the room. There was a fireplace in it—a large one, and Madonna Caterina—for that was her name, Lodovico had said before he left them—seeing her eyes on it, said in her calm voice, 'The winters can be cold here, lady.'

Bianca's room was smaller, with a low bed, almost a couch, covered with a spread whose embroidery was so fine that Bianco exclaimed on it, and the little maid, Giulia, said, 'That is Madonna Caterina's work.'

'Oh, you must teach me,' said Bianca eagerly. 'It is as beautiful in its own way as Father Luca's illuminations.'

There was a big chest, exquisitely painted, with a Virgin in her glory, far finer than the one she had left behind at San Giorgio, and Caterina began to lift the most elegant garments from it, saying, 'Your lord wrote to me from Trani, said that you would need clothing proper to your station, and told me that you were small. Let us hope that some of these will fit you.'

Bianca suddenly had a terrible impulse to cry. Piero had done that, in the middle of the campaign—sent letters by the courier so that she would not be disgraced when finally she reached her new home! She blinked, and said in a hollow voice, 'But I need a bath. I have been living in the camp, in the fields, and it was difficult for me to wash myself properly, me being a girl, and no one to know, as I hope the Lord Piero explained.'

Caterina nodded, went to another chest, and began to produce towels, and an over-robe, and told Giulia to help the lady out of her clothes. Bianca looked around for the wooden tub to bathe in, and Caterina, guessing what she was doing, smiled a little, and said, 'Through the lord's room, there is another, where there is a bath, and the servants will have filled it with warm perfumed water, and you will bathe there.'

A separate room for a bath! San Giorgio, wooden tubs, coldish water and Agneta's grumblings seemed far away. Bianca allowed herself to be led, wearing only the overgown of fine wool, and a pair of slippers with turned-up toes and more beautiful embroidery, to the room where the bath was, and, for the first time, began to understand what marrying Piero had brought her.

'No,' said Piero. He was standing in the large dining-room of his villa, talking to his housekeeper. 'No, I do not agree with you, Caterina. You must remain here as my housekeeper. I trust you and I need you to help my wife. She is strong, I know, but she has no experience of the great world—or the jungle if you prefer—of Florentine society, and your assistance will be invaluable to her.'

'But you know the gossip about us, lord. . .someone is sure to tell her. . .'

'That you were, and probably still are, my mistress? But you and I. . .and Lodovico. . .know that that is not true.'

'Yes, but will she believe you if you tell her so? Let me go, lord. I know that I can find employment elsewhere.'

'But of what kind? Caterina, I trust you. And if my wife is never to meet anyone who has been my mistress, she will not be able to go out into society at all.'

'But they do not live in your household, lord.'

'You were never my mistress, Caterina. And I need your discretion and your skills. If there prove to be difficulties—well, they will be overcome. You have helped her already, I hope.'

Caterina sighed. It was useless to persist; the force of his will compelled her, as it had compelled others.

'Yes, she is sleeping after her bath, and after being groomed and dressed as a noblewoman should be. I think that she is very tired and does not know it. Her life as a boy has been hard?'

'Yes,' said Piero. 'But she has been equal to it.' He hesitated then said gravely, 'You understood what I told you earlier?'

'Fully. That she is not yet a woman, and I am to inform you when she becomes one.' Caterina paused. 'You saved me from the gutter at Ludovico Orso's behest. It is not for me to refuse you what you wish, but I must question your wisdom a little concerning myself remaining here.'

'So long as it is only a little, and you do not do it too often, I give you leave to have doubts,' said Piero cheerfully. 'Now I must go to her to reassure her when she awakes.'

Bianca had enjoyed her bath, and had particularly admired the room it was in. For the bath was of pink-veined marble, and was partly sunk in the floor, and there were flowering plants growing in stone urns set about it, and their scent filled the air. There was a bench of the same marble on which Caterina set the towels, hairbrushes, and more perfumes and oils. The little maid had carried clothing through with her, and took Bianca's loose overgown, and she and Caterina had helped her into the water, which was, as Caterina had said, both warm and perfumed.

On the wall, facing the bath, was a fresco: a clearing in a forest, where nymphs and satyrs sported before a temple in a way which left little to the imagination. In the distance was a pale blue mountain with the sun declining behind it. It was almost as good as really being in the open, Bianca thought drowsily as she reclined in the water. Recline in the water! How they would stare at San Giorgio, where they were only used to tall wooden tubs, and bathed in one another's used cold water—except on special occasions, like getting married.

And then she was helped out again and dried, and the

little maid rubbed oil into her skin as she lay face down and naked on the bench—to replace what the water had taken away, Caterina said. It was so soothing that Bianca fell into a doze, and must have slept some little time.

And after that her hair was dried, and brushed and brushed, and brushed again, the last time with a little—a very little—of the oil, until it was as lustrous as fine velvet, and her curls sprang out around her face as though they possessed a life of their own. Further stuff was smoothed on to her face—a kind of cream; and finally more perfume was applied by the maid, under Caterina's directions, which nearly had her asleep once more.

She was conscious that her body had changed again. The little buds of her breasts had grown, were no longer buds, and she had acquired a waist and hips, and had almost a woman's proper shape, gained during the last few weeks of exercise and good eating, and hidden even from herself, by her padded doublet and lack of a bath.

Her new clothing, which the two women now dressed her in, with the most loving care, quite unlike Agneta's roughness, was so fine that she wished Agneta were there to admire her. Undergarments which she could almost see through, and a gown of lemon silk, with a high waist and a low neck—which further betrayed that she at last possessed a bosom—tight sleeves which came down below her wrists, and a skirt which trailed on the floor, hiding her beautiful slippers, which was a shame, really. When it was on, and Caterina had teased, tweaked, and whisked it into graceful folds, she had thrown a gold chain, with an elaborately worked pendant of topazes and pearls, around Bianca's neck.

Finally, her hair was dressed—'We will compensate for its shortness with a little cheating,' Caterina said briskly, producing something which looked uncommonly like a large mouse, or a small rat, but was actually false hair, and was artfully assimilated into her own, high at the back, her short curls being allowed to frame her face at the front.

'And now for the ghirlande,' said Caterina, and gently placed on Bianca's head a little garland of silk flowers between tiny seed-pearls, mounted on a rolled pad, with fine gold thread ornamenting it. And after all that she was led back to her room, Caterina first, then herself and the little maid behind her carrying the used towels, the overgown, and all the oils and perfumes, brushes and knicknacks in a rush basket. Walking in, in semi-darkness, for the shutters were half closed against the sun, she suddenly saw another girl coming towards her. A pretty girl in an elegant dress, a crown of flowers on her head, with glowing cheeks and great dark eyes.

Bianca wondered who it could be, and put her hands to her own cheeks. The strange girl did the same. She looked again, as Caterina, seeing what was happening, said with a smile, 'You are looking in a long mirror, lady. That is yourself. Do you like what you see?'

A mirror? It was huge! And herself! Was that what people saw, were going to see? Did she like herself? More importantly, would impossibly perfect Piero like her, now that she was no longer a page, but a girl again? Could that pretty girl—who could not be herself, plain, flat-chested Bianca—possibly throw tantrums, assert herself? Or would she do what everyone else bade her? Somehow she hoped dazedly that essential Bianca would still be there; that Dino, who had, in the end, so enjoyed being a boy, would not be entirely lost.

This fashionable girl felt tremendously weary—so much had happened to her so quickly. One moment she had been wild, bad-tempered Bianca, the Lord of San Giorgio's plain shrew of a sister, then the Falcon's wife, and, after that, naughty Dino—a boy, joining in a boy's activities, and holding her own in them, even to taking part—almost—in a battle, or a skirmish, really; and now she was this exquisite, slender creature, with a bosom and hips, looking like the most elegant noble-woman who had ever graced a court. It was too much.

'I would like to rest,' she said. The couch looked so inviting, and perhaps once she had slept a little she could come to terms with this new Bianca before she met her lord again.

'So you may,' said Caterina briskly. She drew back the embroidered cover of her couch to reveal snow-white linen sheets and a great fat pillow. 'Assist the mistress, Giulia; remove her slippers and the ghirlande.' There was a little bell by the couch. 'Ring the bell, lady, when you wish to rise again. Giulia will be near by, waiting to assist you.'

Bianca lay down on top of the sheets, her head propped up against the pillow, and almost before her ladies had left the room she slept.

Piero de' Manfredini, having bathed and changed, and refreshed himself, looked into his wife's bedroom—only to discover that she was no longer there. Coming from his own room, he met Caterina, who answered his unspoken question. 'She is in the gardens, with Giulia, lord.'

So she was, seated on yet another marble bench, beside a statue of Pomona, before yet another fountain, looking down on Florence, which lay far below her, blue in the distance.

Bianca was not aware of his presence, did not hear him coming until he said to Giulia, 'Run to Caterina, child. The lady and I would speak alone.'

The lady. Yes, she was no longer Dino. He had gone—for good, perhaps. But Piero was still with her, looking even more handsome than ever, in scarlet and cream, the bruises fading from his face, a ruby in his ear today, and rubies in his belt—a gold belt. If she was dressed to the last inch, so was he. Everything about him made her feel breathless. He sat beside her on the bench, and took her right hand in his own, then half turned towards her.

Her heart began to beat so violently that she thought it must be visible to him.

'Will I do, lord?' she faltered.

What could he say? For Piero, too, was affected by her nearness, and the changes which Caterina, and time, had wrought in her. As a boy she had been attractive, her face vital and handsome, once good food and kindness had softened it. But as a girl—nay, a young woman—she was suddenly enchanting. It was not only the face, even more alluring after Caterina's attentions, but the blossoming body revealed by the tight fashionable gown, the gently swelling breasts, the tiny waist and the lovely line of her hips, which drew his eyes, and worked on his body. And when she spoke she still had the artless charm which had been Dino's, so different from the spiky aggression which had been hers at San Giorgio.

He wondered if she knew how much she had changed—and how desirable she had suddenly become. His body began to betray him, urging him insistently to make her his true wife on the instant, to kiss her there, where the faint shadow between her breasts showed a dusky mauve, to pull down the shoulders of the elegant dress, to reveal the treasures within, to kiss the soft mouth, parted slightly in her anxious questioning of him, to. . . And this really must stop. She was still the child he must not yet touch, but how strong must he be to deny himself?

The potential beauty he had seen at San Giorgio was suddenly there before him, his for the taking.

'Caterina has worked wonders,' he said, surprised to find his voice normal, that his desire for her was not so plain that its presence would frighten her, virgin as she was.

Bianca looked at him, lips quivering, eyes huge. She knew, without being told, that her husband was hungering for her, as she was for him. Living in the camp, as a boy, for only a few short weeks, she had learned more about life than in all the years she had spent in San Giorgio. It was natural, after all, for men and women to love one another, to mate; it was, with war, and suffering, and work, an essential part of life, and she must not be afraid of it and him—especially since so many enjoyed it so much. She must believe that she, too, would joy in their coupling, and now she was no longer afraid.

How easy it would be if she could tell him so, but even as she made to speak Piero, disgusted with himself, and seeing her anxious face as an indication of fear, and not of expectation, sternly exerted his will. I must not frighten her, he thought, and the moment was gone.

'Besides,' he added, 'I don't think that everything is due to Caterina. I think that my wife has contributed a little of her own.' But he was cool, impersonal Piero again, and the intensity of the last few moments had disappeared.

Oh, thought Bianca, anguished. He does not really want me, after all. I was mistaken. The girl I saw in the mirror cannot really compete with Maddalena, and all the other lovely women he has known and loved. I am only his wife, married for convenience, and he sees no urgency in wanting to make me the true lady of his house. She felt as though a huge and terrible wound had been done to her heart.

Piero, his intuition failing him for once—or lacking because his own emotions were so strongly engaged—thought to remove himself from temptation by rising, holding out his hand, and saying, in a friendly voice—to reassure her that he meant her no harm—'Let us walk around our estate, wife, and I will show you all its beauties.'

The repeated word 'wife' assuaged the wound a little, as did the beauty of the gardens through which he led her, talking animatedly of what had been done since he had been given the villa to make it suit his own taste.

They had walked some way from the house when they came to a tall hedge of yews with an archway of stone in the middle, and he stopped and said, 'And here is my favourite spot of all, which only the gardeners, myself, and now you may share. All else are forbidden here. I call it my secret grove. The Grove of the Gods.'

He led her through the archway, and then they were in what was truly a grove, a vast lawn with a pool—a real one, not artificial—with a stream coming down the hillside and feeding it, a screen of trees at a little distance completely surrounding it. On one side of the pool, which was both deep and clear, a small marble quay had been built, with a stone seat on it. Around the pool, but at some distance away, were statues of goddesses on pedestals, and opposite to where Piero and Bianca stood was a building, like a small temple. Behind it, the hillside rose.

With a sudden shock, Bianca realised that before her was the scene from the fresco, minus the nymphs and satyrs. 'The bathroom,' she breathed.

'Ah, my clever wife,' he said, gratified. 'Yes, I asked the artist to paint this for me, with the lesser gods at play. I didn't want Jupiter and his train overwhelming us.'

'It's beautiful,' said Bianca, and they sat there for some time, enjoying the blessed quiet, so different from the perpetual noise of the camp at Trani.

'And are you ready to accompany me to the banquet, tomorrow night?'

'Will I not be recognised as Dino?' she asked.

'Hardly,' said her husband, with a dry chuckle. 'Have you looked in your mirror, wife?'

Bianca blushed. 'Yes,' she said. 'I must admit that I do not look much like Dino—or the Lady of San Giorgio for that matter.'

'No, indeed,' agreed Piero, and looked down at her to see an anxious expression on her face again. 'What troubles you, wife?'

'Your father, lord. I was very rude to him. And it

troubles me that you and he should be at odds. I thought that I hated him, and then I was sorry. For both of you.'

Piero stood quite still, and she became frightened that she had offended him. 'How am I to behave, if we see him tomorrow?'

'As we surely shall,' said Piero drily. 'He is a great man, after all. Behave as a perfect lady should.'

'It is a pity that you should not be reconciled. He seemed to wish it.'

'Oh, indeed,' said Piero, satiric. 'And would he be so desirous of knowing me, think you, if I were an unconsidered monk in the monastery to which he consigned me, or if I had failed as a soldier, and was now a ploughman on Lodovico's little farm?'

There was no answer to that. And it was not for her to tell Piero what to do when he had been treated so grievously. The old impetuous Bianca might have pursued the matter. The new one was silent.

'My brother, his legitimate son, will be there, too, and you must be correct to him. And Messer Bruschini—we both mistrust him, but you must be all charm, and I must try to repair the breach which necessity made between us, though I doubt that it is reparable.'

'I did not like the way he always looked at me,' she said, suddenly able to talk to her husband of such things.

'No doubt,' said Piero, again dry. 'It is notorious that his taste is for boys. You are now a woman, so he will lack interest in you.'

Bianca wondered if that would be true. He had looked at her so hard, and at Piero so wickedly. But she must follow her lord, and do as he said, and all, she hoped, would be well.

If only he would look at her as he must have looked at Maddalena, especially now that the Lord God had given her a woman's body. But he had shown her his secret place, and he had called her wife, and surely, soon, she would be truly a woman—and his.

CHAPTER TEN

THE next great event was the banquet at the *signoria* to celebrate Trani's taking. Once Bianca might have worried over what to wear, how to behave, but, dressed in white and silver, her hair elaborately coiffured with large pearls and silk lilies on the ghirlande, wearing a sleeveless overdress embroidered with more lilies, with a rope of pearls brought in by Piero when she was ready, and thrown around her neck by him, and a tiny, beautiful fan given to her to hold, the roaring camp at Trani and Dino seemed an impossible dream.

And then, when they were ready to leave, Piero, who was his usual impossibly perfect self in white and gold, took her gently by the shoulders with the oddest look on his face and turned her towards the mirror, to see herself reflected as she stood before him, and—behold—she was as impossibly perfect as he was!

'And where has my naughty page gone to?' he asked, and the hands which held her trembled, and he wished. . . But that was impossible, she was still a child, and all Florence awaited them.

And once at the banquet she was the centre of interest. Oh, yes, the Falcon had done it again; here was no plain shrew, as rumour said, but a rare delicate beauty, a very dove for him to fly with. Envious eyes, Bruschini's among them, followed them both.

And Piero? Piero sat there so conscious of her, even when his eyes were not on her, that it was as though she were part of his very body, and lived and breathed with him.

There were entertainments, singers and tumblers, and in between them people rose, and walked about and talked and ate. Piero was led aside to speak with the magnates. Bianca watched him disappear into the throng, and moved away towards a window, almost exhausted, to hear a woman's high voice behind her.

'Well, you would not catch me allowing my new husband's mistress to be my housekeeper, even if he does look as fine as the Falcon.'

Bianca shivered. Kind Caterina was Piero's mistress? No, that could not be. But she remembered what Naldo had said about him having an older woman in Florence, and an armful. And Caterina was certainly an armful! He would not do that, surely? But the bright day was dimmed a little by what she had heard. She needed to speak to him, to see him, and when she looked again she saw him by a window, talking to another man whom she did not know. He moved away, and she half ran to touch him on the arm. He turned towards her—and he was not Piero, but very like him, dressed as he was in white and gold. His face was handsome, but lacked Piero's strength.

'Lady?' he said.

'I thought that you were Piero,' she said, blushing. 'I see that I was mistaken. Forgive me, Ser.'

'Not your husband,' he said, and his smile was a softer version of Piero's, 'but his brother, and you are my new good sister. I would wish to speak with him; he has my admiration. Dare I ask the lady Bianca, my new sister, to introduce me?'

Oh, he was almost as charming as Piero, and so like the old man who was their father, who, she saw, was watching them from a little distance. She remembered what Piero had said and Caterina had advised: to behave with modesty, to remember that she was there to do him, and Florence, honour.

That being so, she must smile and reply, 'If you would but give me your name, Messer Manfredini, and I can find my husband, who is lost to me at the moment, it will give me the greatest pleasure to assist you.' The Bianca still inside her could not help laughing at this diplomatic reply, and the effect it had on Piero's half-brother.

'Why, I am Michele,' he said, and gave her his charming smile again, which was so like Piero's—without the sting in it. 'I have long wished to know my brother, have admired him from afar, but he is estranged from my father, as I suppose you are aware.'

Yes, she was well aware, and felt a little uneasy at the prospect of introducing him to Piero; but he had told her to be good and polite. He could not really complain if she was both these things! Now, Father Luca would say that was an equivocation, would he not? But there was no help for it, and she looked around for Piero while Michele began to talk to her.

He was as approachable and smooth as Piero was hard and challenging, but the likeness to him was strong. He was so kind and pleasant that it was easy for her to answer him, when he asked her how she liked Florence.

'Oh, I have seen so little of it, Ser Michele, that I cannot say. I only arrived here yesterday. What I saw on the way in seemed very beautiful, quite unlike my old home.'

'But San Giorgio has given its best beauty to Florence, good sister, now that you are here,' he replied, and his look and smile were so deferential after her husband's abrasive firmness that she was soothed by it, could almost believe that she was really as pretty as every man's eyes said she was.

She was also conscious that many eyes were on them both, with some few raised eyebrows, for Piero's refusal to acknowledge his father and his family were well known. And then Piero was there, coming through a great oak door, several of the grave and reverend Signors of Florence behind him. He had seen her, and was advancing on them, face impassive.

It was almost as though the twenty-four hours she had spent with Caterina had wrought a sea-change in her, had changed her from unruly Dino to an artful beauty who knew how to use her charm. She put out a hand to touch Piero on the sleeve, and looked up at him with prettily imploring eyes, so that, despite himself, he gave her a reluctantly admiring grin.

'Wife?' he said.

'My lord husband——' Bianca was all submissive deference '—I mistook Ser Michele Manfredini here, your half-brother, for yourself, and I am sure that he will only forgive me for such an error if I am allowed to present him to you. He has long wished to meet you.' And she made a graceful bow, wondering where on earth all that had come from, and wondering, too, what Bernardo and Agneta would make of what their wild tomboy had become.

Piero's smile of admiration grew. He put out a hand to Michele, who had begun to bow in the middle of Bianca's elegant diplomacy. 'Come,' he said, and his own charm had never been more manifest. 'No need for formality. We are brothers, after all. Amd if I regret the sire, I cannot regret meeting someone who looks as though he has strayed from my own mirror.'

Michele's laugh in response to this was both frank and genuine. 'I had heard that your tongue was as clever as your sword,' he said, 'and now I know that to be true. To call the victor of Trani, and a dozen other actions, friend as well as brother would be an honour which I had never hoped to gain.'

Piero hardly knew what to say. It was easy to hate and to hold off, and he had stubbornly refused to meet or to have anything to do with his father's family, but to be pleasant and friendly was another thing. 'Why,' he said, 'I shall be happy to see you at my villa, and there we may talk a little, perhaps, and learn to know one another.'

'An honour,' repeated Michele, 'and a greater one to meet the lady who is your wife. You are a fortunate man, brother, in more ways than one.'

Oh, yes, he possessed all Piero's charm and more, but

where was the ruthless determination with which Piero faced and conquered life, the steel behind the charm? Bianca thought that that was missing in Michele, and wondered how much Piero's hard life had done for him. For the first time she asked herself whether, after all, she also had gained, not lost, by having to strive so hard at San Giorgio, with nothing coming to her by favour, and her learning with Father Luca, fought and worked for, not handed to her as a gift.

She watched the half-brothers talk; she thought them so alike, but so different, and perhaps that was why their father looked so melancholy—that all the strength and endurance had gone to the unacknowledged and cast-off son.

And then at the end, when the final dances were over, and she was with Piero again, Bruschini came up to them. He had spent the evening avoiding Piero, had dissociated himself from the praise and compliments showered on the victor of Trani.

His words to Piero were spoken in a cold voice, and his smile had no warmth in it. 'So, my Lord of Astra, you have gained all that you sought. A wise man might remember the old Roman custom on such occasions as these: the death's head at the feast to remind the victor not to be overproud, that defeat and decay come to all of us in the end.'

Bianca shuddered, as though a killing frost had filled the room. She heard the hate beneath the words, and clutched at Piero's arm for support.

But Piero only smiled, and, knowing that he had nothing to gain, nothing to lose with Bruschini, all hope of mending the breach between them dead with Trani's fall, said, 'No death's heads need to be hired, Bruschini; you have brought your own countenance here tonight, and that will serve to remind me of failure and loss.'

Bruschini's face paled, then reddened. 'You should enter another saying on the tablets of your heart, Manfredini: he laughs best who laughs last.'

'Nothing to that,' retorted Piero. 'Laughter does not engage me overmuch—and you might consider what petards do to those who misuse them. More men are killed by setting and firing bombards than die under their balls.'

Bianca shivered again; she thought Piero not too wise to bait the angry man before them, who turned his feral gaze on her, and said, 'You make your wife fearful, Manfredini, but fail to move me. Why do I think that I have seen you before, lady—and recently? I thought that you had not left San Giorgio, *madonna*, before becoming the Lady of Astra?'

The old fire moved in her again, the fierce spirit which all San Giorgio knew. How dared he threaten her lord, and now herself? She answered him before Piero could speak, dropping the fan which she had been holding modestly to her lips before she spoke.

'You mistake, Messer Bruschini. I shiver from weariness, first find the room overhot, and then overcold. I am not used to such grand affairs as this. We are simple folk at San Giorgio—but honest.'

'Oh, indeed,' said Bruschini, a cruel smile on his lips. 'I am glad to hear it. A word of warning, though. Look to your lady, Manfredini. White doves are an easy prey, I am told. Particularly honest simpletons who fall easily to the wiles of the birds of prey who infest these parts.'

'Ah, but Messer Bruschini,' said Bianca, quickly again, feeling Piero, rigid with anger, beside her, 'my husband is the Falcon who protects his dove. Best remember that all predators fall before him. Besides, the Father who instructed me was wont to say that the Lord God helps those who help themselves, and I always bear that precept in mind. Even doves have claws—and beaks which can peck out eyes!'

'You hear, Bruschini,' said Piero, grinning fiercely at him. 'My wife is a lady whose wits are sharp. And if she beats me about the head with Father Luca's teachings, be sure that she will belabour the heads of others with them, too, if she thinks fit.

'Bianca, my heart, the evening grows late, we are keeping Messer Bruschini from his much needed rest, and now that Father Luca has had his say I think that we might leave him behind us, if we may, to instruct the company.'

'Truly, I had not meant to annoy, only to defend myself, as the fox said, when caught in the hen-house,' offered Bianca sweetly. 'Father Luca preached that we were to forgive our enemies, but confessed that he found the exercise somewhat difficult. Constant prayer helped, he said, but was rather hard on the knees. I commend his advice to you, Ser. It may help you, as it has helped me.'

She had not meant to speak so, to annoy him further, but the hard and ruthless eyes on Piero, the sense that he would do anything to hurt them—herself because she was Piero's—had revived San Giorgio's articulate shrew again. She was a little fearful that Piero might be cross with her, but he was too busy being amused at the spectacle of Bruschini trying not to burst as she offered him such kind and unwanted advice in so artless a fashion. He found it difficult to keep his own face straight.

Bruschini spoke at last, his voice thick with repressed rage. 'I know that a long and vicious tongue is a Manfredini trait, and you have lost no time in gaining a wife who shares that attribute to the full. Enjoy yourselves at other people's expense while you may. Time and chance may not always be with you.'

He strode away, leaving Bianca shivering on Piero's arm. 'Oh, he frightens me,' she said. 'He means us ill, I know it. I should not have spoken as I did, but I would not have him think me afraid—even if I were.'

'Come,' said Piero. 'We cannot expect everyone to love us, and Bruschini is something of a fool. Forget him.'

'Father Luca said that fools are the most dangerous of all men, for they do what you cannot foretell.'

Piero was silent. He did not for once twit her as she trotted out the Father's wisdom, but said slowly, 'The Father spoke true. But we cannot live in fear. What will be, will be, and when it happens we will deal with it. Until then, seize the hour, and the day—for they will not come again. Now, we must take our leave. We have done our duty and the hour grows late. For once, I have acted as my father wishes me to, and I have been kind to my brother. No, do not tell me what Father Luca would have to say to that. He has done his duty by us, and must be silent for a time.'

Despite their late arrival home, the steward came to meet them on their return to the villa, and he and Giulia, blinking a little with weariness, escorted them to their rooms; otherwise the house was dark and silent, one candle in a great sconce burning in the hall.

Another candle was burning by her bed, and Bianca was grateful for Giulia's help in removing her fine clothes. Such magnificence brought its difficulties, she saw. Not for the Lord of Astra's wife the flinging off of shabby garments on to the floor, the unwashed, scrambled leap into bed. But finally she was prepared for the night, and the yawning Giulia was sent to her own rest. But Bianca could not sleep. Her head buzzed and rang, as all that had happened since she had arrived in Florence ran through it.

She slid out of the bed to sit on a cushioned settle, to try to come to terms with her new life, until the door opened, and Piero, also unable to sleep, entered. Part of her own inability to rest she shared with him. Each was conscious of the other, so near and yet so far away.

Piero was wearing an overgown of green and gold, with a light band of cream fur at the neck and wrists, for the night was a cold one. He was carrying two tall metal cups, with tiny jewels set in their sides. He sat on her bed and held one of the cups out to her.

'Come, wife,' he said. 'Water after wine is a saying you might like to add to your store. You will sleep better after it—or so I have often found. Why, I know not.'

Bianca took the cup from him, and he patted the bed beside him. 'Sit with me, wife. I do not wish to sleep yet, and by your looks you are of the same mind.'

She did as he said, conscious that they were alone together as they had not been since their wedding night. In the camp there had always been others present, or, if for a moment there had been but the two of them, someone had been sure to interrupt them. None, she thought, would interrupt them here. She gave a sidelong glance at Piero's face, shadowed in the candlelight.

He seemed not to notice, put down his empty cup, and hers, on the exquisite little table by her bed, another luxury of the villa, and took her hand. Piero did not know why he was in her room at all. Only that, lying alone, he had experienced a sudden longing to be with her, even though to join her would subject him to a temptation which he did not know that he could resist. He had seen the effect which she had had on all the men at the banquet, knew that Bruschini's hatred for him was fuelled because he had acquired such a jewel for a wife. He had always known, from the moment at which he had first really looked at her, all the inherent potential for beauty which she possessed—if only she were properly treated—but was astonished by the speed of the change which had come over her.

But, sitting there beside him, her hair loose, wearing only her simple white nightgown, she was almost the little girl of San Giorgio again—except, and what a big except that was—she now possessed the body of a woman, and was his wife.

He put his right arm around her, felt her begin to tremble at his touch, took her reaction for fear of him, and thought, Yes, but I could make her forget that fear, I am sure, make her love me; I have only to be gentle, I need not wait. He remembered with what fire and passion she had defied Bruschini, eyes glowing—and yes, that passion could be for me, he decided. Forget my vow, why not? And he turned her towards him a little, put his left hand up to cradle and stroke her head, and could feel her breasts under the thin cloth, pressed to his own broad chest.

But there was such simple trust on her face that he swallowed; the hand which had paused in its ministrations to her head, ready to stroke the perfect little breasts, half seen in the beautiful gown which she had worn to the feast, dropped instead to his lap, and the kiss which he had intended for her mouth found her warm cheek instead—and was chaste, not passionate. No, he must not begin their married life on a lie—that he had vowed never to mate with her until she was physically ready, but had broken that vow to take her before that happened.

For once, he was overset, and said the first thing which came into his head, was not his usual careful, considered self at all; and what he said betrayed, although he did not know this consciously, that he was strangely uncertain of her response to him. The man who had always dealt so confidently with his mistresses was shy before his virgin wife, was not sure that she cared for him at all.

'You seemed to be much taken by my brother, lady.'

Surprised and disappointed that he had stopped what he had started, for she had been so ready for him to make love to her that she had felt her whole body responding to his touch, like a flower opening itself to the sun, Bianca replied a little stiffly, and knew after she had spoken that she had said the wrong thing, in the wrong tone of voice.

'Yes. He seems gentle and kind.' It was almost a rebuke.

'Gentle and kind,' said Piero abruptly. He felt the implicit rebuke; there was no doubt. He dropped his

hands, rose, and moved away from her. 'Fortunate
creature that he is, he has had no need to strive.'

'Perhaps it is his nature, lord,' she ventured. But that
conciliatory remark did not answer, she could see.

'As mine is not, I suppose.'

'You are the Falcon, lord, and you make your own
rules. I suspect that Michele is content to follow those
already laid down.'

He swung about to stare at her, his eyes hooded, like
the predator she had named him. 'And what exactly
does that mean? More of Father Luca's wisdom, or your
own conclusions, wife? Explain!'

Bianca felt hurt and helpless. A moment ago he had
seemed on the verge of loving her truly, of making her
his wife in fact, not in name, and now he was all
challenge. Sexual frustration moved in her, as it did in
him, and what should have united them parted them,
making each cruel to the inaccessible loved object. She
spoke defiantly, harshly, to hurt the man who gave to
his mistresses what she could not have.

'Why, I suppose that Michele might find it difficult to
make his mistress his wife's housekeeper, to refuse his
wife in order to visit her bed.'

He moved so swiftly to take her by her hand, to pull
her to her feet, that, despite herself, she let out a
frightened cry, before she recovered her self-control and
pulled away from him, head high, eyes blazing.

'Ah, now we have it. Where got you that lie?'

'Half Florence seemed to know what your wife did
not, and thought it a joke.'

'Half Florence! Half Florence is not aware of the truth,
then. Caterina, is not, never has been, my mistress. Will
that suffice?'

'It is not what the world believes. What am *I* to
believe, lord?'

'Lord?' he said roughly. 'You are no longer my page.
I am your husband, Piero—and Caterina is not my
mistress. I am not making ready to leave you for her. I

have touched no woman since Maddalena, and will touch none another until you are truly a woman, and then that woman will be you.'

'But I am a woman, in all but that one thing. Yet you remain my husband who is not my husband, whether Caterina is your mistress or no.' The rage which she had so often felt at San Giorgio, and had begun to lose over the past few weeks of happiness and fulfilment, was sharp on her again in the face of what she saw as his rejection of her. 'Why *did* you marry me, lord?'

'To make you my page, why not?' he mocked her, as distressed beneath his self-control as she was. 'I had lost mine, needed another. You were useful as Dino. It did you no harm to learn self-discipline. Dino was better than the naughty girl who misbehaved herself at San Giorgio.'

The tears, the bitter tears which Bianca could not repress, were on her, and the rage spoke through them.

'Oh, I think that you only made me your page in order to see that I behaved properly, to break my spirit. That was what Bernardo was forever saying: "You need to have your spirit broken."' And she gave a great gulping sob.

Piero answered her with his best sardonic grin. 'Well, if that was my aim, I certainly didn't have much success, judging by the way you are carrying on now.'

'Oh, men are all the same,' she said, her sobs redoubling. 'And I certainly can't imagine why you married me, and to cheat Bernardo to gain me—that is the biggest mystery of all.'

Piero went quite still, then seized her and caught her to his breast, her face a little below his, and, frightened though she was, her look remained defiant.

'And what exactly do you mean by that, wife?' he snarled through gritted teeth. 'Explain yourself, before I beat the truth out of you.'

She gazed steadily up at him, her black eyes meeting his hard blue ones. 'You know perfectly well what I mean. I saw you change the dice over, that night after you had finished gaming with Bernardo. You played with loaded dice of your own to win me.'

'Did I, indeed?' His voice was ice, as hard as his eyes. He released her, and stepped back. 'You say that you saw me. What did you see?'

She would not be stared down, she would not. She flung the words at him, cheat and liar that he was. Caterina not his mistress! 'You changed them after I came in. Oh, you did it cunningly, but I was watching you, and saw. Afterwards you slid them from your hand into your purse.'

'What sharp eyes you have, my lady wife.' The note in his voice had changed to one of amusement. 'Fetch me my purse, Bianca.'

'Lord?' she said questioningly as she had done as Dino.

'You heard what I said. Fetch me my purse. It is in my room. On my bed.'

She obeyed him. As always, when he commanded it was difficult for her—or anyone—to disobey him. She fetched the purse he had worn that evening, and returned to find him sitting on her couch again, face alight with mockery.

'Open it, Bianca,' he said, and although his voice was stern it was not altogether unkind.

She obeyed him. Yes, there were dice inside. Four of them.

'Take them out, Bianca. Throw them here,' he ordered, and he indicated the little table beside her bed. Again, she did as she was bidden.

'Look at them carefully—and throw again.'

They had fallen in a random pattern, and at the second throw they fell so again. 'Throw them as often as you will, and you will find that they always fall true. They are not cogged,' he said, his voice neutral.

Bianca did as he bade again, then stopped and bent

over them, her hot tears falling on to the dice and the table.

'Come,' he said. And now his voice was suddenly gentle. 'I always carry true dice with me. There are wolves in the world. I learned that lesson as a boy, and have never forgot it. Yes, I changed the dice. *Bernardo's* were loaded, cogged—that was why he won at first. Chance gave you to me, Bianca. The Wheel of Fortune turned—and you were mine. It was meant.'

What could she say? Of course, Bernardo was a swindler. She had always known that, but had not known he would stoop to a trick as low as this. She looked up at him piteously. 'And all along I thought that it was you who cheated Bernardo out of his lands, and then cozened him into giving me to you.'

'No,' he said, 'it was Bernardo who cheated, and he was too drunk to realise what I had done. I underestimated my wife's intelligence, though. I shall not do so again. And think, Bianca, think; I could have asked him for you straight, without the game, and he would have thrown you to me on the instant. It pleased me to give him his lands back in exchange for you. That way, he owed me.'

'So,' she said passionately. 'You remain a trickster, self-confessed, and still no explanation as to why you married me. And all this is nothing besides Caterina, and who she is.'

'Caterina!' His mood had changed when he had seen her tears. 'Oh, my wife, I will not lie. I have had many mistresses. I am a man, after all. But she has never been one of them. I have many faults, too, the Lord God knows, but I do not cheat—unless I am cheated, as with Bernardo—and I would not foist a cast-off whore of mine on you.' He paused—how to tell her that Caterina and Lodovico were lovers?—but he could not breach that confidence, even to save himself.

Bianca saw his hesitation, mistook it a little, and, the rage dying within her, wondered how that earlier moment of tenderness which they had shared had come to this, that they were in arms against each other, as they had hardly been since San Giorgio.

'You have had a long day,' said her husband, seeing the conflicting passions chase across her face, not knowing that what he wanted so dearly she would have freely given to him had he not abandoned his lovemaking to her so prematurely. Bianca had grown up more than either of them really appreciated, and after he had left, careful to keep a distance between them, careful to offer her no word of love, because to do so would open the floodgates of his own passion, she cried again as she had done on her wedding night.

But this time her tears were those of a woman whose rejection was the more bitter because she would have given herself to the man she loved willingly and joyfully, and did not know how to tell him so, being fearful that he might make her his true wife out of a sense of duty rather than a felt, willed passion.

So close together and yet so far apart, husband and wife lived together, both fearful that they did not possess the other's love. Piero's feelings were so strange that the whole world seemed to have changed around him. Each succeeding day told him something about himself which he really did not wish to know. The girl whom he had made his wife, the girl he thought that he could take or leave, as he had taken and left other women, for pleasure without commitment, had wound herself around his heart. The hard and self-sufficient man had acquired what he had always denied himself: a feeling for another, for Bianca, who, having been Dino, had become a part of himself.

Her presences and her absences were full of meaning: a tapestry she was working, left on a bench; her request for materials to carry on the calligraphy and the illumination which Father Luca had taught her; her perfume in the air; her face opposite to him at the table, now glad, now grave, all worked on him.

The little air of constraint which she had adopted towards him since the night after the feast hurt him more than he could have once believed possible. It was, he knew, a sign of her growing up that she was losing the childishly frank and open response which she had brought to life, but it also distressed him. Would the way in which he had met and married her always stand between them? Would the rapport which had blossomed between them when she was his page ever be restored? Foolish to want her a boy again, now that she was a lovely and vital woman, but knowing that he, by his acts, had created her, how hard it was to think that this Bianca might never love him, would lie with him through duty, not through love. And how changed was he that this should disturb him so, and that another's welfare should matter to him so much more than his own.

Compensations there were: work, and the new-found friendship both of them felt for Michele. He visited them at the villa, and dined with them, and occasionally all three went riding together. Like Piero, he played the lute well, and on several evenings they sat together in the gardens—though never in the Grove of the Gods—and made music.

The brothers' likeness was more than that of face and form, and if Michele lacked Piero's steel he shared his quick brain and many talents. Sitting in the dusk and watching them play and sing in counterpoint, the melody lingering in the warm air, the pale moon rising, San Giorgio and Trani far away and half forgotten, Bianca was almost happy. Michele took to visiting the villa frequently, and when Piero was not there she rode out with him, because she had no wish to lose all the skills which she had gained as Dino.

Occasionally she saw Piero's eyes on her as she laughed and talked with his brother—no constraints there, Piero noted wryly, and although she did not know it her husband began to suffer from a new emotion—jealousy. So, she liked the soft man who was his brother! He liked his brother, too, but thought that lifelong prosperity and ease had done him no favours. He bore no marks of the whip on his back as Piero did, put there to teach him self-discipline and forbearance. All that was as nothing, except that not so long ago Bianca had looked at *him* without reservation on her face.

There was one blessing for husband and wife: Bruschini had taken his glum face out of the city, some said merely into the country, others that he was on a commercial mission to Milan—or Venice, perhaps; gossip did not know the truth.

Piero's father held aloof until one evening, sitting over dinner, Bianca, wearing a cream silk dress embroidered with carnations, carnations wreathed in her hair, told Piero of the Marquis's visit to the villa that afternoon. Piero had spent the day in Florence.

'He came with Michele, of course. Their business here is nearly over.' She hesitated. 'I think that he hoped to see you. He spoke of you with admiration, said that he understood your feelings towards him.' She hesitated again. 'I told him what you said—that he would not want to know you if you were a ploughboy—and he laughed and said that was true, and your saying it simply proved how alike you both are. Michele is not like you in that way at all; he is so gentle.'

Piero was silent for a moment, then said coolly, 'You will miss your admirer, and as for my father—why, nothing to that—as Bandelli taught me to say. He made his decision long ago, and must abide by it.'

They had finished their meal, and gone outside to drink wine and eat fruit, Piero carrying the flagon and goblets, and she the dish of peaches, to the Grove of the Gods, where they sat in front of the water, which was silver in the moonlight. Suddenly, there was an ease between them again, and they laughed and talked about their new life together, so that he was sorry to say before they parted for the night, 'I must go to Prato tomorrow, for a few days; the lord there sends word he has a small commission for my troops, and wishes to talk terms. I shall leave tomorrow. Lodovico will stay behind, and between him and Caterina you will not lack company. I shall be gone nigh on a week. These things take time.'

'Caterina will be pleased that Lodovico is staying,' said Bianca demurely.

'You know?' he said.

'That they are lovers? Yes. I seem to see things these days which I used to miss.'

'It is known as growing up,' her husband answered, a smile softening his face, relaxing its usual stern lines, and her heart ached at the sight. 'And you know that I spoke the truth about her and myself. Lodovico is a proud man. He would not take my leavings.'

'Yes, I know that, too. I also know. . .' And then she paused, suddenly shy of him, as he towered above her. How to say that I love you? she thought. That my anger the other night was because of my jealousy of Caterina? That I now want you as a woman wants a man, and, more, I want to know your true feelings for me, and whether you feel for me as I for you? I want to know whether or no you married me as a duty, to get sons, and nothing else. But she could not speak—the words were too hard to utter, and again the moment was gone; but, as they parted, he kissed her on the cheek, which was all he dared to allow himself, so desirable was she, so much the woman he had always wanted, with brains, beauty and a body for a man to celebrate with his own. San Giorgio's shrew had blossomed into a nonpareil.

And, in the night, the Lord God relented at last, and Bianca awoke to find herself a woman, as though her new understanding of life and her changing body had come together to make something truly different of her. She put her hands to her hot face: he could no longer deny her now, and she did not know whether she was glad or sorry, only that she would soon discover what being a woman really meant, and whether her lord loved her or no.

'So, the flux is with you,' Caterina said, 'and your lord must be informed.' Her eyes on Bianca were knowing as she helped her to cope with this new thing in her life. 'It is woman's curse, and woman's blessing. We shall help you to endure it, lady.'

It would have been difficult to be Dino with it, thought Bianca, lying in bed, eating the day's first meal, feeling pampered, laughing to herself at what Agneta's rough and shrieking response would have been to the news. Later, dressed, and feeling little different from the girl she had always been, she met Piero in the gardens.

He had risen before dawn, visited the *condotta*, and brought back Van Eyck and some other of his senior officers to the villa, where they sat in the kitchens, eating breakfast, before leaving with him.

She knew at once that he had seen Caterina, and that she had told him—to spare her, she thought. He was dressed for travelling in half-armour over a leather hacketon and a rough linen shirt. His hair, which he had grown longer in Florence, was confined in a golden net, and he was carrying a broad-rimmed hat to shield him from the hot sun which the day would bring. There was a spring in his step and his eyes were kinder than they had been lately.

He spun the hat on to a stone bench, and took her hands in his, to be nearer to her than they had been since the night of their quarrel.

'It is true, then, lady? What Caterina has told me?'

'Yes,' she said, shy with him. 'The Lord God has blessed me, or cursed me. Caterina does not seem to know which!'

He smiled at that, held her even tighter to him. 'The change has not deprived you of your witty tongue—that is certain. I should not like my clever dove to turn into an idle sluggard.' And he kissed the top of her head, then tipped her chin up to him, as he had done so often when she was Dino, but gently—oh, so gently. 'When I return, wife, you will truly be my wife. You understand me?'

'Thy will is mine, lord,' she said, as on her wedding night. But the emotions and passions which coursed through her were oh, so different. Father Luca would say, Do not deal in exaggerations, child. Ohings and ahings are for fools. Then I am a fool, Father, and oh— oh, I wish that he were not going today! she replied silently.

'Only that?' Piero answered. 'Then let me try to fire you before I go.' And he bent to kiss her. Such a kiss it was—not brotherly or chaste as all his previous ones had been, but a kiss given by a man to the woman whom he loved and wanted. Her whole body felt it, and as his tongue opened her mouth, so that he might caress her there, too, her own responded to him, as though the Lord God had taught it what to do, during the night when he had blessed her.

Piero gave a little groan, deep in his throat, his hands rose to hold her head, and the kiss deepened, so that their first union was through the mouth, and her whole body offered itself to him. He pulled away at last, denying himself further tantalising passion which could not yet find fulfilment.

'I cannot stay. They are waiting for me, and it was I who demanded urgency. No matter; I would have had to be patient, and my wife will be ready for my return, to perform her wifely duties at last.'

'Yes,' she said, her senses still reeling. Ah, God, how powerful love was, that it invaded and took over all the body. She yearned for him, and saw with wonder the tender expression on his face. I do believe that he yearns for me, too, she thought. Can it be? Can it really be?

'And your pleasure, wife, I hope,' he said softly, as if to confirm the impossible thoughts she was having. 'In a week, then, a moment or an eternity—farewell.' And he was gone, picking up his discarded hat, leaving her there, to stride away, not to Maddalena this time, but to his military duties. War, she knew, was his constant mistress, with whom she must share him. And that night her tears were for his absence, with a prayer to the Lord God to bring him safely home again, and soon.

The week which he had said he would be away was the eternity that he had suggested. The flux left her early, which pleased her, as it seemed a draining thing which spoiled her active pleasures. She was relieved that it was over, when Michele arrived as he had promised, the day before Piero's return home. She was able to ride out with him, and enjoy the afternoon. Except that Michele was disappointed to find Piero absent again. 'But he is a man of affairs,' he said. 'Not an idler. We leave at the week's end, our mission accomplished. The bankers were kind after all. I hope to see him—in Florence, perhaps, before we go.'

'He said he would return tomorrow.'

'And you will ride with me today, good sister?'

'Indeed. He would wish it. He told me to entertain you when you came.'

The day was a golden one, and their ride was pleasant. They stopped once to dismount and eat fruit, then rode again. They had taken no attendants with them, the hinterland around Florence was safe—the *contadini*, peasants with little farms and small holdings cultivated it to feed the city—and the Florentine notables who had built villas among the holdings—slept well at nights.

It was to be their last outing together, and they went a little further than usual, to the edge of the civilised area, where they lost sight of the town itself, and saw the hills which surrounded it instead. It was at this point that Bruschini and his bravos struck.

He had left Florence, savage in his desire to revenge himself on his successful rival, who had made the pessimistic dispatches he had sent back to Florence from outside Trani seem foolish, and himself a croaking

Jonah, not entirely to be trusted in his judgements. He had hired a rogue *condottiero*—one like Bandelli—who had established himself in a small town in the mountains, and preyed on those around him when opportunity offered.

He knew that Manfredini and his wife rode out alone in what they thought was safety, and his hireling, Maso Marinaro, who had his own reasons for hating the Lord of Astra, provided him with a sergeant and troops to wait for Piero and his wife, to kidnap them, take them to his eyrie, and demand a ransom—and, perhaps, ransom paid, to kill them all the same. Such an act would make Bruschini an outlaw, too, but he felt that he could endure that to see his rival dead.

Michele they mistook for Piero, and when the troop rode up, to surround their prey, the sergeant thought that they had their man. Neither Michele nor Bianca could withstand the kidnappers. At the moment when they realised danger was on them, they put spurs to horse, but were caught by another small group of men-at-arms before they had gone far.

'Dismount, I say. Dismount, Manfredini. This is one snare which the Falcon will not escape.'

Bianca, who was refusing to get down, but was pulled off her horse by a burly rogue, all the same, began to say, 'But this is not the Falcon——' but before she could speak Michele said,

'If it is I whom you seek to capture, take me, but let my wife go free,' and the look which he gave Bianca was a warning one.

'Brave words,' grinned the sergeant. 'They say that you are as hard as the bird whose name you have taken. We may test that ere dawn. As to your wife, we have orders to take her, too. She will make a handsome widow.'

'No,' panted Bianca, beginning to struggle, but it was a useless exercise, hampered as she was by skirts, and held by a man twice her size. 'Do not take us. We can pay you all and more than the man who has hired you. Let us go. Van Eyck and the others will come after you, and I doubt whether you could withstand the might of the Falcon's *condotta*, even without him leading it.'

'A spirited wench,' said the sergeant approvingly. 'But he who has hired us is rich, too, and my own master has a score to settle with your lord. Here he comes—the lord who has hired my master; he may tell you himself what his plans for you both are.'

'My wife says true,' said Michele desperately, watching another small troop, which had been standing by, ride towards them, a richly dressed figure at its head. 'Think what you are doing. All Florence, as well as my *condotta*, will come after us.'

'Useless to speak,' said Bianca, for she had recognised who was leading the troop. 'He will listen to nothing but the hatred and revenge which devours him,' and she was heartsick for Michele, because for sure Bruschini would know what the sergeant did not—that they had captured the wrong man, and she was fearful of what Bruschini would do when he discovered that he had the Falcon's dove, but not the Falcon himself.

For the moment, Bruschini, too, was deceived. At a little distance the brothers were so alike that one might mistake the one for the other, and Bruschini's eyes were on the girl who had taunted him, who stood hacking with her feet at her captor's legs, and using her elbows on him.

'So, the dove has claws,' he jeered. 'But not effective ones. Yes, lady, I hope to cause you to regret your words. And how may I address you? Lady of Astra? Or would you prefer Master Dino the page? San Giorgio's shrew?'

'You need not address me at all,' flashed Bianca, giving Michele a few more seconds of safety, wondering how she could warn him. 'I have no wish to speak with you, or go with you. If you are wise, you will release me at once. My husband will pursue you to the edge of the world, and on to the seas beyond, if you are foolish enough to take me.' She feared he would kill Michele on the instant, without warning, when he discovered his mistake.

'Your husband? What have we here, then?' And Bruschini, whose understanding was sharp, bent to look down at Michele. His face grew ugly. 'Body of God, you fools. You have captured the wrong man. This is the soft half-brother, not the Falcon. Were you deceiving your husband with him already, lady?'

'Let him go,' said Bianca again, before Michele could speak. 'You cannot want him. Let him go.'

'Be sure I do not want him. Nor will I let him go. Beg for your life, pretty boy,' he said cruelly to Michele. 'Before you pay for taking your better's place.'

'Not I,' said Michele, from where he was held by two men. 'The dear God knows that I do not want to lose my life, but I would think shame to plead for it to such a one as you. All Florence knows the grudge you bear my brother.' And he stared defiantly at his captor, his brave manner concealing the fear of the death about to be put upon him.

'You are a fool in the wrong place,' said Bruschini indifferently, and then, to one of the men holding him, 'Cut him down.'

'No,' screamed Bianca, as the man-at-arms did as he was bidden, and, taking advantage of the fact that the man who was holding her had his greedy eyes on Michele's end, she threw herself, as Taddeo had taught her, at the legs of the soldier who was hacking him down.

She did not prevent the blow, but turned it aside a little to leave Michele stunned and bleeding on the ground, his bright hair, and fine clothing, stained.

'No, he has done you no harm,' she cried, shocked at the sight.

'Nor will he now,' said Bruschini cruelly. 'Up with her on your horse, man, and leave the carrion for the birds. The afternoon grows late, and I want none coming after them yet.'

They rode off, Bianca giving one last agonised look back at Michele, dead or dying, dragged a little way into the bushes. When the soldier would have struck him again, Bruschini stayed him. 'Leave him; I do not want him disfigured. Let his brother find him so, and the hurt for him will be the greater.'

Bianca was helpless, tightly and unpleasantly held by her captor, who was delighted to have such a fine lady in his power. But she yet managed, as they rode into the mountains, to try to note and to remember the direction in which they went, recalling what Taddeo had taught her when she was a page. God might be kind, and the knowledge of where she was going in relation to Florence would keep her occupied, might even be of use, though how she could not think.

CHAPTER ELEVEN

PIERO had left Prato early, finishing his business there with dispatch. Van Eyck and part of his *condotta* remained behind, all that were necessary to carry out the lord's commission—the smoking out of *banditti* living in the hills around Prato and preying on the little settlements outside the town itself.

Dressed still in the magnificence put on to impress Prato's lord, Piero arrived back at the villa a day early, the sooner to see Bianca again. The once single-minded warrior was now afire to greet and gain his bride at last, the memory of her always at the back of his mind in his long dealings with the lord and his council. For some reason it was the fiery imp she had been in the hall at San Giorgio, when he had first met her, which occupied him, and made him smile, once, in the middle of the haggling, so that his would-be patron mistook it for secret knowledge, despaired, and agreed to his severe terms. But it was also the beauty the imp had become who drew him back so speedily.

Caterina came to meet him in the entrance—knew what he wanted, and said, with a little, rueful smile, 'The lady is out riding with Messer Michele. They are somewhat late returning, but his party leaves Florence shortly and it is his last visit. He will be pleased to see you, after all.'

It could not be helped. Piero had thought of her pleasure when she heard that his troops had been sighted by the men-at-arms who kept unobtrusive watch. Had seen her as alone, not with his brother. . . But their real reunion would come later, when Michele had gone. . . and he was smiling as he listened to Lodovico's report of all that had taken place during his absence.

216

'And the business went well?' Lodovico asked.

'Very well.' He was suddenly restless. 'They should have returned by now. Come.' And he walked Lodovico from the garden-room, out through the great doors, into the forecourt, where they would see the riders returning.

But the riders did not return, and the joy he had brought with him from Prato evaporated during the wait. As he sat on a stone bench, by the doors, the beauty of the scene before him slowly became invisible. He rose, and called for Lodovico, who had left him to resume his duties. 'I have a mind to take horse and seek them. I am beginning to dream of a mischance.'

Lodovico said, 'Do not go alone. . . Take myself, and some of the men.'

'Prudent always,' answered Piero, trying to speak lightly. 'You know in which direction they went?'

'North-west,' said his uncle. 'They would follow the trail to the foothills, but Michele is no fool; he would be wise enough to go no further, I am sure.'

Well, either Bianca and Michele were delaying because they were taking the opportunity to become lovers—a possibility he could not, dare not believe—or some mishap had befallen them. 'Then give the order to saddle up, and bring along Niccolo Tenda and his men. Best, perhaps, had they not gone alone.'

'But they were not going far, Caterina said.'

'Then all the more reason to search for them, and urgently,' said Piero anxiously.

They took the route which Bianca and Michele had followed earlier, the ground so dry in the summer's heat that no hoofmarks could help them, and finally came to the spot where the trail petered out, and Bruschini's ambush had been laid, and began to search the scrub.

Despair was growing in Piero now that there had been no sign of the missing pair, and his despair became the greater when one of the men-at-arms called, his voice sharp, 'Here, Lord Captain, here, at once!'

Ah, *Dio!* What had he found? Heart thundering, Piero,

Lodovico following, pushed his way to where the trooper was bending over Michele, holding him gently in his arms, his face anxious at the sight of his captain. Everyone at the villa had known and liked the Falcon's half-brother.

Piero dropped to his knees and said hoarsely, 'Not dead, I hope, Fabrizio?' at the sight of the blood and Michele's livid face on his soldier's arm.

'No, lord,' said Fabrizio. 'But far gone, I fear. By the looks of it, he has dragged himself a little way, after he was cut down.'

'And no sign of the lady—or their horses?'

'None.'

The sound of Piero's voice rallied Michele, who now lay with his head on Piero's arm, Fabrizio resuming his futile search. His eyelids flickered, the livid mouth writhed. Injured though he was, the two brothers had never looked more alike, as though Piero's anxiety and Michele's sufferings had marked them as one.

'Piero?'

'Yes, brother.' And, despite his anxious wish to find the lost Bianca, Piero did not want the effort of speech to destroy Michele. 'Have a care,' he told him.

Michele rolled his head then spoke, his voice a thread. 'Bruschini. Jumped on us. Took her.' His eyelids fluttered, closed, but he rallied, spoke again. Piero's ear was by his mouth to catch his muttered words. 'Thought I was you. She. . .saved me from instant death. . . Now I can die.'

'No!' Piero's voice was almost his battle shout, as though by the force of his will he could save his brother.

Lodovico, who had come up, and was kneeling on Michele's other side, took his slack hand. 'He's badly hurt, but maybe not fatally. He has lost much blood, but his pulse, though weak, is constant. Leave me here with him, and two troopers to help me. You must return to try to discover where Bruschini has taken your lady.

Send me a tent and supplies, and I will bring him to the villa if. . .when. . .he is fit to be moved.'

Piero realised there was nothing to do but leave Michele in Lodovico's capable hands; if anyone could save him, his uncle could. He took one last look at them before he left, and the man who had never loved others was distraught with grief at his brother's plight and Bianca's loss.

Fabrizio had found where Bruschini's troops had waited, before they fled with Bianca, and they followed the trail through the scrub, broken by their headlong passage, until it ended in a wasteland of stones and dry earth.

'No point in further search,' said Piero. 'They could be anywhere by now. Bruschini disappeared from Florence a fortnight ago, and none knew where he had gone—or why.' He thought of the many bandit eyries in the hills around them, and guessed that his enemy had hired one of the rogue *condottieri* who ruled them to carry out his revenge for Trani.

Piero cursed himself that in his pride he had thought Bruschini's threats empty, and that he had never thought to guard himself and Bianca from a surprise attack.

And Bianca. Where was she now? And what would her captor do to her? Murder, or a demand for ransom to strip him of his fortune? He must return to Florence, to smoke out Bruschini, and do all without harming Bianca.

He and his little party, full of anger at the taking of their lady, rode at full speed towards Florence.

'Yes,' said Bianca firmly. 'I really should not have made that move, Rafaello. I admit it looked good, but Father Luca always used to say that moves at chess which look good at first sight are put there by the Devil to tempt us. Let me take back my knight, else you will checkmate me, and I shall have lost again. You really ought to be teaching me.'

She was sitting in what had once been the solar room of Marinaro's tower, when it had belonged to a Malatesta lord, now long dead. Bruschini had personally escorted her there, bowed ironically to her, and said, 'And now we shall find out how much your lord values you. All of his fortune, do you think? And when he has paid me, shall I send you to him piece by piece, or would you rather I gave you to Marinaro and his soldiers to play with before I send you back? Amusing for him to think that you had been the garrison's whore. As you know, I have little use for women, particularly for noisy, rude ones. Gossip says that you are still a virgin. Interesting for Marinaro to find out. He will have you first.'

She had sat down, folded her arms, and refused to answer him, and he had laughed at that. 'Gossip also says that you have a mind—strange to find one in a woman. A pity for the Lord God to waste it on you. You may use it here to ponder on your wisdom in aiding your husband to insult me. No, I shall not treat you harshly— yet. I wish to speak true when I send word to him that you are not harmed. You shall feed well and go unmolested—for the time being.'

She was silent, understanding for the first time what Father Luca had once said: 'Silence is a weapon, too.'

Rafaello, one of the pages, brought her food. Once a day she was allowed to walk on the battlements, a man-at-arms behind her, Bruschini at her side, his taunts swirling about her. Once she turned to him in the middle of a tirade against her husband to say, 'There is a chess set in my room, and I am bored. I would like to play a game against someone. You, or another, would do.'

He had gazed at her with unwilling admiration. 'Body of God, lady, you are cool. Almost, you compel admiration.' He gave a burst of laughter. 'Teach the page to play. He may spend a little time with you each day, when you have dined. Having been one yourself, you should find in him a brother.'

This was better than she had expected. So, on her third day, when he came to take her empty tray, he stayed for her to teach him. 'Be on your best behaviour,' Bruschini had said to him.

Rafaello, fifteen years old and conscious of his lack of physical attraction, blushed angrily. To be taught anything by a girl was demeaning, but the lord had given his orders, and he dared not tell him that he could already play a little. Be taught by a girl, indeed!

But Bianca was kind to him and soothed his ruffled spirits, telling him how rapidly he was improving, asking him questions about his duties and admiring his ability at chess.

'I have always wondered,' she said, looking at the board, making a foolish move herself, to prolong her time with him, 'what pages did. I know that you are the third part of a lance——'

'Oh, everyone knows that,' he interjected, 'even girls.'

'Yes, but what else do you do? Here, for instance. Do you work with the Lord Marinaro's horses? I heard pages were required to do that.'

He looked up at her, lip curling a little. 'I am the best of the pages with the horses,' he said. 'When I have finished with you, I shall go down and exercise Hannibal, the Lord Captain's best black. I do that most afternoons.'

'Difficult in the castle courtyard,' sighed Bianca. 'I fear that you are being too good for me today.'

'That is because you are a girl. Of course I don't exercise him in the tower. I am allowed to take him through the gates, and give him a run outside on the days when the lord does not ride him.'

'Only you?' said Bianca idly. 'That is a great honour.'

'Indeed, and now I have beaten you. See, it is mate. Messer Bruschini did not know that my father taught me the game. But then, beating girls is nothing. One expects it.'

'Oh, yes,' said Bianca. 'We are poor creatures. It grieves me to say it. Frightened by things that boys hardly notice. To ride a warhorse——' And she shuddered delicately. 'And you do it every day—and no other?'

'Well, sometimes when I am training at weaponry one of the other pages takes over. Even Messer Bruschini gives me best on a horse, though. I thank the Lord God that I am not pretty enough for him, but I wish that he would use his tongue on some of the other pages. It is not my fault that I am ugly.'

'I do not think that you are ugly,' lied Bianca, flattering him so that he chattered artlessly on about the tower, and the land round it, and told Bruschini and Marinaro that night that the Lady of Astra was a nice girl, who deserved better than the Falcon for a lord.

'Indeed, so,' grinned Marinaro, the burly man who had been promised Bianca first after Manfredini paid her ransom, but like Bruschini agreed that, until then, they would go easy with her. 'Perhaps she will gain a new and better lord,' he added, and he laughed at the thought of having her.

Their victim was at that moment standing on the wooden bench in the solar, looking through one of the slits high in the tower wall at the landscape below. She had watched the sun rise and set, knew in which direction she was looking, and from which direction she had been brought.

The map in her head told her where Florence lay, and she had questioned Rafaello to find out how the tower was disposed in relation to the town in which it stood.

She had torn a long strip from her chemise, twisted it and hidden it in the chest at the bottom of her bed, and at night she thought of all that Taddeo had taught her— but never of Piero, for no, she would not cry, and to think of him, out there, looking for her, wondering where she was, and whether he knew Bruschini had her, was torture.

And Michele, whom she had left in the undergrowth, she must not think of him, either. Later, she promised herself. Later. And please, Lord God, make Bruschini pay for what he has done to poor Michele, and to Piero and me.

Piero de' Manfredini was a madman—controlled and organised, but a madman none the less. The thought of Bianca in Bruschini's power drove him to act with more speed and determination than even he had ever shown before.

After visiting Florence—questioning, arguing, trying to discover where she might have been taken—he returned to the villa to discover that a messenger had arrived with a letter demanding ransom. He read Bruschini's message.

This to Piero de' Nobody, temporary Lord of Astra. Know that I have your wife safe and will deliver her to you only on presentation of the sum of fifty thousand florins to my agent Roberto Ricardi at the Medici Bank. . .

He read the thing with a dreadful mounting rage, helpless to do anything but rail at the messenger who brought it, who knew nothing—had been paid by a man he did not know to deliver a letter to the villa of the Lord of Astra.

The Medici could not, or would not, help, either. Confidence towards their clients was their watchword; to breach it would destroy their reputation. They might deplore what Bruschini had done, offer their sympathy, but Ricardi himself was sacrosanct. Behind their apparently heartless behaviour was the belief that these acts would happen in a society not yet completely civilised, and that their neutrality helped the victim as much as the criminal.

Reason might say that they were right, but to Piero, as to others in a similar plight, reason had little to do with it. What was worse was that he could not discover exactly who it was whom Bruschini had hired to help him kidnap Bianca.

Four days after her capture, still in ignorance of her whereabouts, with the ransom unpaid, he came home to the villa, face grey, clothing in disarray, a parody of his usual cool self. Those who met him at this time were astonished at the change in him. The impassive young man whose cold control of himself was a byword, whose lack of feeling for others was notorious, had quite gone. Instead, despair rode on his shoulders, and it was plain that his whole world had shrunk down to one thing and one thing only: a frantic determination to recover his lost wife.

Lodovico met him. He had returned with Michele the previous day. Michele was out of danger, recovering slowly.

'You have visitors, nephew,' said Lodovico, 'and I have advised that they be placed in separate rooms.'

'Visitors. Who, then? Are they important?'

'For you to judge,' said Lodovico. 'Your father—and Bandelli.'

'A strange pair. My father to see Michele, I suppose.'

'He wishes to see you, too,' Lodovico told him.

'Then let him be the first—who is least. Lead me to him.'

Lodovico had put the Marquis in the garden-room after he had visited Michele. He rose to meet Piero as he entered and saw immediately that his son, who had always mocked at all human passions, now knew that he, too, was human, had joined the ranks of those who felt and bled and cried for salvation, for surcease from pain.

'So, the iron man suffers. The emotions which you have rejected are taking their revenge.' The Marquis did not speak unkindly, but with infinite pity.

For the first time since he had lost Bianca tears swam

in Piero's eyes, as though his father's words had shown him the stark reality of his situation.

He made a negative movement of his hand, and said, voice stifled, 'You wished to see me. In the face of Michele's sufferings, I cannot refuse you.'

'I wished to thank you for your care of him.'

'My care! He only suffered because that villain mistook him for myself.'

'But you helped him—and he loves you. You have your revenge on me, you see. He admires you, says that you are the brother he has always wanted.'

Piero saw that his father had suffered too—feared that Michele would die, felt for his legitimate son what he, Piero, felt for Bianca.

'I accept your thanks. And, Father—although I may never forgive or forget what you did, there is no hate left in me. In the face of Bianca's loss, such feelings as I had for you seem petty. You are but a man, after all, not a monster. Michele loves you, and what he cares for I cannot entirely reject.'

It was as far as he could go, and he saw his father's face change in pleasure that he had relented at all. And when his father spoke, he made no reference to himself, but said, 'I am sorry that Bruschini has taken your wife, and hope that you may soon recover her safe and sound. She is a gallant creature, most fit for such a one as yourself.'

Piero passed his hand over his face and said, 'I thank you, and now I must leave you. I have other duties. Bandelli is here, and must be seen.'

His father put out his hand, a hand which Piero took. 'I shall arrange for Michele to be moved to Florence as soon as possible. And then we shall leave when he is fit to travel the distance to Alassio. If we do not meet again, my blessings on you both go with you.'

Piero could not speak, and he dropped his father's hand. It was a strange, silent parting, but one made in amity, at last.

* * *

'Such a fine house you have, Pierino,' roared Bandelli. 'Who would have thought that the ragged lad I took in would have achieved such splendour?'

He was standing in the dining-room where Lodovico had left him, an uncouth figure beside the villa's sophistication. The feral eyes met Piero's with pity. 'So, that pen-pushing villain has taken your wife, your page who first took off and then resumed her skirts for you.'

'Maddalena told you?'

'Not she. *You* told me, Pierino. I saw your face when you carried her away after I had made her drunk. Until then you had both fooled me. But I know the expression on the face of a man in love—and you never liked boys. After that, I watched Dino, and the truth was plain. A pity to lose a woman so gallant.'

Gallant. Twice in a few moments. His Bianca. Whose worth he had only realised when he had lost her. Piero wanted to scream against the gods, but reined in his helpless rage, and said as levelly as he could, 'Why are you here, Agostino?'

'Business, Pierino, what else? It goes on though the world falls about our ears. I came to collect what you owe me for Trani—and offer you another proposition. One I think that you will like.'

'I am not thinking of business at the moment, Agostino. You should know that.'

'You will like my offer, Pierino, and for the love I bear you I shall offer my services to you at a discounted fee.'

Why am I standing here, bandying words with this fat villain, when I should be looking for Bianca, my lost love? Nevertheless, Piero answered wearily, 'You shall have your payment—and I can see that you are determined to make me your proposition. Make it, Agostino; I owe you that.'

'No, I owe you still, my Falcon, and one day the debt may be finally paid, and we shall meet as equals, you and I. Bruschini has taken your wife, you want her back, and I need employment, Pierino—money: I have many mouths to feed, and Agostino's people are hungry wolves. I have, too, a bombard I have bought, a big one which I need to test in battle. You will help me?'

Would he ever come to the point? 'If I am able. But my wife comes first, you understand?'

'And so she shall, Pierino. So she shall. Look you, I know where she is, and for the smallest of fees will help you to get her back.'

Dino would have recognised Piero's speed. He advanced on the grinning Bandelli, grabbed him by the collar, and hoisted him off his feet.

'You wicked bag of lard. To haggle and cheat while she suffers. Tell me where she is, or I'll let a hole in your guts.'

'Gently, Pierino, gently,' said Bandelli, no whit abashed. 'Of course I will tell you, and you will hire me, will you not? I could have said nothing, let you squirm, but for the love I bear you——'

Piero threw Bandelli from him with a crack of sobbing laughter. 'Love? I'll hire you, you villain. Now, tell me where she is, or, by the living God, I'll hang you at the villa's door as a message to all *banditti* not to palter with me.'

'Oh, she has not softened you, then, boy—little vixen that she is. Marinaro has her at Vercelli. Why, that fool, Bruschini, offered the commission to me first—me, your loving friend, Pierino.'

'But you never thought to warn me?'

'Warn you? I thought that you knew his fell intent. Were prepared. After all, you are the Falcon.'

'But you turned him down?' said Piero, still impatient.

'Turned him down? No, not I. No, no. I named a price for hire so high that even the Doge of Venice would have blenched at it. He called me a vulture and left. But not before I had told him that only the highest price he, or anyone, could offer, could make a Judas of me. I would not sell you for nothing. You would not like that, Pierino. And now I collect any way. We shall ride against Vercelli together, try my bombard and rescue your lady.'

'Not so fast,' said Piero. 'When he sees us arrive he may kill her—or worse.'

'La, la, Bandelli thinks of everything. I know a trick or two to prevent that. Trust me, Piero. Trust Bandelli.'

'Trust you? I suppose I must.'

'Then summon your men to march at once. It will be like old times. You and I together against the world. Tell your Lodovico to make all ready to start on the hour. I wish that I had a battle-master half his worth. You are at permanent stations for action since this occurred, are you not?'

No gainsaying the old rogue, thought Piero, as he half ran to give his orders. Bianca at Vercelli—in Marinaro's hands, as well as Bruschini's. He shuddered; it did not bear thinking of.

Unaware of what was happening in the world outside, Bianca knelt by her bed, the day after Bandelli had told Piero of her whereabouts, and prayed to the Lord God for assistance. Before she had done so, however, she had prepared herself for an attempt to escape, for if the Lord God blessed you He only did so when you had made and laid your own plans. So far as she could tell, His intervention was never direct.

She had tied the twisted linen rope around her waist, set out the chess board, and waited for Rafaello to bring her midday meal.

He came in, the smell of the food creating nausea in her rather than hunger, as on other days, but she forced herself to eat a little, while he examined the chess board, trying out moves. Yesterday, in the middle of the game, she had given a high-pitched cry, stared into the dark corner of the solar, and said fearfully, 'It is there, I know it. Oh, I am so afeared.'

'What is there in the corner?' Rafaello had said, grinning. 'A wild boar, or a wolf?'

'No, a rat,' she had said. 'I cannot abide rats.' He had risen, looked about, but could see nothing, so sat down again, and laughed at women's fears. 'I wonder girls can bear life at all,' he had said, 'so much frightens them.'

'Oh, we need you to protect us,' she had said, and afterwards could not concentrate on the game, looking fearfully across the floor, once drawing up her skirts, to his great amusement.

'No rats today,' he said, as she finished her meal, and sat down opposite him.

'They woke me in the night,' she lied. 'They live in the walls and between the floor and the ceiling below. I can hear them.'

'Well, I can't,' said Rafaello, and pushed forward one of his pawns. For the next half-hour Bianca was silent, until suddenly, as he advanced a bishop down a long diagonal, she gave a great cry, jumped on to her chair, and screamed, 'It is there, I can see it. Oh, kill it for me.'

'Girls!' said Rafaello, and, picking up the heavy brass candlestick, advanced to the corner, to bend over, saying, 'I can see nothing.'

Bianca jumped down, came up behind him, untying the rope round her waist as she did so, and held it as Taddeo had taught her. 'Of course, you cannot see it. Go on your hands and knees, and hit it as hard as you can.'

She had some regrets about what she was going to do to Rafaello, who had been kind, but she must try to escape, and if she failed—well, she would think about that when it happend.

Still grinning his maddeningly superior grin, he went down on his hands and knees, and as he did so Bianca knelt swiftly behind him, flung the garotte around his neck, and pulled. . .hard.

She had to hurt him enough so that he could not resist. He gave a strangled cry, before the force of the pull overwhelmed him, and as he fell on to his knees she thought for a moment that she had killed him outright, and slackened her hold on him, so that his hands came up to claw at the cloth which choked him, and she was compelled to pull again, until he fell forward, semi-conscious.

'Oh, Rafaello, I am so sorry,' she whispered, which was stupid, and Taddeo would have been ashamed of her. But she pulled the dagger from his belt, and took the napkin which had come with her food, twisted it, and gagged him—another of Taddeo's tricks—then loosened the garotte, so that he could breathe a little again.

Rafaello's whole world had dissolved in pain, and he had no clear idea of what had happened to him. One moment he was on his hands and knees, laughing, looking for the silly girl's rat—which he thought was imaginary, a product of her imprisonment, but it tickled him to humour her—the next, he was gasping for breath, in great pain, eyes popping, tongue protruding, and the whole world going dark.

He came to, to find that he was gagged, half undressed—he had lost his hose, his mutande, and his short cloak—and someone was pressing a dagger into his stomach.

'Can you hear me, Rafaello? Nod, if you can,' she whispered.

He nodded, to please the creature who had treated him so cruelly, and wondered what had happened to Bianca; what was she doing, while some assassin half killed him?

As though she knew his thoughts, she whispered in his ear, 'It is Bianca who has strangled you, Rafaello, and she needs your clothes.' Disbelieving, terror-stricken, he nodded at last.

'Good,' she whispered in his ear. 'Now, I am going to untie your hands, so that you may take your shirt and doublet off, but first I shall tie your feet together, and blindfold you, so that you cannot easily attack me.' All this was part of Taddeo's instructions—how a cunning weakling may surprise and overcome a larger foe. She prayed to the dear God again that it would work, as she loosened Rafaello's hands.

'Remember, I have your dagger, and shall not hesitate to use it on you if you try any tricks.'

Try any tricks! Between the searing pain in his throat and chest, which made breathing an agony, the tightness of the bonds round his ankles, and the cruel gag in his mouth, Rafaello was quite undone.

Sobbing through the gag, he stripped off his remaining clothing to lie naked on the floor. What a fool he had been, and if she succeeded in escaping Bruschini would surely kill him, if Marinaro did not. How in the name of all the devils in Gehenna had she known how to do this—the soft, pretty thing she had been, sitting demurely opposite to him, bleating and crying, upset by every wind that blew? He shivered from more than his nakedness, as he lay in the dark.

Bianca pulled on Rafaello's stinking clothes, picking up the keys on their ring, keys which would take her out of this claustrophobic cell. She flung her own garments over the naked boy, and then, regretfully, cut off her new growth of hair, before putting on her head Rafaello's conical *berretta*.

Rafaello was struggling and writhing on the floor, able to breathe a little more freely, but still in pain. Before she left, Bianca dropped on to her hands and knees beside him and said earnestly. 'Oh, I'm so sorry to do this to you, but you do understand that I had to.'

That eased her conscience a little, but not much, and she opened the door which the page had earlier locked behind him, and looked out.

The corridor and stairs were empty. She relocked the door and started off, falling into the page's trot. Now, what was it that Rafaello had told her? That he exercised Marinaro's horse each afternoon, and, without meaning to, he had told her where the stables were, and as she reached the courtyard she consulted the map in her head again. Yes, they were that way. Now, all she had to do was say that Rafaello was detained, and she was to exercise Hannibal in his place.

She knew that she had one huge fact in her favour. No one but Bruschini knew that the delicate Lady of Astra had been Dino, the page, and even he did not know that he had been an apt pupil of a cunning sergeant. She had only to hope that it would be some time before Rafaello was discovered, so that she might, the Lord God willing, get clear away.

Ercole, the liveryman in charge of the horses, stared at her as she trotted up. 'I've come for Hannibal,' she said, offering no explanation for Rafaello's absence.

'Where's Rafaello, then?' asked Ercole, doing her job for her. 'And you're a bit of a midget to look after Hannibal, aren't you?'

'Rafaello? He's been a naughty boy, sentenced to help clean the latrines, so they've sent me instead. I'm a bit of a wonder with horses,' she offered, immodestly, but truthfully.

'Can't say as I've seen you afore,' said Ercole, as he gave her a leg-up. She tried to avoid too much physical contact with him. Rafaello's padded doublet obscured her woman's body, but she was conscious of it—so different from being a boy outside Trani.

'Wouldn't, would you?' she said. 'I've been waiting on the lord, and dodging Bruschini.'

This brought a cackle of laughter, and while Ercole was enjoying the joke she began to school the horse. Watching her, Ercole said, 'You have the right of it, lad. You know how to master a horse, for all your pretty face, and lack of size.'

She swept off her *berretta*, glad for her shorn hair, gave him a salute, and made for the main gates, praying that no one would guess who it was who rode Hannibal. Now, only the sentries to pass.

And that was easy. They were bored, had watched

Hannibal ride out every day at this hour, and, as she had thought, one page was very like another to them. She rode the big horse slowly down the street, swept off her hat again, to the sentries who guarded the gates in the little town's wall, and passed safely through them. She walked Hannibal slowly round in a big circle, in front of them, before setting off at a sedate trot down the trail which led from the town. Once well away from it she took off into the scrub, consulting the map she had made in her head, which told her where Florence was and where Vercelli, and prayed that she had got it right, and was not making for Milan in the north, Rome in the south, or some place even the Lord God had never heard of.

A little way into the scrub she stopped, wrenched the ring of keys from her belt, and threw them as far as she could, thinking of the wretched page from whom she had stolen them, and then forgot him, as she tried to make for home—and Piero.

Bianca's disappearance was not discovered for some time. It was Ercole who first became disturbed when Hannibal and his rider failed to reappear. He was pacing the courtyard, trying to summon up courage to inform the short-tempered Marinaro that some mischance must have befallen his charger and rider, and that he had let an unknown boy take the lord's precious charger out, and had disappeared with it. The time for return was long past.

He found Marinaro and Bruschini talking together in the tower's main hall, and endured their anger at his tale.

'That fool, Rafaello,' said Bruschini contemptuously to his captain. 'I told you that he was not responsible enough to school your horses.'

'Begging your pardon, Messer Bruschini, but it was not Rafaello, but another—a little fellow—who rode Hannibal out for exercise this afternoon. And, look you, the page who came for him lied, said Rafaello was doing what he was not. And, more, Rafaello's not to be found. He's not been seen since he took the lady's meal to her. The kitchen says he has never returned her tray, and the other pages have not seen him. The lad who took him knew how to ride. Controlled Hannibal like a master.'

A dreadful suspicion grew in Bruschini's mind. He remembered Dino, the page, whose skill with horses had become known throughout the army camped outside Trani. And Dino was none other than Bianca, the Lady of Astra.

'To the lady's room, at once,' he roared, and both men ran up to the solar, Ercole following, to find it locked against them, and that banging on the door and shouting for it to be unlocked brought no answer.

'Search for Rafaello and the keys,' howled Marinaro at Ercole. 'I want him found.'

Lying on the solar floor, helpless and fearful, Rafaello heard the noise, and Marinaro's angry roarings, wondering what had passed, and whether it would not have been better for Bianca to have killed him on the spot, rather than leave him to face what was sure to come to him now. He prayed silently as the door was battered down by two troopers, and Marinaro and Bruschini burst in to find him trussed, gagged and naked on the floor.

Marinaro turned to Bruschini after they had untied the quaking page, and heard his cracked and fearful explanation. 'My horse! The whore took my best horse, my Hannibal! By Satan and all his devils, I'll hang this witless fool from the battlements for the crows to peck at!' And he directed a savage kick at poor Rafaello's ribs.

'Your horse!' almost shrieked Bruschini. 'The girl's a goldmine and my revenge as well, and you prate of horses. Forget the horse, and the page can wait. Later he can die slow. Leave him locked in here to think of his doom as he waits for us.' And he, too, kicked at the wretched Rafaello.

The two men ran down the stairs together, shouting for search parties to be made ready, but a worse Nemesis was on them, for the tower's look-out reported that an army approached them, and by the banners it bore it was Agostino Bandelli's, and what that could mean stopped all possibility of any men leaving the town, for the gates were to be closed and battle-stations taken up.

'Look you, Pierino, I have hired you—or so we will tell the world. I will approach Vercelli with my pennants flying, and you shall be anonymous under my command with no banners to give you away. No, do not seek to argue. That way, they will not know that you are with me, will not harm the lady. I shall have come, or so I shall hint, to share in the massive ransom all the world knows that Bruschini is claiming. When they refuse, my black dragon will belch fire at them——' he meant his bombard '—and you will bring up your reserves, which we will keep hidden until then. Together we will go through the hole my dragon will burn for us in their walls, take the town with ease, and only after they have sued for surrender will they discover that you have come for your lady. Until then it is merely poor Agostino, trying to share in their spoils, or take them over. You like it, Pierino?'

Piero gazed at him in fascination. 'So fertile a brain for such base trickery as yours, my old master, I have seldom come across. Will it work, do you think?'

'Why not? They must know I am aware that Bruschini went to Marinaro after I refused him. They think that you have no idea where your lost wife is. They know I would sell anyone—my grandmother if it paid me.'

'And when we reach Vercelli, will you then sell *me*?' said Piero.

'Oh, that is a risk you take, I can see that. But remember, not only do I owe you, but there is Maddalena. Foolish creature that she is, she would not have you harmed, even if you have got a wife!'

What else to do? And the next afternoon found them nearing their destination, slowly, because they could only travel at the dragon's pace. 'A snail,' Piero said once, exasperated, 'not a dragon,' watching it lurch slowly along on its wooden wheels.

'But think what it can do for us, Pierino,' Bandelli roared, and then, at last, Vercelli was before them, and Bandelli sent out a herald to bray to the men on the walls that the Lord Agostino Bandelli would speak under a flag of truce with Messer Bruschini, or his herald.

'Suppose he accepts you as a partner?' said Piero, standing anonymous, his uncrested helm on, by Bandelli's side.

'Not he,' said Bandelli. 'He doesn't need me to hold your lady. He'll not want me. The gold grows smaller with each who shares it. Besides, I shall pitch my demands so high, he will faint with shock, and think it better to hold me off. He cannot see my dragon. It is well hidden.'

Bruschini rode out himself—he had no mind to tell Bandelli the lady had gone. He had a troop behind him, and stood close before the gates. 'No treachery, mind.' Piero watched them haggle, then suddenly Bruschini clapped spurs to his horse, and shot back inside Vercelli.

'As I thought,' said Bandelli gleefully. 'The old fool thinks I cannot sustain a seige. Defies me. Wait until the dragon spits at him.'

Battle now engaged, the dragon was wheeled forward for Piero to inspect her, and to see where she got her name: her mouth and body were dragon-shaped, and the gunners began their deadly work, ramming the giant ball down her gaping throat, after running her forward to stand in direct line to the little town's gates.

'Not a pretty way to wage war, eh, Pierino? But when the gates finally collapse, be ready to storm through them. I see your reserve troops are ready. That should shock them. They thought that they had only mine to contend with.'

He spoke true. Marinaro, suddenly seeing a huge contingent of men-at-arms, lances and archers, appear at the sound of a trumpet, turned to Bruschini and said, 'If the gates go, and go they will, we are doomed. By your leave, we must surrender before they enter, or we are all cat's meat. We cannot stand against a bombard and such superior forces. God knows who Bandelli has down there with him.'

'No need to call on God,' snarled Bruschini. 'Ten to one he has the Falcon with him. And his woman would be cat's meat now, if only we had her. I'll not surrender.'

'By God and his angels,' said Marinaro, 'but I will. Our cause is hopeless and the girl is gone. Nothing to fight for, and nothing to bargain with. At least Bandelli will gain little from this. He'll not want Vercelli, and when the gates go I shall hoist the white flag.'

And so Vercelli fell. When the dragon's last shot blew away the gates, and Bandelli and his followers prepared to stream in, a trumpet sounded on the battlements, and the flag of surrender was flown.

Bandelli halted his men, rode forward, Piero at his side, his helm off, golden hair streaming free, to see Marinaro walk through the broken gates to meet them.

'Vercelli is yours, Agostino, but what you hope to gain by this I cannot imagine.'

'Why, Messer Bruschini is the man I want; bring him forth, and we'll talk terms. You are his sword, not his voice.'

Bruschini came slowly forward, his face grey, to glare at Bandelli, and then at Piero, Bandelli bellowing, 'There, Pierino mine. He's yours, as I promised.'

'Mine,' echoed Piero, voice grim. 'And you know what I want, do you not? My wife. Bring her out, Bruschini, safe and sound, and I'll spare your worthless life.'

Marinaro burst into mirthless laughter, and Bruschini's ashen face turned yellow. 'Bring her out!' Marinaro roared, before his master could speak. 'There a joke for you, if only we could, eh, Messer pen-pusher? If only we could.'

'You'll laugh at the end of a rope if you've killed her. . .' threatened Piero, his own face ashen now.

Bruschini spoke at last. 'Killed her? That's rich, Manfredini. Killed her!' And even in his frustration and baffled hate of the man before him the grotesque humour of the situation struck him, and Marinaro echoed him, bellowing,

'Aye, Manfredini; not content with three-parts killing the page who was guarding her, the impudent vixen has fled Vercelli, and made off with my best horse—even had the gall to ride through the main gates with it, kissed goodbye by the fools put there to guard it. We only discovered that she was gone as you arrived. You have broken us for nothing. The wench you married has saved herself before you even reached Vercelli.'

Bandelli gave a great gleeful shout at the news. 'By the Lord God, Pierino, a woman of spirit. Took your horse, did she, Marinaro? Showed good taste there. Little but choice, little but choice.'

Piero was disbelieving, feared a cruel trick. 'You lie, Marinaro. What have you done with her? By God, I'll butcher the pair of you slowly if it takes that to make you talk! Could not you think of a better tale than that?'

Fear overwhelmed Bruschini as Piero leapt from his horse, drew his great broadsword and advanced on him. 'As God is my witness, I am speaking the truth,' he cried. 'The page, fetch the page! He will tell you what she did, and the liveryman will tell you how she went— nigh on three hours ago now. She is halfway to Florence if she's as cunning at finding her way as she is at tricking men.'

There was truth in his voice at last; Piero lowered his sword, which he had lifted high above his head. Thought of Dino the page, and said, 'Bring him out, then; one of my men will go with you to see that you do not brief him to lie. But, I warn you, I'm ready to slaughter the lot of you if you've harmed a hair of her head.'

But, once he had spoken to the wretched boy who had been the victim of the same trick with which she had overcome Tavio, he knew that somewhere, out there, in the Tuscan countryside, the gallant child he had married was trying to find her way home to him, and, once alone with Bandelli, with Marinaro and Bruschini waiting outside for their fate to be determined, he dropped his bright head and wept.

'Nothing to that,' said Bandelli. 'Why are you hanging around here, Pierino? Be off with you to find your lady. I have never seen you unmanned before. Love, is it? Well, by the sound of her, she is worth it—strangling pages, stealing chargers. Of course, she'll find her way home. Take your men and go.'

Talking so, he pushed Piero out of the room to find Bruschini arguing angrily with his chief lieutenant, who was guarding him. Bandelli said coolly to him, 'I mislike your tone, do not wish to hear your voice again. You are a traitor to friend and foe alike. Be quiet, or worse will befall.'

Bruschini glared at him. 'I'll not be spoken to by such a treacherous dog as you, Bandelli. Prisoner I may be, your serf I am not, nor that of the disowned bastard who walks beside you. I hope his wife lies dead in a ditch, under the horse she stole.'

'Do you so?' said Bandelli, and his voice for once quite indifferent he added, 'Such misery as you live in, best out of it. Never say I did not warn you,' and before those with him knew what he was about he had drawn the long dagger at his belt, and slid it between Bruschini's ribs. 'You'll not worry yourself or others now.'

There was a terrible silence as, face disbelieving, Bruschini fell dying to the floor.

'For God's sake,' said Piero, roused from the depression which had followed the news of Bianca's flight. 'You've murdered him, Agostino. Was that necessary?'

'Necessary?' Bandelli's smile was wry. 'Of course it was necessary. You heard him, man. He would have pursued you to the ends of the earth. You were not safe while he lived. And if he stole your wife unpunished, why should not another?'

'And I,' said Marinaro. 'Will you murder me, unarmed as I am, too? Where is honour in this?'

'Honour?' said Bandelli, and laughed. 'You hear him, Piero? Men who talk of honour have none. No, no, I don't ache to kill you! Keep your worthless life—you were but his tool. I've done you a favour, Piero, and paid my debt to you for saving me from hanging five years agone. Go, boy, go to your wife, and when you find her kiss her for me, and tell her she may sleep safe with the pen-pusher dead.'

Better to have Bandelli for friend than enemy, thought Piero, running through the gathering dark to his horse, and telling his troop to ride with him to Florence, and thence to quarters. And may the Lord God prove him right, and that she will be home when I get there.

CHAPTER TWELVE

BIANCA lay in her bed at the villa, sleepless for the moment, one thought and one thought only running through her brain—where was Piero?

She had arrived back at the villa, long after night had fallen, to joy mixed with sorrow that Piero and his men were not with her, and now she waited for him, sleep eluding her. God grant she might not wait long!

Sleep finally came and she awoke at first light. All was silent outside: *he* had not returned, and she could only think of him. Lodovico had told her not to worry. 'You know that your lord never does anything foolish,' he had said, but she knew, instinctively, that a Piero who had been robbed of his wife might do anything.

She was restless, and then she knew what she wanted to do. She began to dress herself as though she were Bianca di San Giorgio once again, and not a great lady with servants all about her. She put on the gown decorated with crimson carnations: it was one which *he* liked. Then she slipped on a sleeveless overgown of light wool, trimmed with silver braid, and her best slippers—but left her poor shorn hair unbound.

Bianca opened the door and began to make her way through the quiet house—she could just hear the servants beginning to stir—out along the corridor to the door which led to the gardens at the rear, and then she slipped out into the silvery grey of early morning, walking slowly along to the Grove of the Gods, thinking of Piero and their last trip here together, before Bruschini had shattered their world.

She sat for some time in the temple as the day grew brighter, thought of poor Michele, who was, to her great

241

relief, now recovering, and had been taken to Florence in a litter the previous afternoon. She was sorry to have missed him, but the sorrow was lost in her gratitude for his survival.

Standing by the edge of the pool, she suddenly felt a distaste for herself, and even for the beautiful clothes she was wearing. The taint of Vercelli seemed to be on them. Secure here, where none might visit, she entered the little temple and opened the huge, beautifully painted chest there; lovely, like all Piero's possessions, it was where clean towels were always kept, and slowly she stripped off her elegant clothing until she was quite naked—a strange sensation—and, picking up two of the towels, walked outside into the heavenly, scented peace of the Grove.

She put the towels down on the small marble quay, and slowly descended a flight of marble steps into the warm and inviting water. It was almost, she thought, with amusement, enjoying the warm air on her body, as though she were Mother Eve, sunning herself in the garden of Eden. Her ever-present humour told her, In that case, I must beware of serpents, but surely with Bruschini I have already had more than my share of them! On second thoughts, perhaps I am one of the nymphs in the painting in the bathroom! And the thought made her blush a little, but did not spoil her enjoyment of the water.

Slowly, she grew accustomed to this new sensation, and began to splash and play, as though she were Dino, clearing away all the nastinesses of the last few days, trying to forgive herself for what she had done to poor Rafaello, cleansing herself against the return of her lord. . .

Bianca had been correct in her judgement of her husband. The normally cool and rational man who was fully in control of himself, the people around him, and the world he lived in, had disappeared. He was frantic to recover his wife, the wife whom he had taken half in jest, and who had suddenly become the whole of his world.

Tired though he was, he set a punishing pace back towards Florence, but the night was on them, and, as he and his company fled westwards, Niccolo Tenda, the captain he had taken with him to Vercelli, suddenly rode up level with him, put out a hand and said, 'Lord, forgive me, but you must stop. I beg you, halt a moment to allow me to speak.'

His captain turned a face on him which Niccolo had never seen before, so ravaged was it. But he was not totally lost to the world. Piero nodded his head, and slowed down, the troop slowing behind him. 'Well?' Piero said curtly.

'Forgive me for speaking, lord, but we should leave off the chase, and rest until morning. We cannot find your lady in the dark, and so gallant is she that by now she is like to be home before us. You have not slept these last two nights. You cannot help her by driving yourself into exhaustion and illness.' He did not say, This is quite unlike your normal behaviour, lord; he did not need to.

Piero stared at him. He shook his head as though to clear it. His instincts told him, Ride on, but the reason which had always ruled his life until Bianca's arrival in it suddenly reasserted itself. He smiled wearily at Niccolo, whose anxious face betrayed that he feared he might have offended his captain, then put out his own hand and said, 'You are not only brave, my Niccolo, but you have the saving grace of common sense. It is true that I cannot help my lady by plunging about in the dark. We shall make camp at once.'

Lodovico ran to meet him as he rode in; the look-out had reported the troop riding up the hill from the valley floor. There was no sign of Bianca, but the expression on Lodovico's face told all. It was grinning, triumphant—the iron man, like his nephew, was at last allowing his feelings to show.

'She is back, Pierino. Safe and sound. Brought Marinaro's best steed home for you into the bargain. You may claim him as ransom. Your lady is a jewel of price.'

A cheer went up from the men behind Piero, and for the first time his *condotta* saw the Falcon show emotion, too. He turned away from them all, hid his face on his horse's saddle, then lifted it to show the tears standing in his eyes. 'Praise be to the Lord God,' he said. 'She is resting, I suppose?'

'Resting?' cried Lodovico. 'Not she. She awaits you in the Grove of the Gods, Caterina says. Has been there since before dawn. Go to her, lad. Her thoughts have only been of yourself.'

Piero was suddenly grateful for the night's rest which Niccolo had compelled him to take. He threw the reins of his horse to a waiting page, and walked into the villa to find Caterina waiting for him, to reinforce what Lodovico had already told him. 'Towels,' he said to her, 'bring me towels,' and when she brought them to him began to run towards the Grove, as though the last agonising week had never happened.

He did not know what he expected to find when he reached there, but, as he walked through the archway, and then around the screen of trees which hid the Grove from watchers, he heard the noise of her play, and then saw her.

Bianca had her back to him, and was splashing the water with her palms, so that it rose in a great fan beyond her. He called her name, and without thought she turned to see him standing there, still booted and spurred from the journey, the towels in his hand. She threw herself, again without thinking, into the age-old gesture of modesty, her hand covering her sex, and the curly black fleece which hid it, her blush mounting not only over her face, but her whole body.

Before she ducked into the water to hide herself he saw her fully, and caught his breath. In the months she had spent with him she had turned into a beautiful woman, better than any statue he had ever seen—rosy, shapely, with proud little breasts, pink-tipped, a tiny waist and delicate swelling hips.

'Well met, Lady of Astra,' he called. 'Or are you the nymph of the Grove? Lodovico tells me that you have brought me a splendid warhorse. What shall I do to thank you for it, lady?' All tiredness gone, his face was alight with loving mockery as he threw down the towels and began to strip off his clothes.

'W-what are you doing, lord?' she stammered, straightening up a little.

'Why, I mean to join you, wife. The Grove needs its satyr. Surely you were awaiting me? There are other games we might play in the water. Would you like me to show them to you?'

He was seated now, pulling off his boots, removing his hose, until he, too, was completely naked. Bianca stared at him. Stripped, he was, if anything, more remarkable than in his full panoply either of war, or of pompous ceremony. No wonder the women fell before him in droves. He was exactly like the statue of the beautiful marble man she had once seen, with the advantage that he was living and breathing. There was golden hair on his broad chest and it ran down beyond his stomach into a fleece above his sex.

His sex. She tried not to look at it, and him. He crouched, put his arms above his head, and sprang with a long low dive into the pool to come up beside her, having sprayed her with silver droplets of cascading water. He stood up and caught her to him for a moment. His hair clung to his skull, he was rubbing water from his eyes, and laughing at her. 'So, wife, you have played your naughty tricks on yet another unfortunate page. And cheated your husband out of the chance to rescue you into the bargain. I would be pleased if any of my captains showed half the initiative you did in rescuing yourself. Come, let me see this Amazon I have married.' And he took her under the arms and lifted her clear of the water.

Again, she tried to hide herself from him. Oh, she desired him, yes, she did; else why wait for him here naked? But now that she had him naked, too, the instinctive modesty of the untried virgin she was overcame her. Her hands rose to hide her breasts, and, laughing, he removed them gently.

'All of you, wife. All of you.' His eyes drank in what he saw. 'The scrubbing wench has become a woman behind my back.' Oh, what were his eyes doing to her? And his hands, which he placed over her breasts? 'Come, if you must have them hid, then give me the pleasure of hiding them.' And he was stroking them, and the sensation was so delicious that Bianca thought she would faint with the pleasure of it. She felt so weak that she reeled against him, wondering what she was doing to *him*. She could not, indeed, avoid seeing and feeling what she was doing to him as his hard sex rose against her. She gave a faint cry, half desirous, half fearful, and pulled away from him a little.

He caught her to him the more tightly. 'No escape now, my dove, my wife. What, shall the lady who did not fear Bruschini fear her husband? Have you no idea what pleasure it gives me to find my brave lady here, safe and well? I have nigh run mad this last week, thinking of you in that villain's hands.'

'No, lord. But this—is different.'

'Ah, my little one. My sparrow who has truly turned into a dove. Of course it is different. Do you know, my dove, my white dove——?' And each time that he called her dove he kissed her on the lips—oh, so gently, but she shivered and trembled at his touch. 'Do you know what men and women do together?'

'Oh, who could not know, lord?'

'Not lord, my dove, thy Piero, thy love. And you have

never done it, have been as virtuous as a maiden should be; that is plain.'

He had taken her hand while he spoke, and held it against him, so that she could feel his manhood, live and throbbing in her palm. 'Ah, but I desire thee, my white dove. Do but feel how I need thee, burn for thee. For sure, you know what this is for, too?'

'To give you pleasure, Piero mine,' she said timidly, but could not say, I burn for thee, too, although surely he could feel her melting against him, as though she were dissolving. Instinctively she stroked the velvet thing she held, and heard him gasp. He put his hand on hers.

'Not yet, my dove, not yet. And it is to give thee pleasure too, my life. You understand that—or my pleasure is nothing.'

Oh, he could see that she was trembling and shaking for very desire: that their love was mutual, that what he had suffered this last week she had suffered, too. 'I love thee, Bianca.' There, it was said. 'I say again: I have near run mad since I knew Bruschini had you. My men thought that I was crazed. I, who cared for nothing and nobody, was unmanned by your loss.' And now his hands were stroking her, her whole body was on fire, and as he spoke her hand moved against him, so that he whispered, 'Do not pleasure me yet. No pleasure for you. We shall die together, I promise thee, the sweetest death a man and woman may have.'

And now his stroking hand ran down her belly to where she ached and trembled the most, so that she welcomed the hand to the place most secret to her, and the world swung about her at his touch.

He began to walk her backwards to where a mossy bank ran down to the water, compelled to hold her up— she was faint against him. 'Come, we shall be man and wife at last, where the gods sport.'

'Here?' she asked. 'Here? In the open?'

'Where better?' he said. 'None will disturb us, as

we celebrate our union, and our reunion. This is my private place, my love, and I have brought no other woman here before you, before my wife.' And he ceased to speak, running his hand down her back, her spine to the cleft at its base. He cupped her there, and then stroked the inside of her thighs, so that her legs parted for him involuntarily to give the loving fingers greater access.

Piero bent his head, kissed her on the mouth, whispering before he did so, 'The Falcon greets his dove, and for once the birds will fly together in love and peace.' And now they had reached the bank, and he laid her down upon it, half in and half out of the water.

'My goddess of the bath,' he said, and she saw over his shoulder the cloudless blue of the sky, and the line of mountains, a grave mauve in the distance, until suddenly there was only the sky, and she felt the soft bank against her back.

'No clothes to dispose of,' he said, and his kisses were travelling downwards, having first penetrated her mouth, so that as once before they were deeply united there, and then wandered down, down, and her body trembled beneath him, but not with fear. It felt full, yet empty, and she lifted herself towards him and said, 'Please, oh, please,' and knew not what she asked for, except that it was *him* she wanted.

She had always been a little fearful of him, ever since she had met him in her brother's tower, but she was not afraid now. Except, who was Bianca? She had gone, quite gone, leaving behind only something female which ached to fulfil itself, and her tremblings and vibrations now were not caused by fear. She shuddered from head to toe as his teeth caught her earlobe, nuzzling it gently, producing the strangest sensations elsewhere in her body.

'I honour the ear with which I first met you,' he whispered, and let it go. 'Its owner deserves to be well rewarded.' And now the little bites and lickings, which did not break the skin, but caressed it, travelled downwards with his hands, and she cried out as the sensations began to overwhelm her.

To her astonishment she found that not only were her hands wantoning with his body, but she was thrusting herself at him; her body seemed to know better than she did what it wanted.

'Oh, at last, the dove is ready to mate with her Falcon, and I must hurt you a little, at first, my white bird, but afterwards—oh, afterwards, I promise thee, all will be celebration and pleasure. You are so ready for me.'

Bianca wondered how he knew. She knew quite well that he was ready for her, had been more than ready for some time, but had delayed to calm her fears, with such success that now she was as desperate for him as he for her. She opened herself to him, his hands were on her flanks, lifting her to receive him, and she cried out in pain at the shock of entry—there was nothing he could do to save her that; but, once joined, he held and stroked her, not fiercely, but gently, as though she were a child.

'Better soon, I promise,' he said, and he was right, so right. For it was as though something had broken inside her, something not physical, but that which belonged to the essential Bianca, the spirit, not the body, and it was not really broken, but changed, and what had gone was the desire to be separate.

All that mattered was that they were one, that she and he were together, that he was pleasuring her with such careful and loving affection that she was suddenly calling his name—'Oh, Pierino, my Pierino'—using for the first time the loving diminutive. Oh, who and what were he and she? The blue sky disappeared beneath a silver rain. She was part of a great wheel which turned and, turning, took her—and him—with it. The only external thing she knew was him in her, and then there was nothing but *it*, and at last *it* was satisfied, as he shouted her name, and it was as though a giant note of music chimed in the air between them, and vibrated on, long after the sound had gone. And fulfilment and the intense pleasure which came with it had been necessary, desired, but, once achieved, she was but Bianca again, and he was Piero, and what they had been together had gone. . .but would come again.

'And now you are truly my wife,' he said, and kissed her gently. They were still lying half in and half out of the water, which had cascaded about them as they had achieved climax together, and that had been the silver rain in which Bianca had been consumed only to be reborn. She was no longer beneath him, but on top of him, where he had turned her after their ecstasy was over.

The air caressed her body. Her very skin seemed alive. 'You enjoyed your first flight, my dove,' he whispered in her ear. 'Who would have thought that the scrubbing wench would soar so high, so anchored to the earth she seemed?'

Oh, his voice was as cunning as his body. He had used it as a whip to her and to others to command, to deceive, to charm, but when he spoke again the truth rang in it. 'Oh, my dove, few have flown so far and fast with me; I do not lie. You are a nonpareil.'

'And thou, Pierino,' she said. 'My love and my lord.' She was silent a moment, then asked, 'Thou said thou lovest me. Since when, my lord? Thy dove would know.'

'Why,' he said, after a moment, 'I think it was when I saw the dirty wench in the hall, on her knees. So different from all the women I have known. So full of fire and spirit and passion, and lost in your brother's tower to be wasted on some coarse fool who would use you and break you—or barren in a nunnery.'

Bianca was silent, feeling his strength below her, then looked down to meet his blue eyes.

'You speak true? So impossibly perfect as you were, you wanted me?'

'Not entirely seriously, at first; I will not lie. But, on

our wedding night, I found that I desired you most desperately, and could not touch you. And when you were Dino—it was a living agony. And you, my love, my own dear wife, when did you first love thy Falcon?'

'Why, when you did me,' she said simply. 'I thought at first I hated you, you were so far above me, and I so plain and small——'

'Not now,' he said. 'And in a moment I shall prove again how much you mean to me. When Bruschini took you, I nearly ran mad. If proof were needed of what I felt for you, for I had burned for you for months, I received it then.' He hesitated, hugging her to him. 'You were right about impossible perfection, my love. I tried to live without others, and what a barren life it was. You changed all that and the snows melted within me, my heart. And after I found you, and knew that I loved you, truly loved you, I found Michele, my lost and loving brother—and I even found that I could forgive my father a little. That men and women were not simply there for me to use, that Maddalena could truly love me, and could let me go with dignity—because I loved you, she sacrificed herself to please me. And holding off, not taking you, taught me a necessary lesson: that we prize what we may not easily have, must earn by sacrifice. Love is not easy—is giving, not taking, and by the end I loved you so dearly—and could not have you. I even feared that you might prefer Michele.'

Bianca kissed the hand which held her, and said in wonder, 'Oh, no. I liked Michele, but he is not you. Never you. I thought. . .' She hesitated. 'I thought that you had no use for your child-wife, Pierino, no love for me. . .'

'Oh, I always loved you,' he said, and his voice was full of teasing affection. 'Even when you belaboured me with Father Luca. What would he say to us now, think you? Would he have a phrase for us?'

'For sure he would, my husband. *Finis coronat opus*— or "The end crowns the work".'

'Well, Father Luca is wrong, then,' said her husband briskly, tucking her beneath him again, 'for I have not yet done with you, my dove, and I doubt whether I ever shall. You are Astra's lady, and my love, and now I shall prove it to you, in case the first demonstration was not sufficient.'

The other exciting

MASQUERADE
Historical

available this month is:

THE CAPTAIN'S ANGEL
Marie-Louise Hall

Despite the bitter Russian winter and Napoleon's threat to Moscow, Angèle's problem was closer to home. She knew it was only a matter of time before her cousin André forced his will on her. She must escape to England!

But taking shelter from the snowstorm brought her face to face with Captain Tristan Beaumaris, one of Napoleon's Chasseurs, wounded and feverish, but intent on reaching his men. Now that they were forced to travel together, their attraction grew—but what hope was there, when they were on opposing sides?

Look out for the two intriguing

MASQUERADE *Historical*

Romances coming next month

THE DANBURY SCANDALS
Mary Nichols

Having been brought up in the Reverend Cudlipp's
household, Maryanne Paynter was both astonished and a
little frightened to be suddenly taken up by Viscount
Danbury. Discovering herself to be related to aristocracy
changed her life completely, and even more mystifying, it
brought her into contact with Adam St. Pierre, who also
seemed to have some connection with the Danburys. The
uneasy peace between France and England in 1814 seemed to
be part of the mystery, where past Danbury scandals could
affect the future. Where could Maryanne seek refuge–with
her new cousin Mark, or Adam?

AN ANGEL'S TOUCH
Elizabeth Bailey

Miss Verity Lambourn found she had no choice about
accompanying elderly Lady Crossens to Tunbridge Wells,
but she didn't mind. Far from husband hunting, Verity had
other plans in mind which would make full use of her vivid
imagination! But dreaming didn't stop her impetuous rescue
of two small children, nor cause her to back down from their
stern father. When she discovered his identity she did
consider she ought to have been more circumspect, not
knowing her refreshing candour drew both children and
father. . .

Available in December

MASQUERADE Historical

Experience the thrill of 2 Masquerade historical romances absolutely free!

*Experience the passions of bygone days
in 2 gripping Masquerade romances - absolutely free!
Enjoy these tales of tempestuous love from the illustrious
past. Then, if you wish, look forward to a regular supply of
Masquerades, delivered to your door!
Turn the page for details of 2 extra FREE gifts,
and how to apply.*

An irresistible offer for you

Here at Reader Service we would love you to become a regular reader of Masquerade. And to welcome you, we'd like you to have 2 books, a cuddly teddy and a mystery gift - ABSOLUTELY FREE and without obligation.

Then, every 2 months you could look forward to receiving 4 more brand-new Masquerade historical romances for just £2.25 each, delivered to your door, postage and packing free. Plus our free Newsletter featuring special offers, author news, competitions with some great prizes, and lots more!

This invitation comes with no strings attached. You may cancel or suspend your subscription at any time, and still keep your free books and gifts.

It's so easy. Send no money now. Simply fill in the coupon below at once and post it to - Reader Service, FREEPOST, PO Box 236, Croydon, Surrey CR9 9EL.

───── NO STAMP REQUIRED ─────

Yes! Please rush me 2 FREE Masquerade romances and 2 FREE gifts! Please also reserve me a Reader Service subscription. If I decide to subscribe, I can look forward to receiving 4 brand new Masquerade romances every 2 months for just £9.00, delivered direct to my door, postage and packing free. If I choose not to subscribe I shall write to you within 10 days - I can keep the books and gifts whatever I decide. I may cancel or suspend my subscription at any time. I am over 18 years of age.

EP30M

Mrs/Miss/Ms/Mr _____

Address _____

_____

Postcode _____ Signature _____

The right is reserved to refuse an application and change the terms of this offer. Offer expires 31st December 1992. Readers in Southern Africa write to Book Services International Ltd., PO Box 41654, Craighall, Transvaal 2024. Other Overseas and Eire, please send for details. You may be mailed with other offers from Mills & Boon and other reputable companies as a result of this application. If you would prefer not to share in this opportunity, please tick box. ☐

mps
MAILING
PREFERENCE
SERVICE